HER

DEADLY

PROMISE

BOOKS BY CARLA KOVACH

HER

DEADLY

PROMISE

CARLA KOVACH

bookouture

Published by Bookouture in 2022

An imprint of Storyfire Ltd.
Carmelite House
50 Victoria Embankment
London EC4Y 0DZ

www.bookouture.com

ISBN: 978-1-80314-361-3
eBook ISBN: 978-1-80314-360-6

I would like to dedicate this book to everyone who is currently going through the menopause or has entered perimenopause. It's an unsettling time, that's for sure, and one that is being spoken about, more and more – thank goodness. May that openness continue!

PROLOGUE

Sunday, 15 May

Billie saunters and smiles while reading from her huge lemon-coloured book of tales that sits on the purple lectern. My heart jumps as her hands slap together to make the sound of the snapping crocodile. She is the storyteller extraordinaire, and the children love her. While watching her work her magic, I can see the attraction of the children's entertainer. Some people naturally have this magnetism, but it's something I've never had. I guess if I'd worked as a holiday park entertainer or indulged in acting classes, I'd be far more confident. She sparkles when she enters a room, and everyone's attention is on her. She makes people happy and warm inside with her sickly-sweet voices. I say voices, as she is a woman of many while she is putting on a show for the children. She is also a woman of many secrets of which everyone here knows but everyone is too polite to mention. Polite society, don't you just love it?

As she reaches her crescendo in the story about the mean

crocodile who eventually befriended a warthog, every child in the garden is transfixed. She places the book down, not needing it for the big finale and she gives each child a glance, not missing one out. They all love her, I can tell. Her crocodile costume starts to slip as she gives the tail a flick before getting her glittery wand out and declaring the end of the story. She winks at her little boy, Kayden, who is clearly in awe of his mother. It's his birthday and she's making it as special as she can.

The easy-to-please crowd of five-year-olds clap and laugh as Billie takes her final bow. Parents, drunk on Pimm's, cheer. The dads can't keep their eyes off her and the mums all want to be her. If ever there was a person who was perfect, it was Billie. So bloody perfect, alluring and beautiful. Only her secret tarnishes her perfect image but we all have secrets, me included.

I spot the top of a head above the back fence, then I see a wide eye peering through the slit of a gap. A prickling sensation tickles the back of my neck and I wonder how many seconds will pass before the watcher realises I've spotted them. Who's watching us and why? With scrunched brows I hurry over, slipping past the trampoline and alongside the shed. I must see who it is. What if they're watching the children or one of us? It's an eerie feeling knowing that someone was looking on as we partied away. What do they want? Stepping between the flowers at the border of the garden, I lean up and peer over, just catching the watcher as they turn a corner. They're gone and I don't know what to think. All I know is this uneasy feeling is churning in my stomach and it isn't down to the summer cocktails.

It's a sweltering day and the sweat patches under my arms are testament to that but I'm left with a shiver. The watcher must have been there for a while and when I approached, they scurried off, not wanting to be seen. One thing I'm certain of is, if I see them again, I'll recognise them. The cat thuds onto the fence and I drop my glass of Pimm's. The glass catches a rock and shatters onto the earth below. Heart banging, I gaze around. People are looking at me and my cheeks redden.

One of the mothers hurries over. 'Are you okay?'

I nod. 'Yes, it's just the heat.' I sigh. Maybe the watcher was just a curious passer-by who heard Billie acting. It was nothing, so I paste on my hugest red-lipped smile and rejoin the party. I shake the thought of that stark staring eye away. Whoever was loitering had now gone.

I glance across at the men as the barbeque is lit and all I see is my friend Nadia's husband, Ed. His gaze falls on Billie as she enters the house. The expression on his face tells me that he could be angry or maybe I'm seeing jealousy? It's hard to tell, especially as he slips his sunglasses on. Nadia turns to see her leering husband too, then she glances at me. I feel her pain but now isn't the right time to talk to her about it. She wouldn't thank me, not with all these people around. Our other good friend, Meera, has had a few too many glasses of Pimm's. She giggles like a little girl as she asks for a top-up. No one else sees it, but I can see that Nadia is crying inside.

The whole situation feels wrong, like we're all acting a part in a play, just like Billie was when she read her story. We're all characters delving into our motivations and our feelings while we assess how the next scene will go. One thing I don't know is how it all ends, but I know it's not going to be pretty. It's going to be explosive.

ONE

Wednesday, 15 June

'Dev, it's time to go.' Dev's mummy, Meera, rushes out of the house holding a lunchbox.

'But, Mum. I want to play with Kayden.'

Kayden glances back at his own house as he steps out of Dev's plastic car and onto the patchy bit of grass out the front. He doesn't want Dev to go to his grandma's. They were playing, having fun. The dark path between their home and Dev's looks like a mouth that wants to swallow him up. Mummy uses it to wheel the bin from the back garden and it's always damp. His house is a bit grey and it's patchy. Mummy said it was from a drippy pipe. Dev's house is bright, and his mummy puts baskets of flowers that hang beside the door. Yellow, purple and pink; all bright colours and some of his favourites. Kayden's forehead is sticky wet, so he grabs the end of his T-shirt and wipes it dry. Mummy doesn't like him dirtying his clothes but it's okay, it'll dry.

'You can play with Kayden tomorrow but right now you know we have to go and take this food to Grandma's before it gets cold, so let's go, now. Damn, look at you.' Dev's mummy shakes her head and pops the lunchbox on the wall. She kneels to tie the laces on his trainers, her long black hair falling forward and brushing Kayden's leg like a tickly spider. 'How's your mum, Kayden? I haven't seen her for a while.'

He picks up his football and shrugs, lips pressed tightly together. Mummy's been weird, she keeps putting him to bed early and telling him he was never to come down until she said he could. That's when he'd hear the noises that scared him. When she'd come back up to check on him, he'd lie there pretending to be asleep or if he got scared, he'd hide in his wardrobe. 'She's okay.' Mummy wouldn't want him to talk to anyone else about the noises.

'That's good.' With a final pull, Dev's laces are tied, and his mummy holds out her hand to lead him to the car. 'I'll watch you go into your house. Tell your mum I'll see her later at Nadia's, if she's feeling better.'

'Okay.' He wants her to strap Dev in the car and go. He's going to have to step into the dark alleyway that smells of bin. Mummy said he couldn't come back in until she came out and since he's been playing with Dev, she's still inside. The curtains are shut, and he knows not to knock on the door. He stares at their dull red front door, wondering if he should peer through the letterbox.

'See you later,' Dev calls out, so Kayden bites his bottom lip and waves.

'Well, go on then.' Dev's mummy straps his friend in and slams the car door. 'I'm not leaving until I see you go in.' Dev's mummy's eyebrows are dark and thick, like they're painted on and while she stands there, they don't move.

He doesn't want her to leave but he also doesn't want Mummy to be upset with him, so he takes one step, then another. The further he gets into the creepy alley, the cooler he feels. There is a smell of bin, which makes him feel a bit sick. He likes that it's cool but not that it's dark. As he passes the creepy cupboard that Mummy said used to be used to store coal, he leans against the wall and takes a few deep breaths. There is nothing to be scared of. He can see the back garden shed and the front garden. The sun is shining, and Mummy said there is no such thing as monsters but that doesn't stop his mouth from going dry as he hugs his ball and presses his shoulders into the damp wall.

The car growls. As soon as it's gone, he runs away from the alley monster. He is alone. The street is quiet as most people are still at work. He sits on the kerb, ball between his legs, and he plays with a piece of loose thread on his top, twirling it around his fingers, pulling it longer and longer. School was fun, he did a painting which Mummy stuck to the fridge. She told him how good it was. It was a picture of their house, but he'd put flowers around the door, and he didn't paint the house grey. It was their house, but it looked nice, like Dev's.

Minutes had passed and his head was boiling. He holds out his usually pale arms that were now red. His bottom feels like it's burning on the pavement. When he glances up the road, past the parked cars, it looks like the road is shimmering.

'Kayden. What are you doing out here alone? It's dangerous to be sitting by the road like this.'

He looks up to see the old lady in the straw hat. Their neighbour, Joanna, grips the lead attached to her little dog as they stop on the shady side of the path, its tongue sticking out of the side of its mouth. It sits at her feet and pants. Kayden reaches out and strokes the dog's white curly hair just like he has done many times. Mummy says that it's okay to touch Digger because Digger is a friendly dog. 'Mummy said I could sit here. I'm just playing.' His voice croaks and he'd love a drink of juice or an ice lolly.

'It doesn't look like you're playing. You look like you're getting burned to a crisp in that sun. You need some sunblock and a drink, my lad.' The ball slips from his legs and rolls into the road. A car zooms past, bursting it under its tyres. Mummy hates it when they drive too fast down our road and now his favourite ball is ruined. 'Come on, let's get you in your house. I wouldn't forgive myself if you got run over. Drivers like that should get banged up.' Joanna grabs the squashed ball.

She can't take me to the door and knock. Mummy said whatever happens not to come in until she called him, and he promised her that he'd be a good boy and do as he was told. She hadn't called him yet. 'I can't go in. Mummy said I must wait here.'

Joanna pulls a face and looks at him in a funny way. 'Did she now? We'll soon see about that.' She throws his burst ball into our garden and holds out her hand, which he takes. She's a grown-up. He knows that he should do as he's told. He is hot and Joanna isn't a stranger. Mummy will understand that he needed to come in. Joanna marches him up to the front door and bangs so loudly, he flinches. There is no answer, so she bangs again. After trying one more time, she treads on the dried muddy front garden and tries to peer through the window. 'The curtains are closed. Is your mum ill?'

He shakes his head. 'She was okay when she picked me up from school, but she gets headaches.'

She leads him through the dark alley. It's not as scary with Joanna and Digger. As the old woman reaches the back door, she knocks. 'Billie.' She knocks again.

Kayden pushes in front of her and goes to open the back door, but Joanna pulls him so hard, he almost falls forward onto the floor. Tears are falling down her cheeks as she drags him and her yelping dog through the alleyway and back out the front. 'Is Mummy in? I didn't see her go out.'

Joanna gasps for breath and leans on the wall while grappling in her bag for her phone. 'Can you be a good boy and sit on the step with Digger?'

He nods and takes the lead off her before sitting on the front step, right by the door.

Joanna walks away and starts to talk. He can barely hear what she's saying but he can see that she can't stop crying. What she said next made him shiver and he begins to cry.

'There's blood everywhere. You must come quick.'

TWO

Detective Gina Harte pushed her office window open to its max as she grabbed her mini fan and set it going in front of her face. Red cheeked and damp under her breasts, she was looking forward to heading home soon and getting into a cold shower. She stared down at the car park as Briggs strode towards the entrance. He moved onto the path as a police car pulled in. Earlier, she'd heard him saying that his car was having work done at the garage so she knew that his new girlfriend would be picking him up. As he glanced back, she ducked. He can't see her watching. If he did, he'd know how hurt she was.

She thought back to not long ago when they were happily continuing their secret relationship, until he dropped the bombshell that he was seeing someone else behind her back. Not only was he seeing a woman from his past, but it was also serious. She thought *they* were serious. They were. But she could never give him a family or even a conventional relationship.

Rosemary was her name, the woman who was making DCI Chris Briggs so happy and the whole team were pleased for him, except Gina. Little did they all know, his happiness was her heartache. He might be happy in his new world where he gets to play father and devoted partner but when Gina asked if he loved Rosemary, he couldn't answer. He loved the idea of normal family life. She clenched her fist and threw her fan across the room where the blades became detached from the base. Great, now she'd have to cook in her oven-of-an-office or head to the storeroom to see if someone had returned a desk fan. Hot flushes were plaguing her and a constant reminder that she could never have given Briggs what he wanted anyway. She'd had her daughter years ago. Hannah was in her twenties, and Gina was a grandmother to young Gracie. If only she'd met Briggs all those years ago and had a family with him. Her life could have been so different.

Should she be happy that he stood a chance at normality? Maybe, but she wasn't. She wanted things to go back to how they were; them having a secret relationship, as neither would be prepared to leave Cleevesford Police Station if it came to it.

Slowly, she peered over the ledge. He stood at the end of the road waiting and scrolling through his phone. Only ten weeks ago, Gina had been in his bed then he'd dumped her, cold. Later, she'd go home alone, and she wouldn't be able to call him, and he wouldn't come over for a takeaway or shower with her.

The red soft-top car pulled up alongside him where elegant Rosemary smiled as she waited for him to get in. Her sunglasses and headscarf gave her a timeless look, a little Audrey Hepburn. Who wouldn't be captivated by the hairdresser's beauty? As she drove off with the man Gina loved, her chest tightened. The only way to release that tension would be to have a good cry.

Someone knocked on the door. She ran and picked up the components of the fan and sat down. 'Come in.'

Detective Constable Paula Wyre pushed the door open. Her black hair was neatly plaited at the back and her fringe as poker straight as ever.

'Could you pop the wedge in? It's so hot in here.'

Wyre nodded. 'Whoa, yes. It feels as though I've just walked into a wall of lava.' As she grappled with the wedge, Gina grabbed a folder and wafted it in front of her face. She'd only closed the door so no one would see her watching Briggs leave. 'There. It's not much better but at least there's a bit of air flow.'

'What can I do for you?' Gina forced a smile.

'I thought I'd come and see how you were doing?'

'Okay.'

'You know, I wondered if you fancied going out for a drink sometime or maybe a pub lunch.'

'I'm err... I'm a bit busy at the moment.'

Wyre shrugged. 'How lovely, what have you been up to?'

'You know? This and that.'

Wyre furrowed her brows.

'Watching TV, sitting in the garden, playing with my new pet rabbit.' After Thumper's owner was arrested, it appeared that she now had a rabbit until she could find him a permanent home. 'Do you want a rabbit?'

Wyre laughed. 'Not likely. I live in a flat and I'm never in.' Sitting at the opposite side of Gina's desk, Wyre leaned in.

'How's your lovely granddaughter?'

'Gracie is doing fine, happy as always. I must go and see her and Hannah soon, but my daughter is always so busy.' Gina furrowed her brows. Although they hadn't always got on, they were fine now.

'I'm worried about you, guv.'

Gina raised her eyebrows. 'Why would you be worried about me?'

'Can I be candid?'

'Please.' Gina wouldn't expect anything less of her colleague but nonetheless, she braced herself for what was to come. Had her team seen her watching Briggs? Could they tell she was pining over him? She hoped not. Their relationship had remained a secret and she wanted it to stay that way.

Wyre swallowed and began to fiddle with her fingers. 'You keep biting your nails. The dark circles around your eyes are almost like bruises and...'

'And?' She took a deep breath.

'You look sad. I just wanted you to know that if there's anything wrong, you can talk to me. You've always been here for me, for the team, and we're here for you.'

'Great, so the team all think I'm losing it.' She threw the file down on her desk and placed a hand on her burning cheek. Her heart began to hum.

'No one thinks you're losing it.'

She stood. 'You can tell them all that I'm fine. I'm well, I'm healthy and I'm happy. What more could a person want? Is that it?'

'Guv, I'm so sorry. I didn't mean to upset you.'

Gina shook her head and held a hand up, not wanting Wyre to say another word. 'Look, it's okay. I shouldn't have snapped but I promise you, all is fine, like I said. It's just the heat and the hot flushes. I keep waking up in the night with the sweats, that's where the dark circles have come from. That's all.'

'Have you been to the doctors?'

'What for?'

'The flushes.'

'No, I'm okay. Really. Now, I have stacks to do. Was there anything else?'

'No, guv. If you change your mind about the pub, let me know.' As Wyre stood to leave, DC Harry O'Connor ran in wiping his bald head with a tissue. 'We've had a call.'

Glad of the distraction, Gina ushered him in. 'What is it?' Wyre leaned against the wall.

'A twenty-eight-year-old woman called Billie Reeves who

lives on Church Road was found by a neighbour. When PCs Smith and Kapoor arrived with the ambulance service, the woman was pronounced dead. She has a stab wound to the chest.'

Wyre fidgeted. 'Best cancel the pub.'

'Is Jacob still here?' Detective Sergeant Jacob Driscoll usually accompanied Gina at crime scenes.

'No.' O'Connor leaned on the door frame. 'He had to leave to pick Jennifer up from physio. I think she's being signed off.' His girlfriend had been hit by a car in one of their last big cases. Since coming off the ventilator, her progress had been steady, and she was keen to return to forensic duties.

'Who found the victim?'

'A lady called Joanna Pearlman. She's looking after the victim's little boy until a family member has been contacted.'

'Where was the boy at the time?'

'Apparently, she found him sitting on the kerb outside the house and got worried. She said that the boy kept saying his mum told him he had to stay there until she called him in.'

'That poor kid. How old is he?'

'Mrs Pearlman said he's about five.'

'Wyre, you come with me and, O'Connor, you follow. Have forensics been called?'

O'Connor nodded. 'They're on their way. I'll meet you both there.'

Gina nodded. 'See you in a few minutes.'

Wyre stood in the doorway, waiting to head out. 'We best go.'

'I'll meet you by the car. I just need a second.'

Wyre nodded and Gina listened to her colleague's footsteps tapping down the corridor. She pulled her window closed as she imagined the tiny boy sitting outside, waiting for his mother to call him in while she was being brutally murdered. Swallowing down the lump in her throat, she headed out of her office. Who could kill a young mother like that, and while her young child was so close? Her heart skipped at the thought of entering the scene and seeing such horror and all she could think about was that poor little boy. She was going to catch the murderer and bring them to justice.

THREE

Silence filled the car as they took the turning into Church Road with its terraced houses on both sides. Gina pulled up behind O'Connor's car, just making it before an outpouring of work traffic began to fill the roads. She spotted the forensics van with its back doors open. Bernard Small, their gangly Crime Scene Manager took large strides while holding his toolbox and evidence kits. He'd tucked his long, grey beard into a beard cover. PC Jhanvi Kapoor stood guard at the open garden gate with the crime scene log, checking in everyone who passed the threshold and PC Smith was positioned outside another house a little further down.

Gina took a deep breath knowing that the best thing she could do for their victim was to find her killer. Her heart sank for the little boy that had been left behind. She stepped out, the heat and exhaust fumes hitting her instantly. Cars began to slow down in the road, their passengers and drivers rubbernecking, causing a queue of traffic. Horns beeped as people inched past. Wyre hurried past the outer cordon that was tied from lamp post to lamp post and met Gina at the gate.

'Alright, guv. I'll get you logged in.' PC Kapoor began to

scribble their details on the log sheet, then she passed Gina and Wyre a forensics suit, hair covers, gloves, masks and booties.

Gina waved PC Smith over and he ran across. 'Is that where Mrs Pearlman lives?'

'Yes, I've just left her and the boy. The woman is in a state of shock. There's a paramedic with her now so I'd give it a few minutes. Her husband has put some cartoons on for the lad.'

'Have you managed to speak to her?'

'No, not yet. She wasn't up to talking when I walked her into her house. It's not every day you see a woman lying dead and bleeding out.'

'And it's something we never get used to. Poor Mrs Pearlman. I'll wait for the paramedics to finish with her before heading over. It'll give me a chance to speak to Bernard. Can you get this traffic flowing?'

He nodded. 'Yes, we could do without this chaos. They're only slowing down to nose. I've already waved two cars on because they stopped to take photos. It's probably all over social media by now and we haven't even managed to speak to the relatives yet. I'll keep telling them all to move on.'

'Thank you.'

'I wonder if we can go around the back yet.' Wyre peered up the alleyway.

PC Kapoor stepped forward. 'Bernard said he'll be out the front in a few minutes. They've got the stepping plates down, but his team are just videoing and photographing the scene. Apparently, it's tight and messy in there. They are also working with officers to secure the back garden and the path that runs alongside the back of the house. Another couple of officers are there, blocking it off as a walkthrough.'

Gina hated the wait. She wanted everything Bernard had and as soon as possible. Then she could start looking for whoever did this. 'Do we know anything about Billie Reeves?'

'No, guv. Only that she lived alone with her son.' Kapoor pressed her lips together.

Gina turned to the alleyway as she heard clunking on the stepping plates and Bernard came out. 'You can come through to the back garden but not go in the house yet. We still have so much to do and there's no room for anything or anyone.'

Wyre nodded and they both followed Bernard. Gina enjoyed the cool alleyway even though the stench made her stomach roll. As they came out into the back garden, she peered around, taking in the old breeze-block shed. A shell-shaped sandpit filled the small patio beside the kitchen window and the back fence looked rickety, like it had been patched up by several different types of wood. The yellowy-brown patches of grass looked like they were crying out for water. One thing stood out, the ground was so hard there probably wouldn't be much, if anything, in the way of footprints.

'Step on this.' Bernard pointed to the large plate under the window. Wyre and Gina joined him.

'What can you tell us?' Gina clunked back on the plate with one foot.

'Victim is a woman, aged mid- to late-twenties. One single stab wound to the neck.'

'Murder weapon?'

'Not at the scene. The blood spatter and volume tell us that she was stabbed in that spot. She fell to the floor and bled out. It's bloody and tight in there, which is why we can't allow anyone but our specialist team in at the moment. The crime scene photos won't take long to get uploaded and sent so you'll be able to work from them for the time being. When we're done, you'll be able to search the house.'

'So, we can't go in at all?'

'Not yet. There's too much for us to process and I don't want the scene tampered with at all. You'll see what I mean when you look inside.'

'Any sign of further assault or sexual assault?'

Wyre began jotting down some notes.

'We haven't examined the body that closely yet, but I can't see any more bruising and her clothing is all intact. It looks like there was a bit of a struggle but not much. There are a couple of smashed cups and a few other kitchen items on the floor. I'd say this was quick and unexpected. The house is a mess. Items have been flung out of drawers, things like that.'

'Was the back door unlocked?'

'Yes. When we got here, the keys were on the kitchen table. The sliding lock on the gate was open.'

'Any phones or devices?'

'We haven't found any yet but if we do, we'll get them bagged immediately.'

'Time of death?'

'As always, this is approximate but given the state of the body, I'd say within the last three hours. There is another thing. Look through the window.'

Gina swallowed and stared through the smeary glass and spider plants on the window ledge. On the back wall of the kitchen was a word written in red that made her shiver. SLUT in capital letters. 'What is it written in?'

'Pen.'

'Any sign of the pen used?'

'Not as yet.'

Her heart sank for the bluish-tinged woman lying on the floor. Her chocolate-brown fringe matted with blood made Gina look away. In her mind's eye, all she could then see was the woman's little boy. The child at the neighbour's watching cartoons, oblivious to what had happened to his mother. His world was going to be turned upside down.

FOUR

NADIA

Nadia dragged William into the house, sitting him at the kitchen table while she made him a squash. 'How was school today?'

'Mrs Hallam brought in a guinea pig to show us. He had sticky up hair, and I stroked him.'

'Wow. That sounds wonderful. I love guinea pigs.' She grabbed several packets of biscuits from the cupboard and slid open the bifold doors that led to her pride and joy; the perfect golf course lawn that her husband always lovingly tended to. As promised, he'd put the parasol up and cleaned the large table. She'd promised the other mums a fun evening of tea and biscuits. They all knew that meant a glass or two of wine while their children played on the jungle gym and in the tree house. They could catch up on school news, sort out who was doing what at the summer fete in a couple of weeks. She'd promised Mrs Hallam she would help and that's what she'd do. This year's fete was going to go down in school history. It was time to put her bad day behind her and paste on her happy face.

'Mum, can we have a guinea pig?'

'No, honey. We already have Fluffball.'

'But Fluffball doesn't like me.' William went to pick up the long-haired tortoiseshell cat and she hissed at him before darting away.

'Fluffball is hot, that's all.'

Nadia gasped as someone rang the bell. The other mothers were here already. If only her session hadn't run over with her client who wanted to lose another stone before her holiday. It was only meant to last an hour. All that running in the park, turning over tyres and shaking the ropes had taken longer than Nadia had thought, but her client was thrilled with the burn as she called it. Then she had other things to do, things that couldn't wait. If she'd have been on time, William would have already had his snack and she'd have prepared more than a few packets of biscuits. She'd had all day up until her session but something else had cropped up. Something more important. She swallowed down the anxiety that was threatening to overwhelm her.

Opening the door, Candice stood there calling her daughter over. The little girl's pink cheeks flushed with heat and looked like they were burning. With their red-haired complexions, they preferred to stay out of direct heat. She giggled on seeing William before they raced each other to the jungle gym. 'Come through,' Nadia said. She passed Candice a bottle of wine and a couple of glasses. 'I'll be out in a moment; I just saw Meera pulling in.'

'Fabulous. I'll pour the wine. God, it's so hot.' Candice placed the chilled wine on her forehead and smiled as she headed to the garden.

'Hi, Meera.' Nadia waved as Meera unstrapped her son from the back of the car.

'It's so hot. I'm melting. I just went to see my mother and the woman is sitting in her lounge with all the windows shut. Can you believe it?'

'Damn, on a day like this? I hope you're thirsty. The wine has been opened.' Nadia reached over and hugged her friend.

'I'm parched.'

Meera's long flowing summer dress, fitted at the waist, showed off her figure.

'You look lovely. Is that dress new?'

'Yes, present to myself.'

As Meera's son ran through, Meera stepped further into the echoey tiled hallway.

'Have you seen Billie?' Nadia had to ask.

Meera pressed her lips together and scrunched her brows. 'I'm not sure she's coming. All her curtains were shut when I left, and Kayden was playing in our garden. I wonder if she's having one of her migraines. I should have offered to bring him.'

Nadia bit her bottom lip knowing that Billie wouldn't come. 'Don't worry. She might still turn up. Go through. We have so much to discuss, like cakes and hook-a-bottle. Damn that teacher, she had the nerve to bring in a cute guinea pig today and now William is pestering me for one of those crazy-haired rats.'

Meera laughed. 'But they are so cute.'

Nadia led her friend past the staircase, through the long, open-plan kitchen with its table for eight, couches and bifold doors, out to where Candice was sipping a glass of wine. Nadia felt saddened knowing that their group of three friends should have been four. She missed being close to Billie but too much had happened. As Nadia grabbed a jug of juice off the worktop, she heard Meera's phone ring. 'Hello. Say that again but slower this time.'

Nadia watched as Meera's smile turned into a deep-lined frown. Her hand flew up to her mouth as she gasped.

'That can't be right. Kayden was playing with my son only an hour ago. She was in the house. She wasn't well.' A few moments later, Meera ended the call.

'Meera, what is it?' Candice put her glass down, came over and placed a caring arm around her friend's shoulder.

'I-I—'

'Here, sit down.' Candice led her over to the table and sat her down.

'Meera, has something happened to Kayden?' Nadia felt her heart booming as she waited for her friend to speak.

'It's Billie. She's been murdered.'

Meera began to sob, and Candice frowned with an open mouth.

'That can't be right, no.' Nadia shook her head. A tear trickled down her cheek. Her friend was dead. All their shared memories flashed through her mind. Their children's birthdays, playgroups, boozy fun-filled nights. Gone forever.

How many people knew Billie's deepest darkest secret? Her stomach churned with guilt, and she almost lost her footing. It was all her fault.

FIVE

Gina and Wyre were walked back by Bernard through the alley and away from the scene. 'Right, I'll crack on. Those photos should be with you very soon.'

'Thanks, Bernard.'

Gina and Wyre nodded to Kapoor who would mark their exit on the log. O'Connor approached, dabbing his balmy forehead as he spoke. 'Mrs Pearlman is okay to talk now. The paramedics offered her something to help but she refused. She's much better. Her husband has made her a cuppa and the lad is still watching telly in their lounge.'

'Thanks, O'Connor. Can you organise and collate any information from the door-to-doors? Gather the officers. We need bins, alleyways and pathways searching. The murder weapon must be somewhere. If anyone has CCTV, secure it.' She glanced up and down. 'I can't see any cameras, but you never know.'

'I'll get onto that now. Thankfully the traffic is beginning to thin out as well and we have a team of PCs heading here.'

'Any luck in locating the boy's father or a family member?'

'An officer is on their way over to his grandparents' house, that's the victim's parents. As soon as they've broken the news, we're hoping that they will look after him.'

Gina shook her head. 'I don't envy them.'

PC Smith came out of the house, two doors down from Billie Reeves's. 'Mrs Pearlman is waiting in the kitchen. I said you'd like to speak to her. Also, we tried the neighbour but there's no one in.'

Wyre pushed the gate open, and they passed PC Smith. As they walked through the Pearlmans' door, Gina felt a lump in her throat as she watched the little boy sitting on the couch transfixed by *PAW Patrol*. A mature man with glasses and a grey rim of hair around his head sat on the chair. 'I'm Pete, Joanna's husband. She's through there.'

Gina followed Wyre into the kitchen. 'Mrs Pearlman. I'm DI Harte and this is DC Wyre, are you okay to talk to us now?'

The woman nodded as the little dog on her lap licked the salty tears from her cheek. 'So horrible,' she muttered as she wiped the crumpled hanky under her creased eyelids. 'I can't get her out of my mind. That poor woman; the blood. I've never seen anything like it.' She paused. 'I was about to go in there and give her a piece of my mind for leaving Kayden out by the road all on his own and I saw her. She must have known what was going to happen or that she was in some danger. I thought it wasn't like her. She's such a good mum, I can't believe I was going to have a go at her, then...'

'It's okay, take your time.' Gina and Wyre sat at the table of the small kitchen. If Gina held her left hand out, she could do the washing-up if she wanted. They waited for the woman to blow her nose and wipe her eyes. 'How well do you know Billie Reeves?'

She shrugged as Wyre flicked to a fresh page in her notebook. 'Not well. I say hello to her if I see her coming or going. My great-granddaughter has played with Kayden a couple of times. I don't suppose she'd see an old biddy like me as friend material. She was pallier with the lady next door, the one who lives between us. Her name is Meera, and she has a little boy who goes to the same school as Kayden. Those boys are always playing together in Meera's front or back garden.'

'Do you know if Billie had a partner?'

Mrs Pearlman scrunched her nose in thought. 'She lives alone. There is a man that comes and stays sometimes but…'

Gina remained silent, hoping that Mrs Pearlman would continue.

'I've seen a couple of other men too.'

'Others?'

She nodded. 'Yes, maybe they are friends, or it's possible she's having work done on the house. Maybe they're relatives.'

'Can you describe any of her visitors?'

Mrs Pearlman shook her head. 'No, but I can describe the man who stays as he said hello to me a couple of weeks back. It was early one morning while I was walking Digger, so he must stay the night. He's tall, must be close on six feet. Blond or light-brown hair, a full head of it, in fact. I'd say he was about thirty at the most. Clean-shaven and such a handsome young man. He has a little scar under his left eye. I remember that as I kept trying not to look at it.'

'Do you know his name?'

'No, I'm afraid not. As I say, Billie was friends with Meera. I'm sure she would have spoken to her about the new man in her life.' Mrs Pearlman began lifting and returning the lid to the sugar bowl.

'Did you speak to him?'

'Yes, I said, "Good morning" and he smiled and said the same back. He commented on the beautiful weather, then he dragged Billie's bin through the alleyway. He had a local accent, if that's any help. I wonder if he knows yet.' She paused. 'I think I heard them arguing when I was walking past the house.'

'Did you hear what was being said?'

'No, but it was definitely last week, and I heard raised voices. It was a school day; I remember that much. I thought it was good that Kayden wasn't there to hear it.'

Gina waited for Wyre to catch up with the notes. 'What time did you walk your dog today?'

'Oh, I don't know. Time is irrelevant to me. I've been retired for years. Pete,' she shouted. 'What time did I take Digger out?' Gina wondered if the man had heard her calling over the loud television.

'Did you shout?' The old man walked in, using a stick for support.

'Yes, when did I take Digger for a walk this afternoon?'

The man checked on the boy and pulled the door to. 'It was about half three, love, maybe a few minutes later.'

'That was it. The kids had finished school, in fact, I think they got home earlier than usual today. Anyway, they were playing in Meera's front garden. When I got back, Kayden was on his own, sitting on the kerb. I suppose that was about fifteen minutes later, so before four. I have a regular walk where I head to the high street, go for a walk through the church grounds and then walk back. It takes about that long.'

'Did you see anyone suspicious hanging around?'

'No, only the boys were playing and there was no one hanging around at all.'

Gina leaned forward and wiped her glistening nose, the heat becoming unbearable. She wished that Mrs Pearlman would open the back door. 'How about the back of the houses?'

'Billie's visitors tend to use the back, but I didn't hear anyone come or go today. I don't tend to be looking out for anyone though. Our gate is always locked. That path running along the back of the houses is a bit creepy, so we like to keep people out, don't we, Pete?'

He nodded. 'Yes, love. That's why you made me put the

barbed wire along the top of the fence. Kids like to cause trouble back there. They graffiti our fences and drink.'

Gina undid the top button of her shirt. She glanced out of the window and noticed the back garden was in the shade. 'May we look around the back?' Treading through Billie's garden was a no-no but she could access the path that led to it from the Pearlmans' place and that would save her and Wyre walking all the way to the end of the terrace.

'Of course.' Mrs Pearlman stood and grabbed a bunch of keys. 'Follow me.' She led them down a crooked path, lifting the cord washing line as they went, and she unlocked the back gate. 'There is something you should both know, and I didn't want to alarm my husband with it as he can be a bit old-fashioned.' As the gate unlocked, Gina watched the officers and crime scene investigators working away. The woman grabbed Gina's arm. 'I think that Billie had more than one boyfriend. I don't like to tell my husband things like that, but fair play to her. She's young and having fun.'

'What makes you say that?'

'From our bedroom, I saw a man enter through the back gate. It was dark so I couldn't see what he looked like, but he went up to Billie and grabbed her. They were in a clinch of sorts before going into the house. I'm not sure if it was a passionate clinch or a little argumentative. It was hard to tell.'

'Could it have been her boyfriend?'

'No, this man wasn't as tall, and he was stockier. Either that or he had a thick coat on, maybe one of those puffer coats.'

'Can you describe him?' Wyre jotted down what the woman was saying.

Mrs Pearlman shook her head. 'I'm afraid I can't. It was too dark. All I saw were outlines under the moonlight.' Wyre raised her eyebrows, pleased with the information they were getting.

Gina enjoyed the slight breeze that caught the back of her hair. 'When was this?'

'Last night. I couldn't sleep. Sometimes, I sit on the upstairs window ledge and look out until I get tired again.'

'And what time was that?'

'Around eleven thirty. It had to have been then as I was back in bed by midnight, and I wasn't up for too long.'

'That's really helpful, thank you. Did you hear anything?'

'No, the window was closed, and I kept my earplugs in.'

Gina waved at the investigators working the scene.

'How long will they be here for?' Mrs Pearlman asked.

'Hopefully not too long.'

'I'll offer them a drink in a bit. It's so hot and they must be parched.' The dog began to yap from indoors. 'There's someone at the door. It must be Kayden's grandparents.' The woman hurried back through the door.

'We need to find the boyfriend and this other man urgently.' Gina wondered if jealousy was a motive with a new boyfriend and another man in the mix. She needed to interview both but first, she had to find out who they were.

Wyre made a note and closed her pad.

'We need to speak to Billie's parents, see if they can help us with a name. We also need to speak to the neighbour. What was her name again?'

Wyre flicked back a couple of pages. 'Meera.'

Gina felt as though she was trudging through treacle as she and Wyre went back to the house. It was all becoming too real now that Billie's parents had arrived and there weren't many things worse than seeing the distraught look on a parent's face after losing a child. Their heartache and the fact that they'd have to share such devastating news with Kayden made her think of her own granddaughter. It would break Gina if she was in the same position. She couldn't bear to imagine life without Hannah.

'You coming, guv?'

She didn't want to go back in. She didn't want to move any

closer to where the sadness was centred. Swallowing, she forced back the choking tears that wanted so badly to escape. She would ride through this funny stage she was going through, and she would do the only thing she could do to help. She had to find the evil person who killed the young mother who had her whole life ahead of her.

SIX

As Gina ended her call with Briggs, she glanced at Wyre. 'I've updated him on the case. He's preparing a press release.' They'd been back at the station only half an hour and Billie Reeves's father had already taken his wife and grandchild home, before coming back to speak with them.

'O'Connor has settled him in the family room.'

'Great. Let's get this done. Maybe Mr Reeves can shed some light on who one of these men are.'

As they walked along the corridor, passing the interview rooms, Gina couldn't stop thinking about Billie's mother's face as the woman wrapped Kayden in her arms. Confused by his grandmother's state, Kayden asked if he was going to their house for tea. Gina wondered if he knew what had happened to his mother now. She could only imagine how they were going to get through the next few days, and she hoped that the family liaison officer could offer them some comfort. She cleared her throat and gently opened the door. 'Mr Reeves.'

He went to stand. 'It's George.'

'It's okay, please stay seated, George.' Gina sat in the comfy chair opposite and Wyre sat beside her. Her colleague gave a sympathetic smile. The man's paunch reached over his knees and his loose shirt had unbuttoned by his belly. The lemon-coloured walls seemed too cheery for what they had to discuss.

'I can't believe that someone did this to her. Billie was so gentle, and everyone loved her. And Kayden... he didn't deserve this.' The man turned to face away, trying to hold his emotions back.

'We're really sorry. I can't begin to imagine what you're going through. Are you sure you're okay to speak with us right now?' Gina sat in hope that he wouldn't change his mind, but she could see how distressing it was for him. The constant fidgeting and the twiddling of fingers was making Gina uneasy, but she guessed it was his way of coping; a distraction so that he could think.

He ran his fingers through his full head of grey hair and stared at his feet. 'I want to speak to you. The sooner you catch whoever did this, the better.' He paused. 'I don't know how to feel, what to do. I left my wife to tell Kayden. I couldn't be there.' He snatched a tissue from the box and wiped his eyes. 'I'm a coward.'

'George, you are not a coward. You are here, now, doing something difficult and we appreciate exactly how hard this is for you.'

He exhaled. 'I'm sorry. I need to pull myself together. Put a brave face on it for my wife.'

The amount of times Gina heard this kind of talk from a man saddened her. His daughter had just been murdered and expressing strong emotions was a part of the process. 'You're entitled to your feelings. The anger, the grief – all of it. Your wife and Kayden will need you and you will need them too.'

'What is it you'd like to know?' He shook his upset away and sat up straight.

Wyre sat back and tilted her head.

Gina tucked her hair behind her ears and used the remote

to turn up the air conditioning a little. 'Can you start by telling us a little about Billie?'

'Anything?'

Gina nodded, trying to put the man at ease.

'She was always like a ray of sunshine, even as a girl. She'd dress up in thrown together costumes and force her sister to be in these funny plays that she'd written, and they'd perform them for us. It was all castles and fairy tales. She'd dress her sister up in quilt covers and her mother's old nets. They were delightful children. That's what Billie was good at, making people smile. All she ever wanted was to be a performer. When she left school, she worked at a holiday park as an entertainer for a few years before coming back home. Soon after, she met Kayden's father and accidentally became pregnant. With all of her ambitions, it should have seemed like it happened at the wrong time, but she was thrilled and couldn't wait to be a mother.' He went silent as if recalling the past.

'And after that?'

'We supported her in every way we could by finding her a house to rent and helping her get ready for the baby. She settled into parenthood with our support and a few months later, she declared that she wanted to set up her own business as an entertainer. She did children's parties mostly and she also has several candy carts that she keeps in our garage, which she sets up at weddings and functions.' He paused. 'Used to set up. I know she had it hard, making ends meet but she worked like a trooper. We last saw her a week ago and even then, she still lit up the room for us. She always had a smile. That was Billie.' He took a deep breath. 'Whoever took her life has taken one of the world's loveliest people. I'm not saying that because she's my daughter. Everyone who knew her would agree. I don't know how we're meant to get through this.' He shook his head.

Gina swallowed and exhaled under her breath. 'Can you tell us who Kayden's father is?'

'Shaun Brock. He's from Cleevesford but has never had anything to do with Kayden. Billie tried to get him involved but he went travelling for the first three years of the boy's life and he never got in touch when he was back. He's never given her a penny but it's not all about the money. Kayden is a wonderful child. I've tried to be there for him, be the father figure in many ways, but it will hurt him one day when he knows that his dad doesn't want to know him.'

'Could Billie have contacted him again?'

'I doubt that. He left the area about a year ago to work in Australia. As far as I'm aware he's miles away.' Gina watched as Wyre made a note to check on Shaun Brock's whereabouts.

Gina cleared her throat. 'Was Billie in a relationship?'

'No, she was happy being on her own. She said she didn't want to complicate her life. I tried to tell her that not everyone was a let-down like Shaun, but she wasn't having any of it. It was her job and her life to make everyone else happy but when it came to herself, I feel like she used that big smile as a disguise. She was lonely, I could tell. It saddened me that she wouldn't let her guard down and give others a chance. Me and her mother have been lucky in that we're so happy together. I wanted that for Billie, one day.'

Billie's father had no idea that she was seeing someone, possibly two people. Gina could understand Billie not telling her parents, especially if her relationships were brief or casual. It was more important to speak with her friends, they might be able to shed more light on who Billie was involved with. 'I know this is hard, but I would like to speak to Kayden with you present.' Gina wondered if he knew something or heard things that went on behind closed doors, but what she was asking was a lot. The boy would have just heard about his mother. He'd be distraught and confused, and Gina didn't want to make things worse.

'Can I call you after I've seen how he is? He's just finding out about his mother. It might not be a good time.'

'Of course. If you feel that he's not up to it, we understand. It just might help the investigation.'

Mr Reeves nodded. 'I know, and we want to help in every way we can, but I can't put that boy through any more.'

Gina noticed that it was getting late into the evening. She needed to hurry up and get the rest of her questions out. 'Can you tell me about Billie's friends?'

'She was friends with some of the other mums. They'd met during pregnancy and stayed close. I've met them a few times, mostly at Kayden's birthdays. There's Meera next door to Billie, lovely lady. Candice also lives close by, but Billie's best friend was Nadia. She lives in a huge house on Mockingbird Avenue. It's the first one you see as you turn into the road and it stands out, you can't miss it. She let Kayden have his fifth birthday party there, that's how I know. Me and Kathleen were invited.' Mr Reeves furrowed his brow. 'I don't like Nadia's husband.'

Gina sat up straight, suddenly feeling more focused. 'Why is that?'

He shrugged. 'It's just me, I think. Ignore me. I can be a miserable git sometimes.'

'Please, it might help us. It doesn't matter how irrelevant you feel it is, it might help us to know.'

He bit the insides of his cheek before speaking. 'I kept catching him looking at Billie, which just seemed odd.'

'In what way?'

'The other guys were standing by the barbeque drinking and cooking, but he sat alone. Just after Billie told all the children a story dressed up in this funny crocodile outfit, she left to get changed. Nadia's husband put his drink down and went to follow her in, but then he saw me looking and he went back to his drink. It's as if he was watching her or was going to go after her. I did ask Billie what was going on, but she laughed it off and said that I'd had too many beers. I know what I saw, and that man was behaving weirdly.'

'When was this?'

'Only a month ago, May the fifteenth.'

'Do you know his name?'

'No, sorry.'

'What does he look like?'

'Muscular, he plays rugby, I remember that much. He was throwing a rugby ball to the kids earlier that day, showing off a bit as he dived and rolled over the lawn. He was definitely looking at Billie. I don't care that she thought I'd just had a few too many. I know what I saw.'

'How tall is he?'

'I don't know. Taller than me but not huge. I'm five ten.'

'Is there anything else you can tell us that might help?'

'No. All I want to say is, please find who did this to Billie. They deserve to rot in hell. Nothing is ever going to be the same again.' He glanced at his phone. 'I need to go home. Kathleen needs me.'

Gina stood. 'Thank you so much for coming. I know this must have been hard.'

'Do you have children?' He stood and pressed his lips together.

Gina nodded. 'I have a daughter in her twenties and a granddaughter too.'

'Make sure you tell them how much you love them.'

Gina nodded and bit her bottom lip. That was something she hadn't done for a long time. When this case was over, she needed to give Hannah a call and arrange to see Gracie. A wash of sadness flashed through her. Their mother-daughter relationship hadn't always been straightforward. They'd had their fall-outs, mostly over Gina's avoidance of talking about Hannah's deceased father but Gina couldn't bear to talk about the man who had been so cruel to her, and she couldn't bear to see his dead body at the bottom of the stairs in her mind. Having a daughter with him made her past impossible to forget, which is why it was easier not to call Hannah sometimes.

She pushed everyone in her life away, including her daughter and Briggs. In the end, they all found happiness away from her.

Wyre nudged past to show Mr Reeves out, while Gina fell back onto the chair and dropped the file on the table. A tear began to burst from the corner of one eye. She didn't deserve to be sad. Mr Reeves deserved to be sad, he'd lost his daughter. Gina had never felt like more of a fraud. She heard Briggs's voice booming down the corridor as he spoke about the press release. She wiped the tear away. She hated how emotional she was feeling. He couldn't see her like this.

She pulled her buzzing phone out of her pocket. 'Bernard?'

'Hi, Gina. We're still working the scene, but I thought I'd let you know that you can search the house in the morning. We're hoping to have everything we need by six a.m.'

'Thank you. Is it still going to take that long?'

'You wouldn't believe how much stuff there is and how many prints are on surfaces. We're literally bumping into each other every time we move in this house. If we stop, it will never get done. There are also smears of blood throughout the house.'

'Did Billie cause those smears?'

'No, she died in the kitchen which is why we need to preserve the scene.'

'I may see you first thing then if you're still there. Did you find a phone?'

'It's odd, but no. There are no phones, no tablets, no laptops, nothing.' He paused to allow it to sink in.

'So, whoever was there, took them.' That was a blow to the case.

'I best go, I'm being called to help. The photos should be with you now.'

'Okay, thank you for that.' He hung up.

Billie Reeves ran a business, there was no way she'd be without a phone at a bare minimum. Gina logged on to Facebook and searched for Billie Reeves. Billie's Parties and Candy Carts came up straight away. Gina checked out the business information and, as suspected, there was a mobile number listed.

SEVEN

NADIA

Nadia lay next to William in his bed, taking the scent of his hair in. She almost mourned for his baby smell as it hit her. He was growing so fast and one day, she wouldn't be able to lie like this and read him a story. She shivered as she thought of poor Kayden, he'd never experience that closeness again.

'Has something happened? You look sad and Dev's mummy was crying. It upset Dev so I looked after him and let him go in the playhouse first.'

She hugged him and kissed his head, touched at how kind and thoughtful her little boy was. 'It's going to be okay, honey. Just go to sleep and we'll talk in the morning.' There was no way she could face telling William that his friend's mum was no longer with them, and she wasn't ever going to tell him that she was murdered. Her innocent son had never come across such horror, and she wanted it to stay that way. She wondered how long it would be before his friends at school talked and she had to explain things she didn't want to talk about, or even think about.

Pulling the thin sheet over his clammy body, she forced a smile as she took in his perfect skin and his tiny porcelain white teeth. She couldn't imagine being suddenly taken from him, like Billie had been taken from Kayden. Curling up next to him, she lay there stroking his eyes until his breathing deepened and within moments, the busy day of play had caught up with her son as he fell into a deep slumber. As his short, sweet breaths tickled her neck, she stared at the lit-up doll's house on the large table against the wall, the one that her own father built for her, and all she wanted to do was go back to a week ago when she was playing with William. They were pretending that the daddy doll was making breakfast and it was fun. Life was fun. But now, a dark shadow was hanging over them all.

She glanced at her watch. It was almost midnight. Slowly, she dangled one leg off William's bed, then she turned onto her back and followed with the other leg over the edge of the bed. He made a slight groan so she remained as still as she could until he was once again breathing deeply. She grabbed Dino, his favourite soft toy, and slipped it under his arm before creeping out of the room, hoping that he'd remain asleep.

As she reached the bottom step, Ed held out a glass of rosé and she took it. 'Where have you been? You didn't answer your phone.' She shook her head. 'I needed you. My friend has just been murdered.' Her bottom lip trembled. 'You should have been here.'

'You're right but I'm here now. I got your message.'

'But you didn't call me back.'

'I'm so sorry for not answering my phone, love, I was driving. Come here.' He wrapped an arm around her.

She sunk into his warmth even though she didn't believe him. 'You weren't driving all afternoon and evening.' A tear sprung from one of her eyes.

'Hey, look at me.' She glanced up and looked into his warm eyes. 'There was an accident on the motorway. It's been chaos on the roads and my phone was also dead at the time. I'm here now.' He kissed her on the head before grabbing the bottle of wine from the kitchen island and leading her out into the garden.

Nadia took a swig of the cold wine. 'I can't believe what's happened. I'll never see her again.' The patio was lit up with fairy lights and the garden that was busy with playing children earlier was now quiet, except for a distant barking dog. They sat, with only the sound of the trickling water feature to fill the void of their own silence as he decided not to say anything. Ed was never good when it came to matters of the heart and right now, that really wound her up. The glass she gripped was itching to be smashed on the patio. That would get a reaction out of him. She wanted him to see how torn up she was.

Nadia's hand trembled around the stem of the glass as she wondered if he had another life going on somewhere. He never touched her any more and he didn't seem to talk to her much either. It was as if they were fulfilling a function, respectable mummy and daddy in a respectable house with respectable jobs. She wondered if that's what everyone did. She wasn't feeling the love and more than anything tonight, she needed love, understanding, and someone to talk to.

'Does anyone know what happened to Billie?'

She shook her head and let out a sob. 'No. All I know is she was murdered in her own home. One of the neighbours called Meera and told her. I keep scrolling through the local news to see if there are any updates but, nothing.' She paused. 'I saw her this morning, when we dropped the kids off at school. She was fine, then...' Loud sobs filled the night air.

Ed took the glass of wine off her and placed it on the table. 'I'm an idiot and I'm sorry. I should have made sure my phone was charged and I should have been here. I love you and I'm here now.'

'But you're not,' she wailed. 'It never feels like you're here.'

She wiped her damp cheek with her hand.

'Come on, don't be like that. You're upset. You're lashing out.'

'Too right, I'm upset. Meera couldn't even go home. She went to stay at her mum's. She was scared. I mean, what if it was a random attack, like a burglary that went wrong? What if it happens to us? We're all scared, and you weren't here.'

Ed placed his wine on the table and unexpectedly hugged her. Maybe their marriage wasn't the shambles she thought it was. 'I won't let anything happen to us. You and William mean the world to me. Anyone tries to come here and hurt either of you, I will literally kill them.'

She pulled away, taking in his square jaw, his shiny dark hair and handsome features and she wondered if she could trust him. 'Were you with someone else today?'

He let go. 'Not this again. No, there is only you. I wish you'd trust me.'

'I saw.'

'You saw what?' He swigged his wine down in one go and topped up his glass again.

'The way you looked at Billie.'

He slammed the glass on the table, making it shake. 'You're deluded.'

Nadia shook her head. He got off on telling her things like that all the time. 'I know what I saw. She was my best friend, and I could tell that something was off. What have you been hiding from me?'

'Best friend! That's what you call it. If she was your best friend, you shouldn't have done what you did. No wonder she seemed off.' He stood. 'You let her down and you've only got yourself to blame, but it's easier to blame me, isn't it?'

Tears erupted down Nadia's cheeks. He was right. It was her fault. Maybe she only saw what she wanted to see, allowing her own paranoia to get the better of her. Billie was perfection in every way and to top it off, she was funny and charming, a real people magnet. She glanced around her big house and at her handsome husband, but all she really craved was to have a personality that lit up a room. But no, Nadia was practical. She organised the school fete with the teacher, she attended PTA meetings and helped with sports days and school trips. She knew how to throw a social event, but she didn't shine.

Fluffball jumped onto her lap and began to purr as she nudged her furry head under Nadia's chin.

Ed began rooting in his pocket. 'This is where I was, and you royally screwed the surprise up.' He threw down a piece of paper folded into quarters.

She reached over the cat and opened it up. 'Hot tubs.'

He nodded. 'It was meant to be a surprise. I was going to get it installed next week while you were out, but it's ruined. All because you don't trust me. That's where I was when I didn't answer my phone. Do you know how exhausting it is, never being trusted?' He grabbed the receipt and stormed back into the house. The patio lit up as their bedroom light went on.

She checked her phone and there was a message from Meera.

We should have kept our mouths shut. I'm a horrible friend. X

Meera would never feel as bad as Nadia did. Best friends should be trusted, and Nadia had let Billie down. She had started it. She wished Billie was here, right now, so she could hug her friend and tell her how truly sorry she was.

She nudged Fluffball off her lap and grabbed her glass and the half bottle of wine before going in and locking up. She dragged the bifold doors closed and made doubly sure they were locked. As hard as she tried, she couldn't get rid of the image in her mind. All she could see was blood.

As she turned each light off and crept up the stairs, she stopped to listen outside William's room, and she heard a shuffle. Gently pushing his door, she watched as he kneeled in front of the doll's house, talking in his babyish voice as he marched the little figures around.

He grabbed the miniature plastic crocodile toy that Ed had bought him and placed it in the kitchen before making screaming and crying noises, then he went back to the boy model in the bedroom. 'Quick, hide, Kayden.' William pulled the blanket over the boy doll, before making crying sounds again from the crocodile. Nadia watched as a shiver ran through her body.

'William, what are you doing?'

'Mummy.' Startled, he dropped the crocodile on the floor. 'I was playing.'

'Is the doll, Kayden?'

William bit his bottom lip and stared up at her nodding.

'Why was Kayden hiding?'

William stood and walked over to his bed and yawned. 'I'm tired now.'

'William, why was Kayden hiding?'

He grabbed Dino and got into bed. She ran over and kneeled beside him, stroking his head. 'He wasn't hiding from anything. I was just playing.'

'William, please tell me. I know there's something upsetting you. Mummy can tell.'

He ducked under his sheet.

She pulled it down to expose his blue eyes.

'Kayden said his mummy told him not to tell.'

'It's okay, you can tell me though.'

William pressed his lips together for a few seconds while weighing up whether to talk. 'His mummy tells him he can't go downstairs when he hears her screaming. It makes him frightened.'

Nadia kissed him on the head. 'Thank you for telling me, William.' She grabbed a book, one about a boy who loves eating cake and William's eyes lit up as she began to read. With each word a silent tear fell as she comforted her son. All she wanted to do was take his nightmares away, as for her own, she deserved every one of them.

There had to be something in what Kayden had told William. Her mind whirred. Even the children knew something was going on. As her mind's eye led her back to Billie, all she could now imagine was her friend's screams as Kayden cowered in his bedroom.

EIGHT

Thursday, 16 June

PC Kapoor was already back at her post as Bernard's team were taking the last of their boxes out of Billie Reeves's house. While waiting to get the go-ahead, Gina stared into the distance. Most of the residents remained asleep. Curtains were still closed, and the streets were empty, a far cry from what they'd look like in about an hour and a half.

Gina buzzed down the other windows in her car and nudged the empty burger box onto the passenger floor. That had been the extent of her evening meal, eaten in a parking space outside a takeaway, alone. The smell of cold grease made her stomach churn, along with what she'd seen. Rosemary had been coming out of a nearby house with a man. She'd watched the woman in her rear-view mirror as she looked into his eyes as they left, one hand brushing his before the woman had checked her phone and left him. The way her finger tickled his hand was not that of a brother saying a friendly goodbye to a sister. She'd come so close to calling Briggs, but refrained. He'd hate her.

For a moment, she closed her eyes and took in the dawn chorus as she processed everything. The birds had no idea of the tragedy that they were dealing with and continued their morning in their usual way. In fact, the rest of the world would continue to work, play, or do whatever it had planned for the day. But not Gina, Gina needed to find the person who killed Billie and she needed to be there for Briggs when his relationship fell apart. Before she could let the crime scene photos get under her skin, she opened her eyes again. She'd spent all night studying them for the tiniest of clues and all night that word, slut, had played on her mind. The crudeness of it, the nastiness and how it was written – someone hated Billie and they killed her. Her murder was as personal as it got.

She flinched at the bang on the top of her car. 'Guv, the team are finishing up. We can go in.' Detective Sergeant Jacob Driscoll stood on the pavement, his hair neatly parted at the side and his face looking brighter than usual.

She stepped out of her car and tried to brush away the slight creases on her black trousers. 'How did things go yesterday?'

'Everyone is really pleased at how Jennifer is doing. She'll be back on the job soon and I know she's missing it. She hates sitting around at home all day, but I keep telling her, she needs to do everything by the book and return at full strength.'

'And how are you?' Gina knew that losing the baby had taken its toll on the couple.

'I've done a lot of thinking and all I know is I love Jen more than anything.' He took a deep breath. 'We've been planning the wedding so happy thoughts.' That was her instruction to not ask him any more. He knew she was there for him if he needed to talk. 'Did you get dressed in a hurry, guv?'

She grimaced and then checked herself. Damn, she'd buttoned her shirt up wrong. Turning around to face the car, she quickly put it right. 'Thanks for that. It was a long evening, and I spent all night ploughing through the photos that Bernard sent through. On top of that, I have a rabbit to look after. You don't want a rabbit, do you? Thumper is lovely but my cat isn't keen on him.'

'Erm, let me get back to you. I'll speak to Jennifer.' He paused. 'I saw the photos too, nasty.'

She nodded. 'They're leaving the house. Right, we need to go in and do a thorough search. Is Wyre on her way?'

'Yes, and here she is with O'Connor.'

Wyre and O'Connor stepped out with a pair of gloves and shoe covers. 'Right, are we going in?'

Gina nodded and led the way to the house.

'Back door's open, guv. I have the key to lock up after.' PC Kapoor held it up.

Gina led the way and before entering they gloved up and covered their shoes. Opening the door, the smell hit Gina first. Metallic, mixed with old food and sweat. The blood patch on the kitchen floor looked to be dried around the edges but still sticky in the middle. She stopped and stared at the back wall. Above a photo of Billie and Kayden, that word stood out like a beacon. She leaned in for a closer look at the photo. The young mother had her arms wrapped around her child from behind. Several of Billie's advertising flyers were piled up on the worktop offering story reading, play production, candy carts. She glanced at the smaller wording and noticed an email address as the main contact.

'Right, I'll take her bedroom. Jacob, you take the kitchen. Wyre, take the lounge and O'Connor, the second bedroom and bathroom. Call out if you find anything, especially a phone. I have her number and we're hoping to be able to get her phone records soon but getting our hands on her phone could get us there sooner.'

As everyone set about their jobs, Gina stepped out of the

tiny kitchen to the equally cramped lounge. Against the back wall there was a fireplace and beside it, two recesses that were filled with shelving – again there were more photos of Billie and her son. Boxes of toys leaned precariously at the one end and a two-seater settee almost filled the lounge. She hurried past the front door, stepping over a load of clutter and up the stairs. Straight ahead she could see the open door to the bathroom. She followed the landing, and the first room was Kayden's. Blue walls were broken up by a castle mural that looked like it had been hand-painted. Gina continued past and pushed open the door to Billie's bedroom, the place where hopefully Gina was going to discover more about her. Clothes littered every bit of floor space, along with books, belts and bits of costume.

She hurried over to the bed, taking in the unmade state. On the bedside table, several scented candles were lined up, most of them almost burned down. She turned away from the sickly vanilla smell. Opening the first drawer, Gina spotted a large box of condoms that looked to be half used. Underneath it, a book. She slid it out and saw that it was a battered copy of *Black Beauty*. She flicked the pages in the hope that a clue would drop out, but nothing did. She placed the book back. Feeling around the drawer, nothing was standing out. Several drawers later, Gina started on the first wardrobe. It was bursting full of standard day clothing – jeans, flowery tops, jumpers, shoes and a few dresses. Gina ran her hands over the different materials and in the pockets. The uneasy feeling of invading another's space during a search never went away. A dead woman's life was contained in the cupboards, in the house. There was nothing extravagant about Billie, judging by the fraying clothes she owned. She threw a half-open packet of chewing gum onto the bed and a couple of crumpled supermarket receipts.

A pink shoebox caught Gina's eye. Reaching down, she placed it on the bed and lifted the lid off. Several exercise books were stacked up. Gina eagerly snatched one up in the hope that it was a diary, but it was nothing more than a work ledger where Billie had recorded her incomings and outgoings manually. All the books were the same. Money in, money out. Nothing unusual except that there was more money going out than coming in. Reaching under the bed, she pulled open a drawer that was full of sexy lingerie. After rooting amongst the fancy stockings and bras, she pushed her hands deeper underneath, and she grabbed a pile of paperwork. Flicking through it, she could see the loose pages were bills and lots of them, all outstanding and all with late payment charges added. A wash of sadness came over Gina as she saw the itemised credit card. Billie had been buying food on it from discount supermarkets, not buying luxuries. She popped them in a bag to examine further after they'd been logged into evidence.

She hurried over to the other wardrobe and was greeted with a bright array of costumes and on the top shelf, boxes of stage make-up and accessories. She began to rifle through the pockets and pouches, searching for anything. After going through each one, she placed them on the bed to make sure she didn't miss any. Nothing in the princess dress, nothing in the Red Riding Hood cape. The mermaid tail was empty, and Rapunzel's hair held no secrets. She grabbed the crocodile suit and inside there was a tiny zip-up pocket. Sliding it open, Gina stopped when her fingers felt a piece of paper.

Slowly opening up the page, what she saw written on it gave her the chills.

SLUT

NINE

'Guv. The neighbour has just pulled up,' Jacob called.

Gina placed the note and the ledgers into an evidence bag and hurried down, passing them to Wyre as she reached the bottom. 'Could you log this in.' Wyre nodded and Jacob followed Gina out.

The young woman leaned into the back seat of the car to unbuckle the child. 'Dev, grab your bag.' He stepped out onto the pavement, book bag in hand, hair sticking up on the one side like he'd just been pulled out of bed. The boy yawned and rubbed sleep out of his eyes.

Gina hurried over with Jacob on her tail. 'Hello, I'm DI Harte, this is DS Driscoll. May we speak to you?'

The woman nodded. 'Of course. I'll need a minute to sort my son out.'

Nodding, Gina stood to the side as the woman ushered the young boy into her house. 'Dev, can you go up and play in your room? I'll be with you in a few minutes, and we can get ready for school together.'

'Mummy, I'm hungry.'

The woman rooted around in her bag and pulled out a

banana. She ruffled her son's hair and smiled at him as she passed it to him. 'Have this for now.'

The boy grimaced at the offering, took it and stomped up the stairs.

'Please, come through.'

They followed the woman through the lounge and into the long but narrow extended kitchen, a far cry from Billie's property. So many people had modernised and extended the old town centre terraced houses. The morning sun bounced off the worktop, reaching right through the skylight above.

'Please take a stool at the worktop and I'll put the kettle on. I really need a coffee. Would you like one?' The woman struggled to spoon the coffee into a cup with her shaking hands.

Gina nodded and so did Jacob. 'Thank you. There was an incident next door, yesterday—'

The woman stopped and began speaking rapidly. 'I know, which is why I stayed at my mother's last night. Joanna next door called me and told me what happened to Billie. I was with friends, and Billie was meant to join us. We're all in shock. I can't believe anyone would hurt Billie.' She took a deep breath, like she was holding back a sob.

'I'm sorry about your friend and I can't imagine what you're all going through. Can I please take your full name?'

'Meera Gupta. Call me Meera.'

'Do you live alone?'

She nodded. 'I lost my husband two years ago.' The woman glanced at a family photo on the wall.

'I'm really sorry to hear that.' Gina took in the young woman before her who looked to be in her late twenties. So young to be a widow.

Meera turned to spoon coffee into the cups. 'I still miss him every day. It's a good job I have my boy to think about. He keeps me going. Milk, sugar?'

'No, thank you. As it comes, for both of us.'

She poured water into the coffee and the aroma made Gina's mouth water. 'We can't believe what happened to Billie. She was such a lovely, wonderful person.' She paused. 'I didn't want to stay here last night. The thought that someone could do that to her right under the noses of everyone living around here scared the life out of me. I mean, I was probably here, in this house while it was happening. I keep thinking of her being attacked, trying to scream while I sat here sipping lemonade with the music on. I could have helped her; I should have heard something.' She grabbed a piece of kitchen roll and wiped her eyes. 'Was it a burglary?'

'That's what we're trying to find out and we were hoping that you could help us.'

She sipped the hot liquid. 'I wish I could, but I don't know anything. I'm kicking myself now for not checking on her, but I thought she was in her house, ill. She could have been dying and I didn't check on her. Why didn't I walk Kayden to the door and knock? It would have taken a few seconds, that's all, but as usual I was in a hurry. She needed me and I let her down.'

Jacob pulled out a notepad and Gina tucked her hair behind her ears. 'Meera, you couldn't have known. When did you last see Billie?'

'Yesterday. We walked home from school together. She said her head was pounding and she looked peaky.'

'What time was that?'

'Around two thirty.'

'Do the children normally finish that early?'

The woman's long black hair almost dangled in her coffee as she leaned over the breakfast bar. 'There was a school play yesterday and it finished about two. We had a glass of squash and the children whose parents came to watch were allowed to leave early with them. We left and walked home together.'

'How did Billie seem?'

'Quiet, I guess. Like I said, she wasn't feeling well. She

gets... got migraines now and again and when she did, I'd let Kayden come over and play with Dev to give her a break. She went in and shut the curtains. I assumed she was lying in the dark, in the lounge. That's what she normally does when she gets an attack. The boys played in my back garden for a bit but then Dev and I had to go to my mother's, so they hung out around the front garden while I was getting ready to leave. That was about three, maybe. I was hoping that hearing them play would stir Billie in readiness for Kayden going home.'

Gina waited for Jacob to catch up and when he stopped writing, she continued, 'Did you see Billie before you left?'

She shook her head. 'No, I watched Kayden run through the alleyway into their garden. I should have walked him to the door.' She paused and bit her bottom lip. 'Did he see her?' She placed a hand on her chest and stared at Gina as she waited for an answer.

'No, it appears that he came back out the front and sat on the kerb. Mrs Pearlman found him, and she then saw Billie.'

Meera exhaled. 'It should have been me that found her. Poor Joanna. Kayden must have hidden in the alleyway, waiting for me to go.' She sniffed and turned away. 'What if he'd gone into the house and found her? Where is he? Is he okay?'

'He's safe. He's with his grandparents.'

'I should have checked on Billie earlier. Maybe I could have found her in time and called an ambulance.' Meera began biting the skin around the edge of her thumb.

'Or you could have been hurt too. You couldn't have known.' Gina always encountered guilt. The guilt of people wishing they'd done things differently, been there more, picked up a phone and made a call – anything. 'Did you see anyone acting suspiciously either around here or by the school?'

She picked up her drink and hugged it close to her chest. 'No. The children were running around screaming and playing so all I could hear was them.'

'Was Billie seeing anyone?'

'Yes.'

'We don't have a name for him. Do you know who he is?'

Meera nodded. 'She introduced us a few weeks ago when I saw him on the doorstep. I don't think they're that serious, but I do know he works as a gardener. I've seen his van around here. Nathan Merry Gardening Services.'

They had a name and a business. Gina knew he'd be easy to trace now. The sooner they could find him, the better. 'When did you last see him?'

Meera scrunched up her nose. 'A few days ago, maybe it was the weekend. I think he stayed on Saturday, but I couldn't swear to it.'

'Did Billie ever talk to you about anything or anyone who might have worried her?'

Looking down at the floor, Meera hesitated. 'No. We mostly talked about school and the children. We'd both been a bit busy lately and we hadn't spoken much. I can't believe I'm never going to see her again.' Her lips trembled as she took another sip of coffee.

'Are you sure? She never confided in you, or mentioned something that might have been worrying her?'

Meera's son interrupted them. 'Mummy, can I come down now?'

'Five minutes, sweetie.'

The boy stomped in the room above.

'Well, there might have been something. It's not something she said.'

'What was that?'

'The night before last, around midnight, I heard what I thought was Billie shouting from inside her house. I thought she might be on the phone, and it was only once so I ignored it and went back to sleep.'

Gina thought back to what Mrs Pearlman had said, about

the man she saw from her bedroom window just before midnight.

'Maybe she was having an argument with Nathan.'

'What makes you say that? Did you recognise his voice, or did you see him?' From what Mrs Pearlman had said, it wasn't her boyfriend, but it was late and dark.

'No, I just heard her shouting and I thought she was arguing with him. Billie did that. When she met someone, it's like she'd sabotage the relationship. I think it stems back to Kayden's father, so I don't blame her for being wary of men. I think I'd be the same. He left her pregnant and he's no help. She struggled to trust. I don't know much but what I do know is, not long after she'd start dating someone, she'd end up dumping them. When I heard her shout, I thought she was dumping her boyfriend. I asked her about it the next day, but she didn't want to talk about it.'

Gina smiled sympathetically. 'Where did you go after visiting your mother yesterday?'

'To a friend's house. We had a meeting to discuss who was going to do what at the school fete. Billie was meant to come but I told them she was ill. We had the shock of our lives when my neighbour called to tell me what had happened to Billie.' Meera wiped her tears away. 'I was too scared to come home so when I left my friend's house about eight, I went straight to my mother's and stayed there.'

'Which friend did you visit?'

'Nadia Anderson.'

Gina had her name down and intended to visit as soon as possible.

'She lives at One Mockingbird Avenue, just in case you need an address.'

'Thank you. Is there anything else you can tell us that you think might help?'

Meera looked out through the patio doors into the garden. 'I know Billie was in a lot of debt. I shouldn't have known but I overheard someone visiting the house from a debt collection agency and I think I heard her talking about weekly payments. I feel awful for listening through the open window, as I know what a private person she was. I also saw her at the food bank, queueing outside the church but that was a few weeks ago. She didn't know I saw her, and I didn't mention it as I knew how proud she was. I was in the café on the high street when I spotted her.' She checked her watch. 'I have to get Dev ready for school, then I have to go to work. I don't feel like going after what has happened, but I'd be letting my colleagues down. We're really short-staffed at the moment.' She blew her nose and rubbed her eyes red. 'I don't know how I'm going to get through today.'

'What is it you do?'

'I'm a care manager, which is why I need to go in. I have a team to organise.'

Gina pulled a card from her pocket. 'If you think of anything else that might help, however small or irrelevant seeming, please call me straight away.'

The woman took the card with her slender fingers. 'Am I safe staying here? I have to ask because I have my boy to think about.'

Gina's mind flitted to the blood-red writing on Billie's kitchen wall. Whoever killed Billie had a personal motive, but Gina would never forgive herself if anything happened to the woman standing in front of her. 'Are you able to stay with your mother for a few more days?'

She nodded. 'I think I'd rather do that. I'll pack a few things. Do you need the address?'

Gina nodded. 'That would be really helpful in case we need to speak to you again.'

The woman scribbled it down on a scrap of paper and handed it to Gina. 'I didn't want to say anything as it seems disrespectful. Billie would be really hurt if she knew I was going to tell you this but... Nathan wasn't the only man in Billie's life.'

'Who is the other man?'

'I don't know. I just heard footsteps and a male voice coming from the back garden on a few occasions as she hurries him in through the back door. It's always late at night. Nathan knocks at the front door, so I thought that was odd.'

'When was this?'

'I've heard this a few times. I can't remember when. Over the past few weeks, I'd say.'

'What did you hear them talking about?'

'I didn't. Whatever was said was in hushed tones. I just know the voice was male.' Meera took a deep breath. 'Please catch whoever did this. Billie deserves justice.' Meera went to say something, then stopped. 'I have to get to work.'

'Was there something else?'

'No. I have to go, or I'll be late.' The look in Meera's eyes told her that she had something else to say.

'Meera, someone murdered your friend. If you know something that might help us, please say.'

'I don't.' She looked away and grabbed her handbag.

As they finished up, Gina couldn't stop thinking about the other man, the caller who came around the back when it was dark. Who was Billie keeping secret from everyone? So secret, he had to sneak in when Billie thought everyone was in bed. Maybe Nadia Anderson or Nathan Merry would have the answer.

'Guv.' Wyre held up an opened email so that Gina could read it. Next stop, they were going to Billie's parents' house to speak to Kayden. A flutter of nerves made Gina stumble over her words as she wrapped up the interview with Meera. A part of her couldn't wait to see if Kayden had something to say that might push the investigation forward, but another part of her was picturing this scared and sad little vulnerable dot of a boy who had just found out that his mother was no longer with him. He lived with his mother. He'd see whatever was going on in her life from the inside.

He might know who the other man was, the one who arrived at Billie's close to midnight on the eve of her murder.

TEN

NADIA

Nadia dropped her keys in the bowl on the sideboard and ran up the stairs into William's room. Opening up the front to the doll's house, she sat down cross-legged and took in the scene that her son had left. The crocodile had been left leaning upright against the toy cooker, and the little boy doll was still under the bed sheet. She pulled the cover back, took the doll and held him tight. She could have done so much more but like everyone else, she stood by and watched as Billie went downhill and Kayden was left scared. She closed her eyes and gave a thought to Billie.

She recalled the conversation she had with Billie a while back, just after they'd dropped their children at school. 'Let me help you,' Nadia had said to her friend.

Billie shrugged her off. 'No, I'm sick of people pitying me. I see the way everyone stares when I drop Kayden off, and I can't handle it. They need to get a life, seriously.'

'Who's staring at you?' She remembered the sinking guilty feeling that had threatened to make her throw her breakfast up, right there and then outside the school. People were staring and Nadia was clearly lying by trying to convince her otherwise.

Besides, they'd soon get bored of staring. That's how rumours work. Next week, it would be something and someone else. Guilt began to reach into her core. The rumours were true.

'Her.' Billie pointed to one of the random mums. 'And her. All of them.' The mums stared in disgust.

Nadia remembered grabbing Billie's arm as she turned to hurry away. 'Billie, stop.' Billie shrugged her off, but she chased her.

'They know, they all know. I can tell. You promised you wouldn't tell anyone. I trusted you.'

'Billie, you can trust me. It wasn't me. No one knows, I promise. They were looking because you seem upset, that's all.'

'I heard them whispering, thinking that I couldn't hear. The thing is, I only told you.'

'Maybe someone saw something. It wasn't me.'

Billie shook her head as she glanced back and forth, taking on one last stare from someone rushing past with a pushchair. 'You're a liar. I should never have trusted you.'

As Billie nudged her to hurry around the corner, Candice almost bumped into them, running late as usual with little Poppy being dragged along. Her friend with the long red nails and fiery hair stopped and stared, open-mouthed.

'You know too, don't you?'

Candice was an awful liar. Nadia couldn't squirm out of the situation now. She knew that Billie would see from the falsely raised eyebrows and pressed lips that Candice knew too.

First, Nadia broke Billie's confidence and now Billie had been murdered. Her friend died knowing that Nadia betrayed her. Shame burned her cheeks. It was only a matter of time before the police spoke to her and she'd have to face up to what she'd done.

She dropped the little boy doll and left it lying on William's bedroom floor as she hurried out of the room, slamming the door as she left.

'What's going on? I was trying to have a lie-in?' Ed came out of their bedroom with a white towel wrapped around his middle.

'I was just tidying William's bedroom.'

'Great. I was hoping for a relaxing day off and now I'm up at the crack of dawn. I thought you had clients this morning.'

'I did but I cancelled them. I can't go to work, not after what happened to Billie.'

'No, of course.' He wrapped his arms around her and stroked the back of her neck. As she laid her head in the comfort of his chest, she felt him harden under the towel. 'Maybe we could both go back to bed?'

She pushed him away like she had done a lot recently. 'My best friend has just been murdered. What bit about that don't you understand?' It didn't help that she didn't trust him.

He held his hands up. 'I don't understand why you've spent the last couple of weeks bitching about Billie and now you call her your best friend because she's been murdered. I don't understand why you always tried to help her when it was clear she didn't want your help. You interfere, that's your problem. You talk too much to the gossips at the school gate. You add up two and two and get a total of five.'

'My adding up was just fine. I think I should tell the police.'

He grabbed her arm, sinking his nails into her skin. 'Leave well alone, okay.'

She swallowed. 'But—'

'Shh.' He placed his firm hand over her mouth. 'You know it will be you they'll come for.' She landed on the floor as he pushed her backwards onto the landing. Tears began to run down her cheeks. 'Don't be such a bloody drama queen.' He rolled his eyes and walked away. The worst of it was, he was right. The police couldn't be involved. She had too much to lose. Ed was wrong about one thing. Her adding up of the situation was correct but she wasn't going to try to convince him of that. It had come straight out of Billie's mouth, and it should have gone no further. Her heart ached. If only she could go back in time and make everything right.

Nadia swallowed down her sobs. What had she started? Billie was right that day. Everyone had been looking at her. They were all gossiping and sneering, all because Nadia, Billie's best friend, couldn't keep her big mouth shut. Now the world knew, and it was only a matter of time before the police did.

She heard the shower creak and then start running, so she ran into the bedroom and grabbed Ed's work phone. He had been looking at Billie at Kayden's birthday party, she didn't care what he said. Even dressed in a crocodile suit, Billie looked hot. Every man there was staring. She tried another password, but it wasn't right. Maybe she could wait until he was asleep and use his thumb to unlock it. Either she had his thumb or a password. One thing she was certain of, she'd seen a message flash up on her husband's phone from Billie only yesterday. If she asked him, he'd simply deny it, then delete the message. He couldn't know that she knew about the message. She had to find out what was in it. What she did know for sure was that Ed was capable of violence and Billie had been murdered. She had wronged her friend but that spurred her on more to do the right thing. She toiled with telling the police, but she had to be certain because Ed would bring her down in an instant. She wasn't going to let the police go through her things and her life, turning everything upside down when it might all be for nothing. The other mums would never look at her in the same way again if Ed was hauled in for questioning or they found— She put her deepest darkest secret out of her mind. It wasn't going to come to that as long as she toed the line.

'I'm sorry, Billie,' she whispered, dropping the phone back on Ed's bedside table as he turned the shower off. Her husband was a liar about everything. That hot tub receipt proved nothing.

ELEVEN

George and Kathleen Reeves's house stood proud on the roadside. Double fronted, with a picket fence, and a neatly mown lawn with flower beds. Gina imagined a young Billie performing plays with her sister in this house, maybe even on the lawn when the sun shone like it was this morning. She pictured the little girl full of creative energy, lighting up the faces of everyone she came across with her zest for life. Then she pictured her bleeding body lying on the cramped kitchen floor.

A hand appeared underneath a cream lacy voile that covered the inside of the large bay window and a slim blonde woman frowned before dropping it again. Jacob pulled up behind her and stepped out into the morning heat, before mooching in the boot of his car. As she waited, she checked her phone and saw another update. The appeal had gone out and anytime now it would hit the radio and TV. Briggs had sent a separate message. She placed her finger on it. Her stomach began to churn as it opened in full.

We need to talk when you get back to the station.

That's all? We need to talk. About what? About the case? About them? About her work, the vacant look that she'd been displaying for weeks? Maybe he knew about Rosemary meeting up with another man. Could she broach the subject? He might want to confide in her about leaving Rosemary. *Don't get your hopes up, Gina.* She shook her head, hating not knowing what the message meant.

There were no niceties in the message, no kisses that she'd become fond of over the years. It hurt more than she could ever have imagined. Wyre had mentioned that they were all a bit concerned for her. Had that concern reached Briggs? She didn't need his pity. Her face flushed hot. Not now, she couldn't have a hot flush right here, outside the victim's parents' house. She bent over and caught a glimpse of her face in the side mirror. Yes, her cheeks were burning away like beacons and her neck was prickling like mad, a reminder yet again that she could never have given Briggs what he wanted. She opened the car door and got back in, immediately turning on the ignition and air conditioning that had just been pumping out ice-cold air. Thankfully, it was still cold. She leaned back, trying not to panic and make things worse.

She flinched as Jacob stood by the window. 'You okay, guv?'

Nodding, she turned off the engine and got out of the car. 'Yes, I was just hot. Let's go.' As they approached the house, the sticky dampness Gina could feel under her armpits made her flush again with embarrassment. The blonde woman opened the door. 'Mrs Reeves?'

She nodded. 'Call me Kath.' Her nose was red and scabbed underneath from all the blowing and wiping.

'Kath, thank you for calling us this morning. May we come in?'

She nodded and opened the door fully, exposing a hallway that led up some stairs. She led Gina and Jacob out of the kitchen patio doors and onto a small, slabbed area in a large cottage garden. They all sat around the glass table.

George poked his head around, glasses balanced on his head. 'I'll stay with Kayden, love. Are you okay?' There was a girl in the kitchen, pouring a glass of pop and Gina thought how much she looked like Billie, except her hair was a dirty blonde colour and her dark eyeliner had smudged. She looked a little thicker set around the waist.

Kathleen nodded as she pulled a tissue from her trouser pocket and dabbed her red-rimmed eyes. 'My other daughter, Serena, is helping with Kayden too. She came back from uni last night to be with us.' The creases around her lips puckered as she popped an unlit cigarette into her mouth. 'Do you mind?'

'Of course not.' If the woman needed to smoke to process what had happened to her daughter, who was Gina to stop her or judge.

She took a lighter from her other pocket and lit up, inhaling deeply before blowing the smoke out. Gina leaned back slightly on the creaky chair to avoid getting a nose full, her arm brushing a drooping foxglove.

'I stopped for a year but yesterday I needed a smoke more than anything. When can I see my daughter? I need to see her.'

Gina tilted her head sympathetically. 'I can call the pathologist this afternoon and let you know.'

'Thank you.' She sniffed and used the crumpled tissue again.

'I know I said when I called that you might be able to talk to Kayden, but he said he doesn't want to speak to anyone. He's so upset, as you can imagine. It broke my heart to tell him that his mummy was no longer with us.' Tears flooded her face. 'It doesn't feel real. I keep thinking that it's all some nightmare and I'll wake up.'

'We are so sorry for your loss. I can't imagine what you're going through right now.' She glanced around, noticing that she hadn't seen the family liaison officer as expected. 'Is Ellyn still here?' Ellyn always used her first name while around the families. It put the children and the bereaved more at ease.

'No, we sent her home. It gets to the point when a grieving family need to be on their own and that was us this morning. Lovely girl, but nothing she can say or do will bring my daughter back. Nothing can take this emptiness... this pain away.' She took another drag of her cigarette. 'Right, I suppose we should talk. Kayden told me things last night, things that I can't shrug off and I knew I had to call you.'

Jacob took out his Biro and began scrawling a few notes across a blank page.

'Thank you. We want to do everything we can to bring your daughter's killer to justice. My DCI has put an appeal out today, which I know you've been told about. We're hoping someone will have seen something, maybe someone in the area acting suspiciously.' Gina was a little deflated at not being able to speak to Kayden, but she knew that they all had to do what was best for him. His welfare was their priority and if speaking to him would upset him more than he already was, she didn't want that. 'Can you tell me what Kayden said to you?'

'I lay with him for hours last night. He cried, he held on to me, and he kept saying, "Nanny, don't go". He was scared that if I left him alone, I'd die too. It's understandable, so I stayed with him. While he was lying there, he said that Billie had often sent him to his room and made him promise that he wouldn't come down. She said that if he ever heard her shouting or banging, he was to hide at the back of his wardrobe and not come out. I don't know what was going on in my daughter's life, but she was terrified of something... of someone.' A tear plopped onto the patio table as she stubbed her cigarette out. 'He heard her screaming the night before she was murdered. He said he often heard her screaming and when he did, he'd first hide under his bed sheets and when it got scarier, he'd hide in the wardrobe like she told him.'

'Did he ever ask her why she was upset or screaming?'

'She told him it was nothing to worry about and to just do as he was told. He didn't know what was going on. Yesterday, she made him promise that he wouldn't come in the house until she told him to come in. He said she was shaking, and he thought she'd been crying but he heard her telling her friend Meera that she had a migraine.'

'So, Billie was worried about someone, and she knew they were coming to the house, which is why she made him promise not to come in.'

Kathleen nodded. 'She was protecting him from that monster who killed her. My daughter was scared, petrified and I want to know why.'

'Do you know who Billie was expecting?'

'No.' She pulled another cigarette from the packet and began rolling it between two fingers. 'She didn't tell me anything. George, bless him, seemed to think she was happy, but I told him something was wrong. I could see that she was struggling so I used to give her money but, of course, it's never enough. She was struggling for work, and we argued a little and now I wished we hadn't.'

'What did you argue about?'

'Her work. I told her she really needed to get a proper job now. The candy carts and children's parties, it just wasn't making the money she needed to bring Kayden up. I told her that maybe she should try to get a job in an office or shop, get some regular money in and she looked at me like I was the devil for even suggesting it. As an alternative, I said she should move back in with us so that we could look after her, but she insisted she was going to be okay, that she had some good work coming in. She said things were going to change for her and Kayden but when I pressed her, she wouldn't tell me how. I loved her with all my heart, and I just wished she'd moved back in here. We still have her room. We could have looked after her.' The cigarette was shaking in Kathleen's trembling hand and a snake of ash fell to the patio.

'Do you know if she was seeing anyone?'

'She wasn't. She'd have told us if she was.'

'Her neighbour mentioned a new boyfriend and there was another man, someone who visited the night before last. He went in through the back door. Do you have any idea who that might be?'

A bee buzzed by. Kathleen held up her hand and steered it away from her face. 'It seems that I didn't know my daughter at all. Promise me you'll find him, and he'll pay for what he did?'

Gina didn't know if the mystery visitor had anything to do with Billie's murder, but coming around the back in hours of darkness certainly appeared to be suspicious behaviour. 'Who does she rent her house off?'

'It's housing association.'

That ruled out a dubious landlord who was maybe pressing her to pay in unthinkable ways if she didn't have the money.

'They have our details. If for any reason she couldn't pay, we made up the difference. We did everything we could for her, like any parent would and she loved that little house.'

Jacob peered behind as a rumbling noise came up from the side of the house. A lanky young man appeared, pulling a lawn-mower along. They all stared in his direction. 'Hi, Kath, everything alright?'

'Sorry, Nathan, I should have called you. Something terrible has happened.' With that, she burst into tears. Gina took in the writing on his T-shirt. Nathan Merry Gardening Services. They'd found Billie's boyfriend.

TWELVE

'Nathan Merry?' Gina stood, the metal chair legs scraping across the patio. Just as described, the tall blond, gangly young man had a little shiny scar under his left eye.

He stopped by the gate; his gaze fixed on everyone around the table. 'What's going on?'

'It's our daughter, you know, Billie. You've seen her here when you've cut the lawn.'

'Has something happened?'

'She's been murdered. The police were just asking me some questions.' Kath stood, hands shaking before she ran inside. 'I need a minute,' she called back.

'Shit.' The man ran his hands through his loose wavy hair. As he swallowed his Adam's apple bobbed.

Gina cleared her throat. 'We believe that you and Billie Reeves were in a relationship.'

He furrowed his brows. 'What? I just look after her mother's garden, and I've seen her here sometimes.' His eyes began to glass over.

'So, you've never been to her house?'

'No. Why would I go to her house?'

Jacob stood too. 'I think you should come through so that we can talk.'

'I have work to do.' The quiver in his voice told Gina that he had more on his mind than work, like his murdered girlfriend.

Gina shook her head. 'No, you don't. You need to come down the station to answer a few questions.'

'This is bullshit. I'm busy so unless you're going to arrest me, I've got work to do.' He grabbed his mower and began to walk back through the gate as he muttered to himself.

Hurrying after him, Gina called out, 'Either you come in voluntarily, now, or I arrest you, Mr Merry. What do you prefer? We have two witnesses that put you at Billie's house over the past week, so you've just lied to us.'

His shoulders dropped and he stood in silence as if contemplating what she was saying.

'So, what's it going to be?'

'Okay, okay. I'll just put my mower back in the van.'

'Jacob, go with him, I'll let Mrs Reeves know what's going on.'

As Jacob led the young man out, Kath came back into the garden rubbing her eyes. 'I'm sorry. It's too much.'

Gina placed a hand on her shoulder. 'That's okay. Please don't apologise.'

'Where's Nathan?'

'There's something you should know.'

'What?' The wide-eyed woman waited for an answer, mouth open and a quiver on her bottom lip.

'We have two witnesses who said that Nathan Merry was in a relationship with your daughter.'

'But that's not right. I would have known. Billie would have told me if...'

'They named him and described his van being outside her house.'

Kath bit her bottom lip. 'But he's seeing Serena, my other

daughter. They had a few problems and haven't spoken for a couple of weeks but that happens a lot. You're saying that the lying cheat had made a move on Billie?'

'Sorry.'

'Did he kill her?'

'At the moment, he's only a witness but I will let you know if we find anything out.'

Serena stepped out from behind the patio door. As she went to speak, the words wouldn't come out. Within seconds she was stomping through the house after hearing everything. Gina listened as the front door slammed. Without hesitation, she ran alongside the house and watched as Nathan locked his van door. He was about to get into the back of Jacob's car when Serena ran straight up to him and pushed him into the door. 'I hate you.' With fists beating against his chest, Kath hurried over and pulled her sobbing daughter away from the man. 'How could you do that to me and her, how could she? She's my sister.' Tears streamed down the young woman's cheeks.

'I'm sorry, okay. It just happened. You have to believe me. It was an accident. We just—' Nathan glanced at Gina and Jacob and stopped mid-sentence.

The girl shook her head. 'It just happened. You expect me to believe that. I knew there was someone else. You think I couldn't tell. It was you, you killed her.'

Gina glanced up at the little boy staring out from an open bedroom window. She wanted to pick him up, hug him, protect him from what he was hearing but all she could do was watch as he placed his hands over his ears and sobbed. They needed to get Nathan Merry into an interview room now and away from Serena and Kayden. Gina wasn't going to let that little boy down.

THIRTEEN

As Gina and Jacob hurried through the station, Briggs stepped in front of her. 'Can I have that word?' His usually floppy hair had been trimmed neatly into a short back and sides. That would be Rosemary's doing. She couldn't help noticing his well-fitted shirt and that he'd lost a few pounds. He was transforming into a man she didn't recognise but still, being this close to him made her want him more.

Her heart began to hammer away so hard, she was sure he could hear it thrumming annoyingly. 'We, err, there's a witness waiting to be interviewed. The victim's boyfriend turned up at the parents' house to do the gardening.'

'I heard. Come to my office after.'

Exhaling, she tucked her shirt in, relieved that she had a little more time.

'I wonder what that's about, guv,' Jacob said.

She shrugged. 'It'll just be a catch up on the case.' She knew that Jacob could see through that flippant answer. A catch up on the case would be done in the incident room that was being set up as they spoke. O'Connor was happily taking charge of collating all the door-to-door statements and Wyre was chasing up the phone records and arranging all the photos and evidence on the board. 'Right, we best get our A-game on before we go through this door and interview Mr Merry.' She took a deep breath before entering.

Jacob sat and placed the file onto the table that divided police and interviewees.

'Will this take long?' Nathan Merry slouched back in the chair that had been pulled quite a way from the table.

'Mr Merry, as you can appreciate, a woman who you were in a relationship with has been murdered. It will take as long as it needs.'

'Damn, I'm sorry. I've been a jerk, I know I have but when you asked me about Billie, I knew her sister was home, and I wanted to avoid the scene that happened. I'm an idiot.'

Gina saw a man who was only worried about himself. He hadn't expressed any upset on hearing of Billie's murder. 'Right, we're going to be recording the interview. Do you want a drink?'

He nodded. Gina grabbed three bottles of water from one side of the table and passed one to him and another to Jacob. After going through the procedure with him, Jacob hit the record button. 'For the tape, it's eleven in the morning on Thursday the sixteenth of June. Detectives interviewing are DS Driscoll, and DI Harte. Interviewee is Nathan Merry.'

Gina leaned forward. 'Mr Merry, can you confirm your full name and date of birth?'

'Yes.' The man continued speaking, his voice in a quiver as he answered her questions.

'Thank you. Tell us the nature of your relationship with the victim, Billie Reeves.'

'From when?'

'From the beginning.' The more background the man could give Gina, the better. She thought back to what Mrs Pearlman had said. The woman didn't confirm seeing Nathan at Billie's the evening before her murder but in Gina's mind, he might still have opportunity. Maybe he went over a little while later, saw her with another man and came back the next day, still in a jealous rage.

'It was about four weeks ago. Things haven't been going well between Serena and me, that's Billie's sister. The long-distance thing just wasn't working. I was meant to go and move in with her. She's studying at Liverpool, but I didn't want to leave what I had. I confided in Billie, told her all this when her parents were out. She came by to unlock their gate and let me in to do the garden. You'd think that they'd have trusted me with a key considering that I was seeing Serena, but they didn't. Anyway, after I'd tidied the garden up, she sat there at the patio table with a bottle of wine.' He paused. 'We got talking. She was so funny. She said her son was having a sleepover, so she was making the most of it. We opened more wine, and I don't know. Something clicked, we were quite drunk. We kissed and one thing led to another. After, we both felt awful about Serena and decided it wouldn't happen again.'

'And did it?'

He nodded and took a swig of water.

Gina pressed the control and turned the air conditioning up. 'For the tape, Mr Merry nodded. Go on.'

'I went around the following Saturday night, and I stayed at hers. She told me to come when Kayden was in bed. She didn't want him to see me in case he told his auntie. We felt awful, we really did, but we couldn't stop it. It was then I realised I didn't want to be with Serena, so a few days later I called her and tried to tell her it was over, but I couldn't do it. Billie was really upset with me. We agreed that I'd finish it and a few weeks later we could officially start dating. It wouldn't go down well but she said it was all we could do.' He paused. 'It's just hit me that I'll never see her again.' He turned to face the wall and scratched his cheek.

'Where were you, yesterday, Wednesday the fifteenth of

June, between fourteen hundred hours and seventeen hundred hours?'

'I didn't hurt her.' He clenched his fist.

'Mr Merry, we need to know where you were.'

'I was working on a garden on Blackwell Lane.'

'What is the address?'

'The Forge. Blackwell Lane. The man's name is Mr Peel.'

'And was Mr Peel in?'

'No. He leaves the gate open. I do an afternoon for him once a month.'

'Did you speak to anyone while you were there?'

'No, but I was there. Maybe one of the neighbours saw my van.'

'Thank you. We'll check out your alibi.'

He snorted and finished the rest of the bottle of water in one long swig. 'I didn't hurt Billie. I would never do anything so horrible. I'm a cheat, I know, and I admit that, but I'm not violent.'

'Was Billie seeing someone else?' Gina had to know more about the other man.

Merry swallowed, leaned over and stared at the floor.

Gina nodded at Jacob, and he spoke. 'Did you find out about the other man? Maybe you and Billie argued and hurting her was an accident.'

'I did not hurt her.'

Gina saw the vein on the side of his face twitch. 'But you knew about the other man?'

'Yes, okay.'

'Now we're getting somewhere.' Gina watched as he started picking his nails.

'I didn't want to mention him or them because you're going to try to pin this on me. I didn't hurt her; you have to believe me.'

'Mr Merry, I'm not saying you hurt her, but you must tell me what's going on. What are you holding back?'

He exhaled and wiped his clammy forehead with the back of his hand. 'I went over one evening, it was meant to be a surprise and when I knocked, she leaned out of the window and told me I had to go. I could see the shadow of another person and she had a blanket wrapped around herself. I went away in a huff, thinking that we were over. It was the next day that she called. She told me how much debt she was in and that she'd got into something heavy, and she couldn't see a way out. I told her there was always a way out and that I'd help her. That's when she confessed.'

'Confessed?' Gina furrowed her brows.

'To being a sex worker. She promised me that she'd pack it in immediately. I said I'd help her and that maybe we could move in together. After that, I stayed with her Saturday just gone, that's when she told me that she didn't want a relationship with me and that she was going to sort her own problems out.' He put his hands on his head and gripped his hair so hard, Gina thought he might pull a clump out.

'Did she say anything about the other men?'

'No. I wanted to help her. I'd have given her money, but she didn't want me, or my help, so here we are. I don't know who murdered Billie, but I'd say it was one of her clients. I mean, what type of sleazy letch pays for sex anyway?'

'Did she mention that anyone might be harassing her?'

'No, but she was upset with someone.'

'Who?'

'I don't know the woman, but Billie said her best friend had betrayed her. Someone called Nadia. Billie was angry, upset, and we'd been arguing too. She kept saying that she couldn't trust anyone but herself and that everyone had let her down.'

Gina knew that she had to prioritise a visit to see Nadia of Mockingbird Avenue.

As they wound up the interview, Jacob agreed to chase up Merry's alibi. Maybe Mr Peel had CCTV or as the man said, a neighbour might have seen him. Merry wasn't off the hook yet but the revelation that Billie was a sex worker had opened up a whole new side to the investigation. The fact that her phone was missing told Gina that there might be some communications on it that the killer didn't want them to see. Her stomach began to jump and churn as she hurried back along the corridor, passing the interview room and knocking on Briggs's office door. Whatever he had to say was about to be said and she wasn't sure if she wanted to hear it.

FOURTEEN

'Come in,' Briggs called.

She gingerly opened the door and stepped in, not knowing how to stand or where to go. Should she sit? Stand? What to do with her hands that constantly wanted to fiddle with her clothing or pick her nails. She quickly spoke, filling him in on her interview with Merry then he interrupted her.

'Have a seat.'

'Why am I here?'

He stood and sat on the edge of his desk. She wondered if there was some power play going on. He was literally looking at her down his nose and it was setting her nerves alight. His stiff stance softened as he relaxed his shoulders. 'I'm worried about you, Gina.'

'Not you as well.'

'So, it's not just me?'

'Frankly, I wish you'd all butt out. I'm doing my job, so I don't know why people don't just stop hassling me.'

'It's harsh talking like that about people who care about you.'

She shook her head. Harsh it might be, but it was getting annoying.

'I can tell you're not eating enough.'

'Fabulous. I'm on a diet.' She pasted a huge fake smile on her face.

'I care you know. Is it because of me? I didn't mean to hurt you like I did.'

'Don't flatter yourself.'

He paused and bowed his head. 'Feelings don't just go away.'

'But you don't love me. Wait.' She held a hand up. 'Don't say anything to that. It's irrelevant. This is about me, not us. We are no longer an us. All you need to know is that I work hard and I deliver, that's all you need from me as my superior.' She didn't want to discuss her hot flushes with him.

'I won't say anything, you know. Not to Rosemary, not to anyone. The things you told me in confidence will remain with me, I promise.'

Rosemary, her name on his tongue made her want to vomit. 'I don't know if I care any more. Maybe I'll walk right out there and shout out my secrets to everyone. Get it over with.'

'You do care, Gina.'

He was right. There was no way she'd want him sharing her secret. The one where she'd waited for her violent ex-husband, Terry, to die at the bottom of the stairs before calling an ambulance. When a person shared secrets like they did, they were bound for life – so she thought. What Briggs didn't know was why she never wanted that secret to get out. She could take the punishment. She deserved it. But she couldn't bear the look on her daughter Hannah's face when she found out. She'd probably never see Gracie again. That would be the death of her. Their relationship had been rocky enough, but she knew that despite how evil her daughter's father was, Hannah would never forgive that.

'You're right. I do care.' He'd see right through her lies. That was intimacy for her.

'This is coming from a place of love. We have a past, and I'd hate for you to enter a downwards spiral. You're too good for that. Your team need you. This case needs the best of you.'

'I always give my best. You know that. Sir, there's something I need to tell you.'

'Okay.'

Her mouth began to water but now was as good a time as any. However angry she was, she couldn't let Rosemary humiliate him. He needed to see what a liar the woman was. She might rock up with the best hair and clothes, a fun car and a wide smile but she was nothing but a cheat. 'I saw Rosemary with another man. Last night on my way home I stopped at the chippy and saw her coming out of a man's house.'

'You just can't help yourself, can you?'

She furrowed her brows. 'It's not like that. I care about you. I don't want to see you hurt.'

'Well, I suggest you butt out. To think I thought I could help you and all you want to do is sabotage my happiness. She went to see her brother last night. Get out.'

'But, Chris—'

'Call me sir.'

She wanted to say how Rosemary's body language didn't suggest she was with her brother, but she knew better. Now was not the time.

He walked back around his desk and sat back in his chair, ignoring her and taking a deep breath. She'd never seen him looking as flustered before. 'Team briefing in ten. We've had someone phone in, and I think you're going to want to hear what the caller had to say.'

'Sir, I'm sorry.'

He looked up. 'Get out, Gina.'

A lump formed in her throat. She shouldn't have said anything and right now, she wholly regretted it. Brother or not, he'd have found out in his own time but even as friends, they were ruined. She didn't think it was possible to hate herself any more but this new low she'd sunk to was the pits.

FIFTEEN

Gina pulled open the cold can of cola and let it sink down her throat. She needed a caffeine buzz too. As she sat, the back of her shirt stuck to her back. O'Connor pushed the window open as far as it would go, and Wyre wedged the main door open. PCs Smith and Kapoor sat at the back of the room with another couple of PCs who worked closely with them.

As Briggs entered, the hum of voices hushed and Jacob leaned back on the chair next to Gina, fingers linked over his flat middle.

'Right, let's get started.' Attention was now completely on Briggs as he spoke. Gina couldn't look at him. 'As you know the press release is well and truly out and the calls have been coming in at an alarming rate. The team have managed to sift out the irrelevant calls but there is one that you should all know about. One of the residents, a Mrs Kendall, who lives on the street that backs onto Billie Reeves's said that she saw a man loitering outside her house on Tuesday evening, just before our victim was visited by a man who entered through the back gate. We have a description. Would you mind?' Briggs offered a pen to Gina. That was as close as she was going to get to an olive branch.

She took it and stood.

'The man we are looking for is around five nine. Our witness described him as wearing what looked like a tailored jacket and he was of a slim build. It was dark so the description doesn't cover much more but she did have her window open as it was hot. She could hear him on a phone. The woman said that it sounded like he was reading a bedtime story to a child and telling them that they had to go back to sleep.'

Gina scribbled a few notes on the board as Briggs paused. 'So, we're looking for a father, maybe an uncle, someone with a child in their life?'

Briggs nodded. 'Yes. O'Connor, can you shed any light on the door-to-doors on that street?'

The detective constable loosened his wide collar and leaned in. 'We knocked at that street yesterday, but numerous people weren't in. We didn't speak to anyone called Mrs Kendall.' He flicked through his notes to make sure. 'Yep, no one by that name answered. As for the man who was loitering, not one other person reported seeing or hearing him.'

Gina stepped forward. 'Any CCTV from that road?'

O'Connor smiled. 'The library is at the end of that road and there is one camera that is turned on and working. I've requested the footage and I'm hoping to receive it later today.'

Stepping towards the other side of the board, Briggs stared at what they had so far. 'As soon as it comes in, go through it in minute detail, frame by frame. Look for every shadow, any reflection. It might be our best chance of catching this man on camera. We don't have a name, any facial features or any witnesses so far.' Briggs checked his phone. 'Right, I have a further meeting with the press. Gina, you are Senior Investigating Officer. Keep me involved in everything. We need this person caught. I don't need to remind you of that word written on the victim's wall. We don't yet know if it was personal against our victim or against sex workers in general. All I do know is that we're dealing with a callous, cold-blooded murderer. She didn't stand a chance.'

'Do we need to mention in the press release that sex workers might be in danger?' Gina pressed her lips together knowing that there would be repercussions if they did this. Mentioning it would tell everyone that Billie was a sex worker – people would easily link the two. Not mentioning it could put other people in Billie's predicament in danger. At least other sex workers would know.

'I've been thinking about this and my decision is to say yes. Nothing will be said until this evening. Ms Reeves's parents need to be told first.'

Gina licked a slight crack in her bottom lip, knowing that she would be the one to tell them. The family were already suffering, and this would hurt more. 'I'll sort it.'

'Good. Right, we'll reconvene again soon. Do you need anything else?' He looked at Gina.

She shook her head, letting him know that she was fine and in control, glad that he still trusted her to run the case. 'No, sir. I have a few things to go over, then I'll head out to Nadia Anderson's house. She was Billie's best friend.'

Briggs grabbed his notes and left.

Gina kept clicking the pen lid onto the pen until everyone hushed again. 'Right, O'Connor, have we had any news from Bernard as to when the post-mortem will take place?'

'Yes, guv. Tomorrow morning, first thing.'

'Thank you. As DCI Briggs said, as soon as you have that CCTV, let me know. We're pinning a lot on it. Jacob, did you manage to follow up with a call to Mr Peel, to check on Nathan Merry's alibi?'

'Yes.' Jacob unlinked his hands and sat up. 'I spoke to the man, and he confirmed that Mr Merry was booked but he couldn't confirm his presence as he's never in when his garden is being done. He said his lawn had been mowed, though.'

'Okay, so we're looking for witnesses in that respect. It might not have taken long just to mow a lawn, giving him time to still go to Billie's house. Wyre, could you check with neighbours in the area, see if anyone saw Mr Merry or his van during the time of Billie Reeves's murder?'

'Yes, guv. I'll head over that way next.'

She glanced at the photos that Bernard had sent through. The woman that everyone described wasn't as happy as everyone thought she was. On the outside everything seemed normal. She was a mother, daughter, sister and friend but no one knew that she was also in such bad debt that she saw no option but to sell her own body to make ends meet. 'Do we have her phone records yet?' Gina tried to picture her opening all the red letters and then looking through her bare kitchen cupboards while her son waited for his supper. So many people were struggling with the new cost of living crisis. There were so many other Billies around and they too might be in the same danger.

'They're due in anytime now,' Wyre said.

'Same as the CCTV, they are a priority. She may have had client numbers or messages stored. We need to find out what was going on in her world. Ideally, we could do with the phone. We need access to everything. Facebook, WhatsApp... this may or may not be a long shot, but can we check the web, see if she uses any sites to find customers locally? Speak to the vice department, they will know of any new or emerging sites that we should look out for.' She glanced back at the board. 'We need the late-calling visitor. Either she was killed by a client, or someone is really against what she was doing. Why? Maybe it's a neighbour who has noticed what's going on. Maybe she refused a potential client, and it was a revenge attack. Maybe she knows something she shouldn't know. We don't have a clear motive yet, just speculation and speculation means nothing.

What we need now is some hard evidence.' Gina rubbed her hands together. 'Okay, so we all know what we're doing next?'

A hum of yesses filled the room.

'Jacob, we'll go straight to Nadia Anderson's now. We need to find out what she knows and check out what Mr Reeves said about the party. If her husband, Mr Anderson, was watching Billie throughout the day, we need to know why. Everyone else, if you receive any updates, get them over to me immediately.'

'Guv, the phone records have just come in.' Wyre held up her phone with the message open.

'Great. Everyone, let's get to it.' Gina called Jacob and Wyre over to a spare computer in the corner of the room, where she sat, and the others stood behind her. 'Can we locate the phone?'

Wyre scanned the email quickly. 'No. It's completely out of use wherever it is.'

Gina quickly logged into her email and opened the email that Wyre was looking at and clicked into the file, opening the pages of messages and numbers from Billie's phone. One number kept recurring. She highlighted it with the mouse. 'We need to find out whose number this is. They called her around lunchtime yesterday and several times the day before.'

Wyre made a note. 'I'll check it out before I head to look into Nathan Merry's alibi.'

'Great. There aren't many messages surprisingly.' Gina scanned down them and most of them were from Meera asking if Billie needed her to pick Kayden up from school, or asking when he was coming over to play with Dev. 'That's odd.'

Jacob and Wyre leaned in to read the message.

'There is only one from her best friend, Nadia, and all she says is "Sorry." There are no earlier messages. I'd say there are messages but not sent by text. This screams of someone trying to reach out to her and trying all ways possible. She can't have just stopped at "Sorry." We really have to find out what was going on and Mr Reeves seemed to think that Nadia's husband was looking at Billie in a strange way. We definitely can't dismiss that.' Gina continued to scan the messages and there was one that stood out.

Let me see him or I'll swear, I won't be responsible for my actions.

'It sounds like Kayden's father might be closer than we think but we need to be sure it's him.'

'And the number matches the one that made all the calls.' Wyre flicked back to the previous screen.

'Get everything you can on Shaun Brock. Previous addresses, family, everything. That to me looks like a direct threat.'

SIXTEEN

NADIA

'Damn, I've been called into work.' Ed hurried past Nadia as she turned the kettle on, his smart jacket complementing his broad shoulders. The overwhelming smell of his aftershave almost made her sneeze. He pulled his phone from his pocket and pressed a couple of buttons. She placed the crocodile toy in the fruit bowl carefully, as if it were Billie herself. She'd need to put it back in the doll's house before William got back from school.

Nadia wondered who he was texting. 'But you were having a day off. My friend has just been killed.'

'Not any more. Something's come up.' He scrolled down his phone.

'Will you be late home tonight?' She shifted beside him to get a closer look, but he swiftly put the phone back in his pocket before she could see the screen.

He shrugged. 'Not sure yet as I'm heading to the Derby office. Could be but probably won't be. Don't make any dinner for me, I'll grab something on the go.'

With that, he left, leaving her alone and wondering where he was going and when he'd be back. She dare not ask him. If she did, the accusations would fly, and it would end with her getting hurt. She'd learnt her lesson on many occasions. *She's too possessive, she always nags him and she's trying to control him.* All that couldn't be further from the truth. They had a son and she had to be there for him all day, every day. Ed always did as he pleased. Having a child hadn't changed his life at all. As the kettle clicked, she ignored it, her stomach too nervy for more coffee. Maybe the police weren't going to come. Police didn't care about playground chat. She swallowed the disgust she had in herself. Gossip was hardly a crime. She accepted that breaking Billie's confidence was immoral and wrong, but criminal, no. Her husband on the other hand, he was hiding something, and that text was the key to the truth. Whatever happened, she had to get into his phone. Maybe she could keep topping up his glass when he got home. More wine, a couple of brandies and maybe an Irish coffee to finish the night off. Yes, she'd have to make the night so special he'd end up comatose at the end. Only then could she find out what was on his phone. Maybe he'd also tell her other things, things that could set her free from him. She had to come up with a plan.

As she tried to swallow, the lump in her throat protested. Billie was gone and she was never going to see her again. If only her friend were here now. She'd beg for forgiveness.

A hammering knock shook her front door. As her heart jumped, she hurried through the large kitchen and along the hallway before stopping and taking a couple of deep breaths. If it was the police, she was going to stay calm, not say anything and do some detective work of her own first. She pulled her short-sleeved hoodie over her green sports crop top and half did it up. *Deep breaths.*

She exhaled.

'Nadia, sorry about this morning, not stopping. I was running so late that Poppy missed registration. You haven't been picking up. I tried to call you and then I messaged, twice. With what happened to Billie, I was worried.' Candice stepped in and hugged her, like she often did. Now wasn't the best time. She'd rather her friend went home and left her to rummage through Ed's things, that's what she needed to do. She relaxed a little. At least it wasn't the police.

'Come in.' No need to have said that as Candice was already in the kitchen helping herself to a coffee cup. 'Make me one while you're at it.' Strange thing to say in her own home but Candice was the woman who took over. This usually annoyed Ed. She didn't know why her friend was grating on her so much, maybe it was because she was the biggest gossip of them all. Everyone knew Billie's secret because Candice had blabbed, that she was sure of. She thought she could totally trust Meera, but maybe she'd let Billie's secret out by telling Candice.

'Here you go.' Candice placed the cup down, a tiny bit of her nail polish chinking as she did. She laid a warm hand on Nadia's arm and tilted her head. 'I can't stop thinking about Billie and what happened.' She removed her hand and wiped a tear away.

'Me neither. It's all so surreal.'

'And, I can't stop thinking about her and how scared she must have been. When you didn't answer your phone... I panicked.' She let out a small sob.

'Sorry, hun. I really didn't mean to worry you. Ed has just left for work and my phone is on silent. I didn't see that you'd called.'

Candice waved a dismissive hand and sniffed. 'It's okay. We're all in shock. I just had to come over. Staying in and stewing was making me queasy. My heart has been pounding with every noise I hear. Sorry to burst in like this. I didn't want to be alone. I keep thinking, what if whoever did this to Billie does it again? What if it's one of us?'

'We both know why this happened to Billie. No one is coming for us.' Nadia sat at the breakfast bar while Candice turned to the cupboards and rummaged around for a packet of biscuits like it was her kitchen. Nadia wanted to tell her that there were no biscuits, but she left Candice to find out for herself.

'When I got to the school, everyone was talking about her and what had happened.'

'What were they saying?'

'You don't want to know. It was horrible.'

Nadia scrunched her brow. 'Why would they say horrible things? Billie was murdered.'

'I know, but that's people for you. One of them said that they could do without people like her living in the neighbourhood. Others defended Billie, saying how times were hard.'

'It's all my fault, I should have kept my mouth shut.'

Candice rushed over and placed an arm around Nadia's shoulder. 'You were a good friend. You offered to help her.'

'She asked me not to tell. She was so worried everyone would find out, but I told Meera.'

'I can't believe that you told Meera and not me. Maybe we could have all been there for Billie. Times must have been tough for her to do what she was doing.' Candice sat next to Nadia.

'I'm sorry but it was all my bad. I shouldn't have told anyone, it accidentally slipped out. I wish I could turn back the clock and force Billie to accept my help. It's only money at the end of the day. She was too proud to take any and I get that. No one wants a handout but look what happened.' She paused. 'We argued on the day she died; I wasn't sure if she was going to turn up to the fete meeting. I thought the migraine was an excuse to not come. She'd noticed people talking. I could see them looking at her. I tried to tell her they weren't. That's when she accused me of betraying her. I didn't have the heart to tell her that I'd told Meera and I felt horrible. I still do.'

Her mind went back to the message on Ed's phone. She had

talked when they'd had a few glasses of wine, so he knew everything about Billie too. For a fleeting second, she pictured Ed turning up at Billie's. Would Billie have been angry enough with her to sleep with him to spite her? She knew that Ed would go there as he'd never been faithful to her.

'Nadia.' Candice took her hand. 'You were the best friend ever to Billie, and you still are to me and Meera. We have to be strong and help each other through this. We all miss Billie and we loved her.'

'She died hating me.' Nadia sipped the coffee and coughed as it got caught in her throat. 'Someone killed our friend. I still can't take it in.'

'Come here, sweetie.' Candice held her tight. All she could still think about was Ed's phone. She needed Candice to leave. She'd already stayed too long. 'I think I need to be on my own for a bit.'

'Okay, I get that but I'm not leaving you to fester in this cloud of guilt. Why don't you and William come over to mine after school? And Ed, too. Gavin will be there, so he'll have someone to talk to. We need to be with friends at times like this.'

'Ed will be working late, like he always is.'

'Okay, just you and me. Kids can play in the garden, and we'll get a takeaway. Damn, I'm running late. Got a dog booked in for a groom at one. I tried to cancel given what had happened but my client never answered her phone, so I guess I have to be there.' She grabbed her bag. 'Did I tell you I'm going to open a dog parlour and escape my garage?'

'No... Sorry, I'm really happy for you but I just need to be on my own.' Nadia paused for a moment. She didn't want to go anywhere. Her instinct was telling her to hole up and stay at home, but William needed some normality. She'd go out, for his sake, especially as her little boy had Kayden on his mind. The thought of him playing with the doll's house made her shiver. In her head, she could hear Billie's screams as Kayden hid under his blankets. 'That all sounds great. You're right. We'll get through this together. I'll pop by for a while after school. I'll have to be back about seven.' She had plans for Ed and she'd wait with the wine in the chiller for as long as it took. That message he was hiding was going to be out in the open by the next morning. If she was living with a murderer, she wanted to know.

Candice's phone beeped and she stared at it for a few seconds. Her usual rosy cheeks seemed to drain of colour. 'I'd best go, business to attend to and all that. Can I use your loo first?'

'Of course.' As Candice hurried out of the kitchen, heels tapping all the way along the hallway until she reached the toilet, Nadia grabbed her phone. She quickly read the two messages from Candice and as she was about to place it on the worktop, the phone buzzed. After reading the message from a withheld number, she dropped the phone and gasped.

It's all your fault. All you had to do was keep your big mouth shut. Watch your back, Nadia. You don't want to end up like Billie!!

SEVENTEEN

Gina nibbled the cheese sandwich that Jacob had bought for her at the petrol station while Jacob drove them to Nadia's huge house.

The call to Kathleen Reeves had left her feeling like there was a stone in her stomach. Telling a mother that her daughter had been a sex worker was tough. Kathleen had said how it was her fault, how she should have insisted that Billie come and live with them, how she should have given her more money to help and that she'd never forgive herself. A bit of doughy bread got lodged in Gina's throat. She coughed as they pulled up on Mockingbird Avenue. Nadia and her husband had money, lots of it by the look of their house and the sporty-looking car on the drive. They lived in a completely different world to Billie with all her debts.

As Jacob pulled up on the kerb, she stuffed the rest of the sandwich in her bag. They stayed in the car as a woman with fiery-red hair hurried onto the drive and ran past them in her heels, too buried in her phone to notice them parked outside. She got into her SUV and drove off without looking back.

'I'd say she looked distracted.' Jacob opened the driver's door and stepped out.

Gina agreed. The woman was certainly in a hurry and unaware of her surroundings. They walked past the tree hedge at the bottom of the garden and along the perfectly block-paved drive to face a tall double-fronted Victorian house. She glanced through the window. It might look period from the outside but inside, it was all different textures of white and wood, lighter and airier than expected. Jacob pressed the doorbell, and they waited on the huge step.

'Hello,' the woman said as she opened the door, frowning as she tried to work out who they were. She placed one hand in the pocket of her hoodie.

Gina held her identification up and introduced them both. 'Are you Nadia Anderson?'

Nodding, the woman opened the door to let them in. 'Have you arrested anyone?'

'Not yet. We were hoping that you could help us.'

Gina followed the woman through a large reception hall with actual built-in coat and shoe cupboards. It smelled of leather rather than old trainers and there was no evidence that children lived in the house. She knew that Nadia had at least one child. Everything was so pristine; she could almost see her reflection outlined on the floor. She glanced at the white wall with the family photos all displayed in black frames, most in black and white. The central photo was of the woman in front of her with a handsome looking man of a similar age and a little boy with a wide smile. It looked like they only had the one child.

'This has really knocked me for six. I don't know who would do this to Billie.' Nadia sat at the eight-seater dining table opposite the island and gestured for them to sit. Gina felt her neck prickling, so she undid another shirt button.

'We're sorry. It must be hard losing someone you were so

close to?' Gina wanted to sound Nadia out. Would she confess to arguing with their murder victim?

'It's been hard on all of us and my son, William, he knows his friend's mum has died.' She paused and stared at the fruit bowl. 'He's too young to know any more.'

'Could you tell me how you met?'

'It...' Gina thought Nadia might cry but she took a deep breath and continued, 'It was when we were pregnant, at ante-natal classes through the National Childbirth Trust. I went with my husband, Ed, and I would always notice that Billie was alone. I made a beeline for her, knowing that she'd need the support of a friend. It's a scary time and the thought of her being without a partner, even a friend, made my heart sink. She told me that the baby's father had left her and moved out of the country. We clicked. She was so funny and charismatic, telling jokes that made the other mums-to-be laugh. She was like some stand-up comedian, telling it as it was but not in a limelight hogging way. It came naturally to her, and she was like this people magnet. Everyone loved her. We've been friends since, until...'

'It's okay, take your time.'

Jacob turned a page in his notebook and smiled.

'I'm really going to miss her. We spent so much time together and our children are best friends. We've been through teething, walking, potty training and their first days at school together. I can't get my head around the fact that I'll never speak to her again.'

'I'm really sorry to have to ask you this, but did you and Billie have an argument recently?' Gina knew that the woman wouldn't mention it unless she asked.

Nadia began to pick the skin on her lip before removing her hoodie. The crop top showed off her flat stomach and light golden tan. 'It was nothing. Not really an argument.'

'It may seem like nothing but given what has happened, we have to ask for details.'

The woman glanced at her phone and then back at Gina. 'I said something I shouldn't have said.'

Gina smiled sympathetically.

'I, err... she told me something and I told someone else and other people heard me say it. She found out and she was upset with me. Rightly so. I messed up.'

'What was it she told you?'

'She was in debt, not because she was extravagant. She bought most of her clothes from charity shops and I know she used the food bank. That debt was merely for survival.'

'So, you argued about debt?'

'No, it was more about how she solved her debt problems.'

'And how was that.'

Nadia scratched the back of her head and began to fidget uncomfortably in the chair. 'She was a sex worker. Men came to her house, and I stopped allowing William to go over and play with Kayden.'

'Is that what the argument was about?'

'No, she understood my concerns. Kayden came here to play instead. She had a go at me because I let her down. She told me what she was doing, and I should have kept it to myself. I didn't mean to talk about her, it just came out and...' Tears streamed down her face. 'If only I'd kept my mouth shut, she'd still be alive, I know it.'

'Why do you think that?'

'Because everyone at the school knows. Gossip travels fast and some people didn't like Billie. They hated that she was so popular and likeable, they'd enjoy seeing her brought down a peg or two. You know how jealous people can get? I mean, Billie could have written a book on the laws of attraction. She was just that kind of person. Anyway, she could see that they were gossiping about her from the way they peered behind their hands while whispering in friends' ears. She also knew then that it was me who told. She'd only told me. How could anyone else have known if it didn't come from me?'

Gina held back that it was Nathan Merry who had told her and if Billie had told two people, who's to say there wasn't more people she'd confided in.

'I tried to help her. She could have borrowed whatever she needed from me, but she said she was sick of people offering to help and that she had to find her own way out of her debt. She kept saying that it was okay borrowing, but she wouldn't be able to pay it back. Her mother was apparently trying to get her to move back home but Billie didn't want to go back there, saying that she needed her space and that her sister was due back from uni soon.'

'Did Billie get on with her sister?' Gina felt the sun beating down through the glass doors and shuffled a little further back out of the rays.

'She said they got on okay but weren't that close. She felt that her parents favoured Serena a little as she was the clever one. They always boasted about the daughter that was going to be a dentist one day and Billie felt she wasn't good enough sometimes. Her mother went on at her to get a job in an office, but Billie said she could never stick a job that didn't allow her to be creative. She was a bit of a luvvie, bursting with hand gestures and funny faces. She'd put on silly voices that made the children scream with laughter. They all loved her.'

'Was Billie in a relationship?'

'She mentioned someone she'd dated but she didn't tell me his name. She said he was a gardener.'

'Was she happy with him?'

Shrugging, Nadia pulled a ball of tissue from the pocket of her leggings and dabbed her eyes. 'She didn't say much but she said she liked him and was taking it slowly. I don't think it would have lasted long as Billie normally ended relationships after the honeymoon period. She was a happy singleton really.'

'Did she mention any of her clients?'

'No. I told her I was worried about her safety. I said she didn't know these men, but she seemed adamant that they weren't dangerous.'

'Do you know where she found them?'

'Some website, but she never told me the name of it.'

'Did she have a tablet or a laptop?'

Nadia nodded. 'Yes, she had a tablet but no laptop. She had two phones which was weird.'

'Two phones?' Jacob made a note.

'Yes, a smartphone and an old-looking thing that she bought from a pawnshop. One that just does calls and texts.'

Gina now knew they were looking for two phones and a tablet.

'Do you know her phone numbers?'

'Only the one for her smartphone. She said that her other phone was for work, but I know the phone number on her Facebook page is the number we all have. By work, she meant her clients.'

'How did she seem?'

Nadia scrunched her brow. 'She went from my lovely happy friend to someone who looked washed out and tired within a few weeks. What she was doing took its toll. She wouldn't admit it, but it was killing her inside. It was like she was slowly turning to stone. She stopped coming out with us and always said she had a bad head or felt sick. I betrayed her and I begged her to forgive me.'

'What are the names of her other close friends?'

'Meera Gupta and Candice Brent. She wasn't as close to them as she was to me, but we were all good friends.'

'Do you know anyone who would want to hurt Billie?'

Pausing for a moment, Nadia bit her bottom lip before hugging herself. 'No.'

Gina could tell that something was worrying Nadia, her closed-off body language said it all. What worried Gina more was that Nadia's gaze had fallen on the toy crocodile in the fruit bowl. She felt her heart jolt as she remembered the message in the pocket of the crocodile costume. *Slut.* Someone hated Billie. 'Are you sure?'

Nadia picked up the toy. 'Yes. I'd tell you if I did.'

Gina knew she wouldn't, but she didn't know why. She also still didn't know what was on Nadia's mind, but she suspected it was her husband if Mr Reeves's statement was anything to go by. 'Is that your son's toy?'

'Yes. He likes animals.' She threw it back into the fruit bowl. 'My husband bought it for him. I don't know what's cute about a crocodile.'

That was it. Gina was certain that Nadia was covering for her husband, but she needed some hard evidence. 'Is Mr Anderson in?'

She shook her head and sat up straight. 'He's working.'

'What does he do?'

'He owns a scaffolding company.'

'When will he be home?'

She shrugged. 'He didn't know Billie, really. She was my friend.'

Gina had touched a nerve and she was determined to dig deeper, even if it was going to be painful for Nadia. 'We will need to speak to him, though.'

'They've barely met. He wasn't normally here when she visited. Why would he know anything?'

Billie's father had mentioned that Mr Anderson had been acting strangely around Billie at Kayden's party. 'Kayden had his birthday party in your garden on the fifteenth of May?'

She nodded.

'Your husband would have met her there.'

'But he didn't take any notice of her, he barely knew her.'

'Didn't you meet at the antenatal sessions when your husband was with you?'

'Yes, but it was me that did all the talking. He used to slink off, leaving me with her.' She checked the time. 'I must get to the gym. I'm a personal trainer and I have a client who works out there. Really sorry. I'd cancel but I'm trying hard to build my business up and I don't want to lose her.'

Gina stood and Jacob closed his pad. She placed her card on the kitchen table. 'Could you please ask him to come into the station or call us when you speak to him?'

Nadia nodded and took the card.

After a few more words to wrap up, Gina and Jacob stepped back out onto the drive and walked towards the car. 'Did you see that toy?' Gina asked as she opened the door.

Jacob nodded. 'Yes, bit too much of a coincidence.'

'We need to do a background check on Mr Anderson. Nadia wasn't telling us something and I want to know what it was.'

EIGHTEEN

NADIA

As soon as the police left, Nadia ran to the downstairs loo and threw up the coffee that had been sloshing in her stomach. All she could hear was the thrumming of blood as her heart banged. They knew that Ed was a part of it all. In fact, they knew more than Nadia did and this proved that her whole world was going to come tumbling down. She swilled out her mouth and pressed Ed's number, one hand on the washbasin as she tried to steady herself. The phone kept ringing out.

She kept ringing until he finally answered. 'I can't talk, I'm with a client.'

'It's urgent.'

'Seriously, what can be that urgent?' His hushed whisper made her shudder as she sensed the anger that her interruption had caused.

'It's about Billie. The police have just been.'

'Wait, I'll just go outside. Will you excuse me for a minute? Family matters.'

She waited as she listened to a door slamming closed and the sound of passing traffic.

'What did they say?'

'They just asked me questions like how well I knew Billie and about, you know what.'

'Okay, so why are you calling me? I don't even know her that well. I'm sure it was just one of her punters. I mean, doing a job like that, it brings the nutters out of the woodwork. You did your best, Nadia. Don't beat yourself up about it. She couldn't have asked for a better friend.'

'But I didn't. It's my fault because I opened my mouth.'

'Don't be ridiculous. It wouldn't have taken long for everyone to find out in a small town. People talk. Billie chose that path. It was her fault and dressing in a way that everyone can see your underwear is bound to provoke unwanted attention.'

'How can you say that so coldly? She was desperate, Ed.' He could be such a pig sometimes and that was another thing she hated about him.

'Not desperate enough to borrow some money and sort herself out. She was working as a prostitute, for God's sake.'

'Don't say that.' She felt tears welling up in her eyes.

'What, the truth?'

'She didn't deserve to die. Are you saying she did? Because she was desperate, poor, or she dressed in short skirts?'

'Don't put words into my mouth. I'm not saying that at all. No one deserves to be murdered. I was merely saying things like this are an occupational hazard and stating what everyone else thinks. I told you she was trouble. Anyone could see that.'

'And what's that supposed to mean?'

'Come on, don't make me spell it out?'

Shaking she waited for him to continue.

'Okay, look at the way she flirted with everyone. It was over the top, love. It gave people the wrong impression.'

'Did she flirt with you?' She had to know why her husband was messaging Billie behind her back, especially as he was professing that she was her friend, and not his. There was no reason for Ed to have her number, none whatsoever.

'Don't be stupid. Idiot.'

She ignored his insult, hoping not to add any unnecessary fuel to the fire. 'So, you didn't have her phone number?'

'No way. Why are you being like this? I can't live on a leash.'

She was being like this because she knew he was lying. She had proof. She'd seen the message flash up. Trembling, she wondered if she should mention the message. No, she had to keep that to herself otherwise he'd deny it and she'd never get to see it in its entirety. Even if she said she saw it, he'd say she must have seen something else and then delete it. Maybe he'd claim it was the person who sold him the hot tub. Whatever his excuse, Ed was capable of lying, but she could never quite catch him out. 'So, there's no one else?'

'Never, babe. There's only you. I mean think about it, this morning I was horny for you. No one else but you.'

She didn't believe that either. Ed was horny for anyone with a pulse. 'The police want to speak to you so I guess you should call them because I don't want them in our house again, especially when William gets home.'

Her husband paused. 'Look, I'll see you later. I can't leave the clients waiting much longer.'

'They might come back.' She paused. 'Ed, just tell me where it is.'

'Where what is?'

'You know,' she snapped.

'I'm not discussing this again but all I'm going to say is, this time, keep that mouth of yours shut and I'll deal with the police.'

She trembled, almost dropping her phone. The last thing she needed was him coming home later and taking everything out on her. She pressed her ribs and flinched. It would be more evidence for her collection, but it hurt so much. They both had something the other wanted. Maybe she'd exchange what she had for what he had when the time was right. Either way, she didn't want the police interfering in their personal lives. She went to speak, to remind him of what was at stake but instead, she muttered, 'I'll see you later.'

'Give Will a kiss from Daddy when you pick him up and I'll sort out the police.' He ended the call, leaving Nadia as clueless as she was before she called him and angry that she was no further forward.

She gasped as she spotted the time. Her client would be waiting. Grabbing a bottle of water and the car keys, she ran out the door. As she turned the ignition, her phone beeped again.

I see the police have paid a visit. Unless you want your life turned upside down, say nothing.

It was the same mystery messenger as before. She glanced up and down the road as she pulled out of her drive. There was no one around. It had to be Ed playing with her mind. He was the only person who knew that the police had only just visited. He'd also know that she really wouldn't want the police in the house, not with the secret that she was hiding, and no doubt Ed would tell first if it saved his skin.

NINETEEN

'Guv, we've had a call from Nadia Anderson's husband. He said he's working away but will come in first thing tomorrow morning.' Jacob took a seat next to a computer in the incident room.

'I was hoping to speak to him today. Where is he?'

'He says he has business in Derby and he's stopping over.'

Wyre entered, looking flustered as she fanned herself with an A4 notepad. 'It's stifling out there.' She flopped onto a plastic chair and wiped her sticky fringe from her forehead.

'Any luck with Nathan Merry's alibi?'

'Maybe just a bit.' Wyre unscrewed a small bottle of lemonade, which fizzed over the top.

Gina sat up straight in her chair, poised to hear what her colleague had to say.

'One of the neighbour's heard the ride on mower going around the time that Billie was murdered.'

'Did this neighbour actually see him?'

'No, but a man living in a house opposite saw Merry get out of his van on the same day while he was out pruning his shrubs. He said that Merry didn't come back to his van until after he'd finished which was around five.'

Gina leaned back and bit the cap at the end of her Biro while thinking. 'So, unless he had another vehicle parked out the back somewhere, he didn't leave that garden?' She glanced at the large map of the area where a pin marked Merry's alibi. Following the back of the house, she too could see that the nearest road was quite a jaunt.

'That's right, guv. I checked out the back. There are at least a couple of acres to the nearest road or path. It's farmland that has been left to grow naturally. There are stingers and shrubs galore. It would have taken him too long to get to the nearest road where, at a push, he could have parked another vehicle up. I also checked to see if he had any other vehicles registered to himself and he hasn't. He only has a van.'

Jacob sighed. 'That rules Merry out, then.'

Wyre sat and took an apple out of her bag. She crunched as Gina glanced across the board, trying to avoid catching sight of the crime scene photos. 'Let's do that check on Edward Anderson so that we have background on him before he comes in tomorrow.'

Jacob nodded and turned back to the computer.

O'Connor came in and joined them, his nose looking sunburned. 'I've got the camera footage from the library so I'm going to go through it in a few minutes.'

'Great. What do we know about Shaun Brock, the father of Billie's son?'

Wyre smiled. 'That, I can help with. I have an address for his mother. As far as I can see, he's never lived alone in this country, always travelling then going back to hers. I can also confirm that he's been back in the country for several weeks.'

Adrenaline coursed through Gina, almost making her light-headed. The threatening message that he sent was at the fore-front of her mind. She tapped Jacob's shoulder. 'I think we need to pay Mr Brock a visit, now. We could have this sewn up by the close of today.'

TWENTY

As Jacob drove, all Gina could think about was Shaun Brock and that message he sent to Billie. *Let me see him or I'll swear, I won't be responsible for my actions.*

'Do we have an actual description of Brock?' Jacob asked as he indicated to turn into the housing estate.

'No, unfortunately. With no prior and no one really knowing much about him, we don't know if he matches the description of the man seen at Billie's house the night before she was murdered. I checked for him on social media but from what I can see, he's not on the main platforms like Facebook, Twitter, Instagram or TikTok. At least, not under his own name.'

'There could be a simple motive,' he said as he braked at a junction. 'Maybe she wouldn't let him see their son and in a fit of rage, he went over and plunged a knife into her.'

'It could be, but Kayden is his son too. Would a person really do that to their child? Kill his mother while he plays outside? Then, I think of that text. "I won't be responsible for my actions." It's beyond threatening. He was livid.'

'Yes, I suppose speaking to him will hopefully get to the

bottom of it. Text sent in the heat of the moment or a threat that ended in murder? We are here.'

Jacob pulled over. They glanced up at the four-storey block of flats where the greyish paint had part-flaked from the balconies. Washing hung off some, bikes were piled on others. A dog barked and howled constantly from a property in the middle of the block.

As Gina stepped out of the car, a solitary magpie pecked at a clump of unrecognisable carrion that had been dragged out of the road. She suspected it was a badger. The afternoon stickiness sent a wave of nausea through her. She looked away from the roadkill and concentrated on the main door to the block. 'What number is it again?'

Jacob pulled his phone out. 'One.'

'Bottom floor. I didn't fancy climbing a million steps in this heat. Look, around the corner. There are front doors and gardens. We might not need to buzz with any luck.' They followed the building around and an elderly man sat on a kitchen chair outside one of the flats, a straw Stetson over his eyes while snoring.

As Gina tapped at number one, the man pushed the brim of his hat up and knocked his walking cane onto the patio. 'I can't get any peace around here.' He shook his head and turned away from them. 'And I wish that dog would shut the hell up. All day and night. It's enough to drive a person insane. Bloody torture.'

After knocking again, a rotund, grey-haired woman answered wearing the thickest glasses that Gina had ever seen. 'Hello.' She squinted as she examined them both.

'Hello, are you Ms Brock?'

'What do you want? If you're selling anything, I've got no money so don't waste your time and if it's religion, I already have my God. He's here in my heart and doesn't need me to give you money.'

'Ms Brock, I'm DI Harte and this is DS Driscoll. We're here to speak to your son, Shaun. Is he in?'

She scrunched her brow and peered closer at their identifications. 'My boy is good. He hasn't done anything. Why do you want to speak to him?'

'It would be best if we spoke to your son first. Do you mind if we come in?'

'No, of course not.' As they stepped in through the door, battling with the net curtain, Gina gazed around the front room. Small but clean, it had no end of welcoming furnishings from colourful cushions to a mat that said, 'Make yourself at home'. The woman loved hearts, they were everywhere; in pictures, made of wicker and even stone ornaments.

Gina glanced at the photos on the shelf above the sofa and most were of her, a man and a little boy. 'Lovely photos. Is that your son?'

'Aww, yes,' she said with a smile. 'He was just a little 'un then and his dad was still with us, bless his soul.' She made the sign of the cross and continued. 'As you can see, he never ventured anywhere without one of his Matchbox cars and he grew up to build them – cars, not Matchbox toys. I'm so proud. Do you know he's travelled to Australia and New Zealand? He's a bit of an adventurer.'

'Is he in?'

'Oh yes. He'll no doubt be listening to his music with his earphones on. The neighbour gets mad at the slightest noise so he has to wear them. Is that what this is about? Has that busybody next door complained?'

'No, we just need to speak to him about an incident.'

'I'll go and get him, shall I?' She stared as if Gina should elaborate but as soon as she realised she wasn't getting any details, she shrugged.

'That would be really helpful.'

The woman vanished for a few minutes before coming back with her son. 'Here he is. This is my Shaun.'

'What's this about?' He ran his fingers over his buzz cut brown hair and then stood, arms folded over his muscular frame. Yawning, he did up his belt and stretched.

'We need to speak to you about Billie Reeves.'

His eyes widened. 'Mum, I'm popping out.' He aimed a pleading look at Gina and Jacob. 'Let's walk. There's a bench that we can sit on and talk.' The young man opened the door and stepped out.

'Where you goin'?' Ms Brock pulled up her joggers so that the waistband almost reached under her breasts.

'Nowhere, Mum. I'll be back in a few minutes. Shall we have a cup of tea? Maybe you could put the kettle on, I'm parched.' Brock's mother nodded, seemingly more than happy to make the tea.

On leaving, they passed the old man who tutted at the disturbance.

'There's a bench by the road, can we sit there? I don't want to worry Mum, that's all. She's had some heart problems. One shock and who knows what might happen.'

'That's fine.' Gina knew he was hiding something from his mother, and she was going to get it out of him, even if it meant taking him down to the station. A text wasn't enough to arrest him on, she needed more.

When Shaun reached the bench, he stepped on it and sat on the backrest. Gina made a mental note that his short-sleeved shirt was fitted, and he was close on five feet nine inches. He could have been Billie's visitor, the one Mrs Pearlman described seeing but it could easily have not been. Seeing someone from an upstairs window in the dark would make it hard to estimate the height of a person. If it was Brock, maybe Billie had let him talk to Kayden on the phone and he'd read the boy a story. That would tie in with what the other witness said. Maybe that wasn't enough for him, so he stormed around at nearly midnight. The neighbour had seen Billie in some sort of clinch. She had to consider whether Billie was trying to escape or maybe Billie didn't want to antagonise the man any further so went with an embrace. Or, maybe Mrs Pearlman couldn't see what was going on as well as she thought. So many maybes.

'What's this about Billie?'

'Billie Reeves was found murdered in her house yesterday afternoon. We're speaking to everyone she knew and you're Kayden's father.'

For a few seconds he almost choked on his words and had to stop trying to talk. Either he was a great actor, or this was the first he'd heard about it. 'Bloody hell, I had no idea. I don't get it.'

'Do you watch the news?'

He shook his head. 'Nah.' He stared at the bench slats below and closed his eyes for a few seconds. 'I can't believe she's gone. Who did it?'

'That's what we're trying to find out.'

He stared at Gina. 'You think it's me, don't you? I'm an easy target. Father denied access, a bit angry and I've suddenly turned up in her life.' He scratched his head. 'It wasn't me. I would never hurt her. I was just letting off steam, that's all.'

In Gina's eyes, he'd already hurt her by not being a father to their son. 'Why didn't you want to speak in front of your mother?'

He spread his legs on the bench and leaned over, his chin almost reaching knee level. 'She doesn't know about Kayden. I've never told her.'

The poor woman had no idea that she was grandmother to a little boy whose mother had just been murdered. Gina felt for her, especially as she seemed lovely. She could never imagine how hurtful it would feel to not know she had Gracie in her life.

'Tell me about you and Billie?' Gina felt the sun's rays penetrating her neck. She took a step to the side, stealing the shade of a mature oak tree.

'I met her when I was eighteen and within weeks, she fell pregnant. She promised me she was on the pill. I wasn't ready to be a dad as I'd bought a ticket to travel to Australia. We were just having fun, that's how she put it. Casual.'

'So, you left soon after?'

'Yes. I was a dick, and I can see that now. I was thinking of my own stupid self. For years I tried to deny I was a dad even though Billie would send me pictures and bits of video of him playing. I just deleted them in the hope that it wasn't real. I can see why she didn't want to speak to me when I came back for good a few weeks ago.'

'What changed? Why did you want to see Kayden after all these years?' Gina couldn't help but judge him. Not only did he abandon his child, but he also tried to deny the little boy's existence by deleting everything Billie ever sent him. Billie had reached out, gave him the opportunity to be involved, even if it was nothing more than a long-distance relationship between her son and his father. The rejection of her son must have hurt her.

'I had an accident. I got into stock-car racing, and I had a smash up. There was a huge fire.' He lifted his shirt and Gina took in the gnarled pink skin that covered his taut torso. 'Anyway, all I could think about was, if I died, Kayden would never have known me. As soon as I healed, I got on a plane and came straight home. I know I should have tried to take things slowly with Billie, but I kept calling her. She wouldn't answer most of the time. She was angry and I got that, but I really had seen the light and I knew I needed to do everything in my power to see Kayden. I'm a screw-up and I admit it, but I hoped more than anything for a second chance.'

'Can you explain the text that you sent?'

'Text?'

'The one where you told her that if you can't see Kayden, you won't be responsible for your actions.'

'Bloody hell, that was sent in the heat of the moment. So, I made a few calls and sent a text, that doesn't make me a murderer. Are you arresting me?'

'We'd like you to voluntarily come to the station for a formal interview.'

'No worries. I'm happy to do that. I made a big mistake, one I will pay for for the rest of my life and that mistake was leaving my son and dumping all that responsibility on Billie. Right now, I want to do the right thing by him, especially as he needs me more than ever now. Can I see Kayden?'

Gina stepped under the tree a little further. 'You'd need to speak to Billie's parents. They're looking after him. He and they have been through a lot—'

'So, you think I should leave it for now? I want to see him.'

It wasn't Gina's place to interfere. The man sitting on the bench had never even met the boy. It wasn't going to be the happy reunion that Shaun Brock was probably pinning his hopes on. He'd have a lot of work to do in that respect and Billie's parents might not take his presence in their grandson's life so well. 'Mr Brock, where were you yesterday, between two in the afternoon and six?'

'Walking and drinking.'

'Where?'

'To the Angel Arms, where I had a couple of pints in the beer garden. I was there during that time hoping to meet up with some of my old friends.'

'And the pub will be able to verify your presence?'

'Yup. That's where I was. I talked to the landlady a few times, Elouise. She seemed nice. There was also a party going on. I don't know who it was for, or what it was about but there were loads of people there. Look.' He pulled out his phone and selected the Angel Arms's Facebook page. 'I liked this earlier.

It's a photo of the party. That's me sitting on a bench drinking beer.' Gina made a mental note of the name he was using. *Brock Man.*

Gina knew that Elouise, the licensee of the Angel Arms, would let them see the CCTV and they were going straight there after. She could see that Brock was in the photo, but she couldn't tell what time that photo was actually taken. It did, however, verify that Brock had been at the Angel Arms on the afternoon he said he had. 'Okay, I want you to head to the station, now, and give a formal statement. We can take you.'

'I really need to speak to my mum first, if that's okay. As I'm not under arrest, I'd rather my mum brought me in her car. Before that, I need to quickly explain to her what's happened without upsetting her too much.'

Gina glanced at Jacob. She'd rather him come with them but there's no way she could force him. Brock jumped off the bench and began walking back to his mother's flat. Gina and Jacob followed, watching as he went in. His mother waved out the door and pulled the net across after closing it.

The old man next door lifted the brim of his hat. 'He's a prick, that kid. If you heard the way he talked to his mother, it would make you sick.'

'Did you see him yesterday?'

'I was sitting here all day and he went out about lunchtime. He never came home until this morning. I heard his mum asking him where he'd been, and he told her to stop going on before playing his hideous music. I feel sorry for Beryl having to put up with that racket, I mean, it's disturbed my peace. I did knock at hers and complain but that got me nowhere. Yesterday morning, I was sitting here, and he had the door open. He kept pacing and whining down the phone. I don't know who the poor lass was on the other end of the line, but I wouldn't let him see the kid either.'

As they got back into the car, Gina took a swig of water

from the bottle. 'I don't trust Brock, but that photo proves he was somewhat truthful. There's no time to waste. Before he gets to the station, I want to verify everything he said with Elouise at the Angel. If we find he had even the remotest of opportunity or he lied in any way, he's our prime suspect.'

TWENTY-ONE

NADIA

Hair still wet from her shower at the gym, Nadia jogged to the school gates. The summer dress she'd changed into clung to her damp legs. As she glanced around, trying to catch sight of William, her gaze stopped on Candice who was waiting for her with William and Poppy in tow. William looked a little sad and Candice tilted her head as she spoke to him. Her little boy's frown turned into a smile and Poppy playfully prodded him in the arm.

Candice waved and smiled. 'Nadia, how are you bearing up?'

'Not good, if I'm honest. I was late for my afternoon session, and it ran over. I've never showered so fast.' She grabbed her knotty hair and clipped it up in the hope that it would dry. The truth was, she'd started fishing through Ed's belongings in the garage in the hope of finding the one thing she really needed right now but, as always, she couldn't find what she was looking for. That had set her back for the afternoon. If only she was as good at searching as Ed was at hiding. A knot formed in her stomach.

'You look how I feel.'

Nadia pressed her lips together. 'I feel empty.'

'Same.' Candice wiped a tear from her eye and exhaled. 'Are you still coming back to mine?'

'Yes, that would be lovely.'

'I popped to the deli and got a selection of salads and scones to eat in the garden.' She swallowed. 'It won't be the same without Billie.' Candice took her daughter's hand.

William looked up at Nadia with big, sad eyes and it made her want to crouch down and hug him close. She couldn't imagine not being around to see her little boy grow up. Instead, she held his clammy hand and squeezed while she mouthed 'Love you,' to him. 'I'll see you at yours, then.'

With that Candice led Poppy by the hand towards her car, leaving Nadia in the middle of the playground, surrounded by parents.

Her hearing tuned into what was being said by a gaggle of gossips.

'Was she really a prostitute?'

'Yes, I heard. I told Sam to keep away from Kayden. You know those types, probably on drugs too.'

'Who told you?'

'I don't know, it's been going round. I just heard something.'

'People have choices, and she made a bad one. Look at her now.'

'Are you sure she was? How am I the last to know?'

'Yes, she was always with men. You could just tell. Weird woman. Loud too, always over the top. I feel sorry for Kayden.'

'Does he even have a dad?'

'I wonder what he thinks of all this. Poor guy.'

'I hear Nadia even stopped William from going to her house.'

'Oh, that gossiping cow.'

Dizzy with everything, Nadia pulled William away from

the nasty comments and back towards her car. 'Don't listen to all that, sweetie. Some people can be mean.'

'Mummy?'

'What?' The car flashed as she opened it.

'What's a prostitute?'

'Nothing. You don't need to know and don't say that word, okay?' She ruffled his hair.

'Okay, Mummy.' She strapped him into his car seat and drove to Candice's. As she pulled up, she could see that Meera's car wasn't there. Maybe it was just the two of them.

Candice opened the door as Nadia walked down the drive, William's hand in hers. 'Come in. The paddling pool is out if you want to go in with Poppy.'

Nadia nodded. 'It's okay, sweetie. You can go in in your underpants.'

Screaming with glee, he ran into the garden. Candice closed the door that led to the garage, the one that had been converted into a huge dog spa where clipped poodle hair covered the floor. 'Come through. Here, have this unless you want something stronger.' She passed Nadia a large glass of elderflower cordial.

'Best not.' They stepped out onto the decking where Candice had placed the food and a few plates down. 'I hope you don't mind me asking Meera too. I thought, we're all grieving, we're all worried, and as you said Ed couldn't come, I've told Gavin to stay in his office.'

'Of course not.' Glancing at the food, Nadia knew that she wasn't going to be able to eat anything.

'Yeah, I don't think I feel like eating either.'

It was as if Candice had read her mind.

Candice's bottom lip began to tremble. 'I keep imagining her in her house and being attacked. My heart feels as though it's about to stop and... She must have been terrified.' She turned around. 'Sorry, I can't seem to control my emotions at the moment. I'm all over the place, as you are.' She puffed out a couple of times and turned back to face Nadia.

Nadia wiped the streak of mascara from her friend's face and hugged Candice. 'It's good that we have each other.'

'It is. What would we do without good friends?' She sat at the patio table. 'I saw two suits in a car when I left yours. They looked a bit out of place.'

'Oh, it was the police.' She instantly regretted telling Candice, then she reminded herself that she was the woman who couldn't keep a secret, not Candice. 'They're speaking to people who knew Billie, that's all. I just told them what I knew. I had to tell them about her work.'

'I see. I hope they catch the bastard quick. Did they say anything?'

'No. It has to be one of her clients, though. Who else would hurt her?' Nadia couldn't keep Ed's name out of her head. She didn't trust him one bit. He was having an affair and he had received a message from Billie just before she died. If he was seeing Billie behind her back and Billie threatened to tell, who knows what he was capable of. He was barely around lately, and he wasn't straight with her whenever she asked when he'd be home but, of course, she had to just put up with it. She'd made her proverbial bed and now she was imprisoned in it.

Candice furrowed her brows and paused. 'I don't know but there's Kayden's dad. Billie said he was causing a bit of a fuss. She said he kept calling.'

'Yes, maybe it was him. It's a coincidence that he came back recently and now this has happened.' Anything to deflect Billie's murder as far away from Ed as possible. She wanted to slap herself. A text proved nothing. Another little voice kept repeating itself. He lied about that text. If she couldn't get into his phone, she had no choice but to stand up to him and demand to see what was on it. Asking might hurt if he had one of his episodes but she couldn't live with the not knowing.

'What's this, love? I found it on the printer.' Gavin came out, his glasses pushed up against his face as he read what was written on a sheet of paper.

Candice took the piece of paper and read a couple of lines. 'Oh, that's Poppy's poem for Billie. She wants me to read it at the funeral.' She paused and a tear trickled down her cheek. 'Kayden's mummy was pretty and funny. Her hugs were the best...' Candice passed the poem back to Gavin. 'I can't read any more of it right now.'

Gavin pressed his lips together as he looked at his little girl. 'She's such a lovely sensitive soul. Terrible news. How are you bearing up, Nadia? You two were so close.'

Candice didn't know how lucky she was having Gavin's support. Nadia wished that Ed cared more. 'We were.' From nowhere the grief hit her. She would never see Billie again. After going through the motions all day and fulfilling a booking after originally cancelling, she couldn't hold back any longer. The friend who had been there for the past few years was gone and she'd never see her again.

Grabbing a box of tissues, Gavin hurried over. 'Here, have a seat.' He and Candice ushered her over to a chair at the patio table. 'I'm so sorry. I hope they catch this monster soon. It's hard to believe that there's a murderer roaming around out there.'

'Me too,' she blurted out and she meant it. *Please let it not be Ed.* She couldn't cope if it were him. She sobbed. 'I caught William playing weirdly last night with my old doll's house that's in his room. When I asked him about it, he said that Kayden was scared and often hid under his bed or in the cupboard because of Billie's screaming. Kayden told him this and it's tearing me apart. What she must have gone through and poor Kayden.'

'It's okay. Billie probably had lots of secrets. We never truly know what's happening in another person's life or what they're capable of. How could we?' Candice wrapped her arms around

Nadia. That was true. She wondered if Candice would be this nice to her if she knew her secret. That's why she had to go home soon and wait for Ed. She had to know if it was him. If it was, she could use it as leverage. It could be her way out of her farce of a marriage.

TWENTY-TWO

For a Thursday the Angel Arms seemed quiet. Gina glanced through the corridor that passed the toilets and she could see that a few tables in the beer garden had been filled. Elouise, the licensee, tottered back in on her strappy kitten heels and placed a tray of empties on the bar. Her black hair was piled high on her head and neatly kept up with a red scarf.

'Ouch.' She peeled the rest of a torn pink nail away. 'Another one gone. Detectives, what can I do for you today?'

'There's been an incident.'

'Not my CCTV again?'

Gina nodded. 'Sorry.'

'I can't believe how this area's going down the pan so fast. I still can't walk down that lane out the back.' Only a short while ago, Elouise found the body of a murder victim there. Gina tried to remember that while speaking to her. The landlady hadn't seemed the same since.

'I know, it's worrying. Can we talk in private?'

Elouise removed her apron and called over the young man who peered over the cellar flap. 'Bradley, can you take over the bar for a while. Just call me if a mad rush of people come in.'

'Yep.' He closed the flap and hurried to the bar.

'Follow me. You know the way.' Gina and Jacob were soon upstairs. 'Take a seat on the couch.'

Gina avoided knocking over the packs of juice and miniature bottles of tonic that were piled up everywhere.

'I need to sort all this out but as you can appreciate, time seems to run away. So, what's happened now?'

'A young woman was murdered yesterday.'

'I heard the news. I tell you something, I checked all the doors and windows three times last night before going to bed.' She splayed out her spotty sundress as she sat on a chair. 'I don't know her, though. I saw the photo that was shared on the news. She doesn't come in here.'

'We're checking out an alibi and the man in question says he was here, drinking in your beer garden.'

'Okay, what time?'

Gina remembered him saying he left at lunchtime and was at the pub the rest of the duration. She knew the walk from his house would take him past the Cleevesford Cleaver bed and breakfast and along the high street, that would take about twenty minutes. 'From around two fifteen, maybe two thirty.'

'We had a busy afternoon with a christening bash, so the place was pretty full. They didn't book the place out so the public could still come in too. They used the garden. Is he a regular? What's his name?'

'He's only just come back to the area so you may not know him.'

'Try me, if I got his name while he was here, I'd remember it. I'm nifty with names.'

'Shaun Brock. Late twenties, buzz cut, muscular and about five feet nine.'

She smiled and squinted, emphasising her long dark lash extensions. 'I remember him. He came in wearing a crisp white vest and tight jeans; thought he was God's gift as he attempted to chat up the drunken baby's mother. There was something odd, the label was still on the top. I told him and he pulled it off.'

'Did you speak to him?'

'Yes, a couple of times when he came up to the bar.'

'What did he say?'

'He was full of stories about his time in Australia and New Zealand, but he said he was back for good and how he was trying to settle back into the area. He asked if I knew of anyone renting a flat out as his mother's fussing was driving him mad. Things like that.'

'What time was this?'

'I'd say around five. I know he pulled up in a car as one of the party had to ask him to move it as he was blocking one of them in. He then left the car on the road.'

'He turned up around five and in a car?'

'That's right. I'll get you a copy of the CCTV in a moment, but I know he did. I remember thinking that I hoped the party would hurry up and go. They'd been there for hours, and some people were starting to arrive for after-work drinks and the party were rowdy. They made a total mess of the garden, and I was eager to clean it up.' Gina watched as Jacob made a note about him driving. She knew from their records that he didn't have a car that was registered to him, but his mother did, Brock even said so himself. Jacob glanced at her.

'Can we get all the CCTV from two until the time he left?'

'Of course. That won't be a problem, but it might take a short while. He was here until closing and he left with a woman at around eleven thirty. Are you okay to wait? I can get Bradley to pour you something cold if you want to wait in the bar.'

'Actually,' Gina stood, 'we need to get on. Can I see it quickly and I'll send an officer to collect it later?' She needed to confirm the man's arrival with her own eyes, and she wanted to see who he left with.

'Yes, follow me through.'

Gina leaned over the desk beside Elouise as she scrolled through the grainy footage. Brock had indeed arrived just after five and in a car. He'd lied to them.

'Can I get the hard drive picked up within the hour?'

'Of course. I should have it ready by then. Give me two to be sure. There's a lot of footage if you want all cameras.' Agreeing, Gina made her way to the door.

Jacob stood and followed her back out. The sun had ducked behind the trees at the end of the car park and Gina was glad that the air was cooling a little. 'He had opportunity, motive, and possibly a change of clothes in the car. Did he buy a new top on the way, knowing that he was going to kill Billie and things could get messy? And he lied to us. We need a warrant to get that car and his mother's flat searched as soon as possible. If he killed Billie, there has to be traces of blood in that car. I'm going to call Briggs with an update. If Brock has arrived at the station, we need to keep him there.'

Jacob nodded. 'I'll make a call to organise the warrant, then we can head straight to the station to collect it.'

'Great, get a warrant for the flat, her car and the communal areas for the block.' Gina headed over to the other side of the car park, leaving Jacob to make his call. Briggs answered almost immediately. 'Gina, have you got something?'

She relayed her conversation with Elouise, trying to forget what had happened between them and remain professional. 'Is Brock there?'

'No.'

'He was meant to go straight to the station.'

'He hasn't been in. I've just caught up with the case after dealing with the press all day.'

She kicked the wall. 'Dammit. We're coming back to collect a search warrant for Brock's mother's flat and car before heading straight there. Jacob is sorting that out as we speak along with a tow truck to take the car. We need to act fast before he gets the opportunity to destroy any evidence. He's already had too long. Can you send someone to the Angel to grab the CCTV in a couple of hours? Sorry to ask but we're rushed off our feet.'

'Of course. I'll get a PC to collect it.'

'And we'll need some officers ready to help with the search of the property and the arrest of Shaun Brock. We now have enough to bring him in.'

After ending the call, she turned back to Jacob. 'Let's go. Brock didn't turn up at the station. We need to get that warrant, find him and arrest him.' The more she thought about it, the angrier she got. They had Brock earlier and they'd let him go. If only she'd seen the CCTV before they arrived at his. He'd have been at the station right now. Instead, a suspected murderer was out there and running desperate. That made him even more dangerous.

TWENTY-THREE

Jacob pulled up outside the flats and Gina grabbed the warrant.

'There's his mother's car.' She pointed at the red Ford that was parked against the kerb.

O'Connor stepped out of his car and ambled over, zapped by the heat. He waved at Gina and Jacob. 'Keith from forensics is on his way to take any samples we might need. Bernard is still going through yesterday's evidence with his team, so he won't be coming.'

'Thanks, O'Connor.'

Heading towards the Brocks' front door, the old neighbour stood against his door frame as he folded his garden chair up. 'Back so soon.' He smiled at Gina.

Great, the last thing Gina needed was a nosy neighbour loitering around. This wasn't going to be pleasant for Ms Brock. She waited for Wyre, Kapoor and Smith to catch up, watching as they took a shortcut over the grass. Gina hammered on the door and waited. Beryl Brock answered. 'What now?'

Glancing at the old man, Gina cleared her throat. 'May we come in? It would be best if we spoke inside.' Realising how hard searches were for families, she didn't want to embarrass or upset the woman any more than she had to. Stepping in, Gina held up the paperwork. 'Ms Brock, we have a warrant issued by Cleevesford Magistrates Court which gives us the authority under the Police and Criminal Evidence Act to search your address and vehicle for evidence connected to an offence of murder which we are currently investigating. You'll be given a copy of the warrant, which provides further details. We're also looking for your son, is he here?'

The woman wobbled a little and grabbed the arm of the chair for support.

'Here.' Aware Brock had mentioned that she had a heart condition Gina walked over and helped her to sit down, while keeping her voice gentle.

'We haven't done anything. Shaun isn't here. Murder?' Her jaw wobbled. 'He said he had to get away, but he wouldn't tell me why. What's happened? I've been beside myself since he left.'

'There is a warrant out for your son's arrest. I'm really sorry to tell you that. Where could he have gone?' Gina tilted her head and crouched in front of the woman. From her confused look, Shaun hadn't told her anything at all. If he had, she'd have known about Billie and her grandson. 'I know this is hard, but it will help Shaun and us in the long run if we speak to him sooner rather than later. Does he have any friends he might visit or places he might stay? Did he mention going anywhere?'

Ms Brock shook her head. 'He doesn't tell me anything. What's going to happen?'

'The officers here will search the flat. We'll be as tidy and respectful as we can, I promise. You won't know we were here. I'm sorry that we have to do this but we're investigating a very serious crime.'

'And you think my Shaun had something to do with it? He wouldn't hurt anyone.' She began to gasp a little.

'That's what we're trying to find out.' Gina looked up at

Wyre and Jacob. 'Can we make you a drink or call anyone to be with you?'

She shook her head. 'No, just get it over with.' A tear slid down her cheek.

Gina could see that Jacob was scrolling through the system on his phone for Brock's number. 'I'll just pop outside and try calling him.'

'May I have your car keys?'

'They're over there in the heart-shaped jewellery box.' Gina stood, opened the box and took them. Nodding, Gina turned back to Ms Brock. 'PC Smith will sit with you and go through everything. Is that okay? If you need anything, just let us know.'

On hearing his name, Smith stepped into the tiny room and removed his police hat.

Gina left her in his capable hands while she regrouped everyone in the tiny back kitchen. 'Jacob, you and I will take the bedrooms and bathroom. Shaun Brock's is the one I want to concentrate on. Wyre, will you give O'Connor the car keys, then carefully search the living room? Kapoor, you stay here in the kitchen and check the washing machine too. Whoever finishes first can check the communal areas. Hopefully we'll have more officers arriving shortly to help. There will be their service cupboards and their postbox. We have to check everything that Brock might have had access to. What we are looking for is the item of clothing Shaun Brock changed into before going to the pub and handle it delicately. We are still looking for the knife that was used in Billie's murder. If we find either, they will need to go straight to the lab and if anything ties him to the scene, we have him bang to rights.' She paused, knowing that he'd had ample time to dispose of evidence. 'Shoes too. There may be something in the tread that links him back to the crime scene. A speck of blood, hair, soil that matches samples from her garden. Right, let's get this done.' Gina snapped a pair of latex gloves on.

They murmured a few yesses. As Gina left the room, she heard Keith speaking to Smith in the living room. Gina headed along the dark corridor to the bedrooms. She stopped, pulled her shoe covers on and tied her hair up. Jacob peered around the first door. 'Shall I take his mother's room?'

'Yes, please.' Gina pushed through the last door, opposite the bathroom. The stench of sweat and mouldy food made her gasp. Several plates were piled up on a coffee table next to the bed, all containing bits of leftover food in various states of decay. A bluebottle landed on a pile of chicken bones. She began to sift through all the items on top first before feeling along the underside of the table. Then, she headed to the chest of drawers, the only other piece of furniture in the room. Sliding the top drawer open, she reached amongst the underpants and unpaired socks, flinching as a moth escaped. The other drawers were as unfruitful as the first. After removing the bottom one to check that nothing was hidden underneath, she glanced around the room. Kneeling to check under the bed, she flinched as a silver fish scurried past her face. Torch shining, all she could see were layers of dust.

After a few more minutes of checking behind furniture and amongst the bedding, she realised that what she was looking for wasn't in this room. She glanced into Ms Brock's bedroom where Jacob had a lot more items to search through, including a huge double wardrobe and stacks of boxes. 'Anything so far?'

'No, guv, but I still have a way to go.' He carefully refolded the woman's clothes and placed them back in a drawer.

'Brock's room is clear. I'm heading to the bathroom.' She pushed the door fully open, and her gaze followed the mould from the corner of the windowless room to the top of the bathroom cabinet. She caught sight of her pasty face and dyed brown ponytail before gently opening it. She peered at all Ms Brock's heart medicine, including a tongue spray that Gina knew was used for angina. Her knee brushed against the tall washing basket. Opening the lid, her heart began to judder. This was high on the list of places where the evidence they needed might be. She pulled out a pink top, then some yellow trousers and a few vest tops, underpants and socks, but there was nothing that looked bloody or even that dirty. She opened an evidence bag and placed all of Brock's clothing in it before labelling it up. After, she bagged up the soap, the contents of the hair catcher in the bath and the flannels. As soon as she was done in the bathroom, she'd send Keith in to swab the bath, sink and floor. They'd take Brock's bed sheets too. If there were traces of Billie in the room that had been transferred from him, they were going to find them. It was still a long shot. Elouise at the Angel had seen him leaving with a woman last night. He may have showered at hers and ditched his clothes before coming home in the morning.

'Guv, O'Connor has found something,' Wyre said. Gina hurried out of the room and gave brief instructions to Keith, before following Wyre outside to the car.

'What is it?'

'One of Billie's flyers that she advertises with. It has a streak of blood on it.'

'There was a pile in the kitchen on the day she was murdered.'

'There is also a small teddy bear next to the smeared flyer and that has blood on it too.'

'We need to get them to the lab urgently. If that blood is a match for Billie's, we can place him at the scene. Keith is just taking some samples in the flat. As soon as he's out, he can go through the car before the tow truck gets here. Any news on where Brock might be?'

O'Connor shook his head. 'No. I've been listening to the radio and checking in. All units are keeping a lookout.'

'Great. We know he's on foot, so we need to make sure we

have officers covering the bus stops and taxi ranks. We need to hurry back to the station and comb through the rest of that CCTV from the Angel. Whoever he stayed out with might be on that footage.'

TWENTY-FOUR

NADIA

Friday, 17 June

Television off and sitting in silence, Nadia flicked the cork from the bottle of wine she'd opened onto the floor. After trying Ed's phone several times, it was obvious that he wasn't going to answer. She perked up on remembering that he had a tablet that he always left in the drawer of the sideboard. Maybe he had left it. She could turn it on and see if there were any clues in his online diary that had synched from his phone. Hurrying over to the sideboard, she slid the drawer open and hit it in disappointment. The tablet wasn't there. As she was about to close it, something didn't look right. What was missing?

Fishing through the tangled leads and chargers, it hit her. The spare back door key was gone. Ed often left his keys at other offices and used it when needed. He must have come back at some time, or did he take it earlier when he left? She shrugged, not really caring.

She turned her own tablet on and began checking his Facebook and Instagram. The last photo he'd posted was of him in sunglasses outside the Cleevesford office, where he talked about working hard, success, and reaping the rewards. She glanced at his likes that were well into the hundreds. As a Facebook message from Ed popped up, she almost dropped the tablet. It was as if he could sense that she was spying on him.

On way back. Need to grab some toiletries as I have to go back to the Derby office again. The alarm is going off and I'll probably stay there.

That was a lie. Her mind boggled with who he was staying with. She flinched as she heard a bang coming from the back garden at the same time the security light flashed on. Heart pounding, she hurried to the bifold doors and trembled as she saw the rolling tennis ball come to a stop on the patio. All she could hear was the thumping of her pulse. The messages she'd received flashed through her mind, the one blaming her for Billie's death and telling her to watch her back unless she wanted to end up like Billie. The one threatening her if she went to the police. It would be so easy if she could call the police and tell them everything but that wasn't an option. Her life as she knew it would be over. She had to protect William, even if it meant keeping her awful secret. The last thing he needed was a mother in prison.

A tingle shot down her neck as she felt the warmth of a body behind her just before a large hand grabbed her shoulder. That's when she screamed. She was going to end up like Billie. The messenger wasn't lying.

TWENTY-FIVE

Lying in bed, Gina ate another jelly sweet, that's all she seemed to crave now – sugar. Frame by frame, she took her time sifting through the CCTV from the Angel Arms. She watched as Brock sat in the beer garden behind the partygoers, even accepting a glass of bubbly from one of them. She flicked back to Billie's Facebook page, then to Brock's. Billie posted her whereabouts and what she had on next every five minutes. There were photos of her and her son outside the school gates. Finding her would have been easy for Brock.

Her phone lit up. She glanced at the time. It was a little past midnight. Her heart began to judder as she grabbed it, not knowing whether to answer Briggs's call. She dropped the jelly snake onto her bed. 'Hello.'

'Gina,' he said in a hushed voice. The closing of a door told her he'd gone into another room so they could talk.

'Is everything okay?'

'I needed to speak to you.'

He'd realised that it was Gina he loved all along, that's why he was calling. Why else would he want to speak to her in the early hours when he should be in bed with Rosemary? He'd confronted her and found out she was having an affair. 'I need to speak to you too.' It was time to tell him how she was feeling and how much she missed him. 'I don't know how to be without you.' A tear slipped down her cheek and it pained her to feel this low and vulnerable. Since Terry's abuse, she'd been emotionally closed when it came to relationships, scared to let anyone in. A twang of guilt knotted in her chest.

'Oh, Gina.'

That voice conveyed pity, not what she expected. Her cheeks began to burn.

'I need to tell you that Rosemary has moved in with me and I don't want you going on about what you think you saw the other night, okay? I accidentally slipped the news to Jacob earlier when he was talking about his wedding plans so I thought you should know.'

'Did you ask her about the man?'

'The man. Here we go again. It was her brother. He's staying with a friend in town.'

'That's not how you touch a brother.'

'Gina, just stop it. You're embarrassing yourself. Seriously.'

A tear sprang from her eye. Unable to speak, she hung up on him and lay back on the bed. As far as Gina was concerned, that was it. Nothing to look forward to, no one to talk to any more. She didn't want to be here, to exist, or face tomorrow. Nothing mattered. She grabbed the sweets and threw them at the wardrobe. He tried to call again but she cut him off. A message pinged through.

Gina. Please, we used to be so close. Can we be friends? We have to work together.

No, she would be his colleague and that was all. She blew her nose and wiped her eyes. The only person in the world who needed her right now was Billie. She needed Gina to find out who killed her. She shook her head. The only person who needed her was a dead woman.

She wiped her eyes. Billie may be a dead woman, but she was brutally killed. Kayden needed her to find out who killed his mother. Kathleen and George Reeves needed her. She didn't have much to cling onto, but she still had a purpose.

There was still so much footage to get through. Her colleagues had been exhausted by the end of the day, so it fell on her. There was no way she'd get much sleep. Instead, she opened the footage showing inside the pub. As she forwarded to ten in the evening, she saw the side of a woman approaching the bar, hair falling over her face. Brock waved and the woman sat by him. Her back remained to the camera. Gina squinted to get a better look at the grainy footage. If only the CCTV images were better quality, it would make her job much easier. It didn't help that it kept stopping to buffer and judder, skipping bits of frame.

Later, the woman and Brock stood and walked over to the door as Elouise collected glasses up. People flooded out and they got caught in a small bottleneck at the main door to the car park.

She clicked on the car park footage. People spilled out. A woman fell over and required two of her friends to help her into a taxi. That's when the woman emerged with Brock, standing to the side. She moved towards a car and Gina could clearly see that it wasn't Brock's mother's car. That was parked on the other side of the car park. She began to hold her hands up and it looked like she was shouting. He went to grab her, but she pushed him away. That's when her long hair flicked away from her face. Gina recognised the woman straight away. A few seconds later, she drove away leaving Brock alone in the car park. He rubbed his head as he got into his mother's Fiesta and drove off the premises, only to park up on the road where most of the car was concealed by trees and shrubs. She watched for ages and the car remained in place but was Brock still in it or had he gone somewhere else and disposed of the clothing he wore when he murdered Billie? The footage Elouise had sent went on to seven in the morning and Brock's car remained in position.

It was still her job to keep Briggs updated. She ignored his last message and typed out another with the latest. O'Connor would have to attend the post-mortem in the morning. There was no way she'd make it with visiting the woman in the footage and interviewing Edward Anderson.

Gina flicked back to the system and clicked on a photo of Billie, one of her in happier times. The mum-of-one had been brutally murdered. Gina made a silent promise to the woman that her killer would be brought to justice. He hadn't gone home with Meera, but what were they arguing about and why hadn't she told Gina about her encounter with Brock on the day of Billie's murder? What was Meera trying to hide?

TWENTY-SIX

NADIA

Nadia screamed as she fought with the man who now had both hands on her, only to turn around and see that it was Ed. 'You scared the life out of me.'

'Well, you were in a world of your own but what's new?'

'Someone was in the garden. The light came on.'

'It was probably a fox. I saw one the other night. You're getting paranoid.' He shook his head.

'But a ball rolled onto the patio.'

'They do play.' Something about his poker expression told her that he was toying with her.

She waited for her heart rate to return to normal. Was she reading too much into him? Maybe he was right, and it was a fox. She could never quite read Ed. 'I tried to call you.'

He tutted. 'I got the three million missed calls. Really?'

'Why didn't you answer?'

'I was working?'

'All evening?'

'Someone has to pay for all this,' he yelled, arms in the air. 'It's not like you bring much into the household with your stupid hobby.'

A lump formed in her throat. She'd trained and studied hard to become a personal trainer, all while bringing William up, and that's what he thought. He could be horrible sometimes.

'I must hurry. I need to get back to the Derby office.'

He dropped his phone on the table and hurried upstairs for his toiletries. Bang goes the plan of getting him drunk and checking out his phone. As she listened to him rummaging above, she picked up his phone and as usual, she couldn't get into it. It rang and she took it to the snug knowing that this was her big chance. 'Hello.'

The caller went to speak, then hung up. It was a woman. Shaking, she realised she now had access to everything in his phone. She checked the last caller, and it was Graham. If the caller had been the Graham he employed, the man would have spoken to her, not hung up. She heard Ed sliding open the wardrobe above. She didn't have time to delve into who the caller was. She needed to see the message from Billie. Nausea built up as she opened it. She grabbed her own phone and took a photo of the message, number, date and time, before hurrying back to the kitchen.

Just as Ed charged down the stairs, she dropped the phone back where it was. He eyed her suspiciously. 'What were you just doing?'

'I, err, I didn't know whether to answer. Graham just called, but I left it. You might want to call him back.'

'Oh, right. He called me about the alarm going off.'

She smiled. 'I tell you what. Call him back and I'll put your bag in the car. You look tired and you've been working so hard.'

He furrowed his brow and passed her his holdall, clearly suspicious of her change in mood. 'Okay...'

As she hurried to the door, she grabbed her tablet and placed it under her arms. She opened the back door of his car and popped the holdall on the seat. After, she sandwiched the device between a couple of William's books. When she first bought the tablet, she'd downloaded a tracker app onto her phone just in case it got stolen. Wherever he was going, she would follow with her phone.

He made her jump as he came up behind her. She slammed the door shut and kissed him. 'I hope everything's okay.'

'It will be, I'm sure. I'll probably have to call the engineer out again. I'll see you tomorrow after I've been to the police station to give a statement.'

He could swing from calm to angry in seconds and right now, she wanted him to suspect nothing. 'Okay, hope it goes well. Love you.'

He got into his car, not saying those words back. It didn't matter anyway. As soon as he pulled away, she strolled back into the house and her phone beeped.

Wanna play a ball game?

Again, the unknown number. Nadia wished she'd had enough time to check more of Ed's messages, but he had more than one phone anyway. She knew he'd rolled the ball to scare her. It was too much of a coincidence. It was easy to think that someone else could be trying to play with her head, but Ed got off on controlling and scaring her. Their whole life was a game. What people and friends saw was a charade. She darted back to the kitchen and shivered as she reread the message that Billie had sent to Ed just before she died.

Stop harassing me or I'll call the police.

What had Ed done? No one knew the real Ed except her and what she did know, she hated. She also hated that there was nothing at all she could do about that message. He would destroy her.

TWENTY-SEVEN

NADIA

She could see from the app that Ed had parked up. What shocked her was, he didn't go back to Derby. He was parked up on Cleevesford Industrial Estate, outside his unit. Nadia paced up and down, itching to go straight there and see what was going on. Something was seriously wrong, and it had to involve Billie. That text on his phone was all the confirmation she needed.

She hurried upstairs and peered around William's bedroom door. Her little boy's heavy breaths told her he was in a deep sleep. Could she leave him, just for a short while? It would take her no longer than half an hour and he didn't normally wake once he'd properly fallen asleep. No one would know. She swallowed. If someone did see her leave, they might report her, and she wondered if she could lose William. No, it was just for a few minutes, nothing would happen. She pulled his bedroom door closed and crept across the landing. Pulling back the curtain, she glanced up and down at the eerily quiet street. Every house was in darkness, and no one was around except for a fox. It darted into a patch of trees and shrubs.

Running down the stairs, she slipped on her trainers, locked up and drove along the deserted roads of Cleevesford. Minutes later, she pulled into the industrial estate, pulse racing and mouth dry. Ed's car was exactly where the tracker said it would be, parked up in the space that was reserved for the managing director. She always thought the sign was a bit pretentious but that was Ed. He always liked people to know who he was. She turned off her lights and continued to drive past the building where she pulled up next to a kerb. The business next door was in total darkness.

As she reached the building, she leaned up and looked through the back windows, but she couldn't see him. Light shone from his office upstairs. That's when she saw two elongated shadows across the grass. He wasn't alone. She shuffled backwards, trying to avoid the light spillage. If he was looking out of the window, he'd see her.

She knew it. Ed was having an affair. Why else would there be two people in his office and why would he lie? The signs had been there, just like last time and the time before. If she confronted him, he'd deny everything and accuse her of being unstable. That's how it usually went, and she had no choice but to stay. He had to be the one to leave as he'd ensured that she could never leave him. He was calling all the shots and it wasn't fair, but then again, when had Ed ever played fair? Whoever was up there with him was nothing more than this month's choice, someone easily replaced by whoever comes along next. Heading closer to the light, she caught the back of Ed's head before he moved away from the window.

His office was double aspect. She had to get to the front window to see who he was with. Snatching her phone from her pocket, she held it up ready to take a photo. If she knew what the woman looked like, she could search through his Facebook friends until she found her. Shaking with anger, she thought, *to hell with it.* She'd send the woman a message telling her to stay away. If he hit her because of that, so be it. She was sick of being walked all over.

As she was about to step past the side of the building, the main door opened and she listened to the beeps as Ed set the alarm, then the woman spoke. 'Let's check into a hotel.'

'My desk not good enough for you this time.' He laughed.

'I want you for the night. For once we can feel like a proper couple.'

'Why don't we go to yours?'

'No, not with all that's going on and we can't go to my mum's.' She paused. 'Ed?'

'What?'

'When are you leaving her? I hate the lying and I feel horrible.'

'Soon, I promise. I only want you.'

Nadia shook her head and held a hand over her mouth as she gasped. That was a total lie. He was up for sex any time. Peering around, she watched as Ed closed the door. His bulky frame covered the woman completely as he leaned in and began kissing her hard, pressing into her as she backed up against the wall. *Please don't have sex now*, she thought. A part of her wanted to storm over there right now but another part held back as she caught sight of the woman whose tongue was in her husband's mouth. She'd recognised the voice, but she didn't want to believe it was true. Seeing her made it real and it pained her to the core.

Swiftly retreating, she placed a hand over her banging heart and clenched her fists. All this time, Ed's affair was happening close to home. She trusted her friend, and she'd been welcome in her home. Ed had never given her a second glance when he'd seen her in passing. How dare Meera betray her like that?

The central locking flashed on Ed's car. He couldn't know that she'd left William alone. Confronting him would have to wait. As he pulled away with Meera, she remained stiff against the wall, hoping that he hadn't seen her or the car but then he stopped for a moment too long at the junction, the engine turning like her nervous stomach was. He knew. He didn't stop or turn around, he continued turning right and out of the industrial estate. She could look at her tracker and find out which hotel they were going to but there was no point. Why torture herself any more?

She stood there for a couple of minutes and waited for the shaking to subside. Stomping over to the car, she beat the bonnet with her fists until they hurt, then she kicked the bumper. Her phone beeped.

Little boy all alone. How soundly you sleep.

She replied.

I hate you, Ed!

The text bounced back. She rushed into her car and crunched the gears before speeding back home. How dare he humiliate her and then send her horrible messages. He was the one in the wrong, but he'd twisted everything again.

What if it wasn't Ed? She gasped for breath and almost crashed into the road sign at the entrance to her close. As she glanced up at her house, the landing light was on. She didn't leave it on. William – something had happened.

The keys jangled in her trembling hand as she opened the front door. Legs like jelly, she crept through into the kitchen and could see that no one was there. The bottle of wine she opened had been placed in the middle of the table and a full glass had been poured. Next to that lay the missing door key. Ed had been back.

She hurried up the stairs, getting more light-headed the closer she got. Almost paralysed, she pushed William's door open, and she could see that her son was still sleeping. Her gaze was drawn to the light in the doll's house. A doll had been seated at a table and she was drinking a glass of wine. Silent cries exploded from her chest as she left her son to sleep, throwing every door in the house open, checking every cupboard. There was no one in the house except her.

'Mummy.'

She flinched. 'William.' She pulled her sleepy boy close and hugged him. 'Couldn't you sleep?'

'Daddy woke me up.'

'When? Earlier? I saw your light on in the doll's house; that was all. I turned it off.'

'Daddy turned it on. I heard him when I was sleepy.'

'You heard me just now.'

'No, before when he came in earlier and turned the light on, silly.' He paused and smiled. 'Can I sleep in your bed, Mummy?'

She nodded and tucked him into her bed. As he nodded off, she eased herself away from his sleeping body and paced the room. Ed couldn't have turned the light on in the doll's house, she'd been watching him. Either she was losing it, or Ed was finding other ways to drive her to insanity. Maybe that was his plan and someone was helping him. Take her mind, take her child and then move Meera in while she festers in some facility. It wasn't going to work. She could convince herself that she left the landing light on or even poured the wine, but the doll's house light – she couldn't explain that William thought his dad had been in the room. Fear prickled across her shoulders, sending a shiver through her. She would not go down without a fight and she would search the house high and low. That way, she could remove Ed's threat against her, and she would then leave him.

She stopped rigid and held her breath as she heard a tap, low down against the bedroom door. 'Ed?' she said in a whisper.

Hands trembling, she could barely grip the door handle as she gently opened it onto the silent landing. Placing her arm over her mouth to stop a scream from escaping, she stared at the ball that had rolled onto the patio earlier. She grabbed her phone and checked the app. Ed was driving out towards Leamington right now and was nowhere near the house. Closing the door, she grabbed a chair and wedged it under the handle before running back to the bed and guarding her precious son from the danger that lurked outside the room. Silent sobs escaped from her mouth as she tried to call Ed repeatedly, but his phone went straight to voicemail. She was alone and no one could help her.

TWENTY-EIGHT

Stupid, stupid, stupid. Those were the words that kept attacking Gina's thoughts. She should have let Briggs speak first but no, she went and wore her heart on her sleeve and now, she didn't want to face him again, and he hated her.

Jacob pulled up on time. Gina glanced at Meera's mother's house to see if she could see any sign of life. Turning up at seven in the morning would catch her off guard and hopefully encourage her to tell them everything she knew. The double-fronted house on the new estate stood proudly at the end of a small drive that was shared with three other houses. As she was about to get out of her car, she spotted someone getting dropped off at the end of the long road before turning off.

'Alright, guv?'

She nodded. 'All brilliant. We've got Ed Anderson coming in at nine thirty, he got one of his employees to confirm that time yesterday, so we need to work fast. I want to get back to interview him. O'Connor confirmed that he will attend the post-mortem, so we'll chase that update later. How's Jennifer?'

'Frustrated and bored. She's joining Bernard tomorrow, but

she'll start back on shortened hours, until she gets her strength back up. Taking it one step at a time.' He looked away.

'And how are you?'

'You know?' He shrugged. 'Losing the baby was hard on both of us.'

She reached over and squeezed his shoulder. There was nothing she could say to take his pain away, so she wasn't about to try.

As they walked down the path a little, she heard the approaching pedestrian's steps come to a halt behind the hedge. Gina held up a hand and pressed her finger to her closed lips. Jacob stopped dead in his tracks. Creeping back, Gina glanced around the corner to see Meera trying to hold back a clump of leaves to peer through a bush. 'Meera, we were just coming to speak to you.'

'Oh, I was just... err...'

'Have you just got home?'

The young woman's hair was a little tangled at the sides and her mascara smudged. Her deep crimson dress flowed from her waist and the little floral bag she carried looked beautifully matched. 'Yes. I stayed with a friend.'

'Shaun Brock?'

Meera glanced up and waved at a neighbour who was shaking his head in the window opposite. 'Looks like we've woken him up.' She walked past them and opened the front door. 'Can we talk inside, somewhere Mr Smith can't spy on us from?'

Gina nodded. She and Jacob followed Meera into the small hallway and through to what looked like a studio. Art supplies littered a huge bench, and an easel contained a painting of a Red Setter.

'Sorry about the mess but no one sleeps in the room above. I don't want to wake Dev or my mum just yet.' She removed her shoes and grabbed a jumper from the bench, pulling it over her dress. 'She doesn't know I went out all night. Please don't tell her. She constantly worries.'

'Where were you?'

'Am I in trouble?'

'We just have some questions, that's all.' From the answers Meera gave, Gina would decide if she was in trouble. 'Where were you last night?'

'Has something happened?'

'We're looking for Shaun Brock. We have CCTV footage that shows you and Mr Brock together at the Angel Arms. Where is he?'

She shrugged and sat at the easel. 'I seriously don't know. If I did, I'd tell you.'

'You saw him on the day of Billie's murder?'

Her shoulders dropped. 'On the day Billie was murdered, I was scared. I decided to stay with my mother before returning home the following morning at the crack of dawn to get ready for school and work. That's when you came to speak to me.'

'Take us back to the evening of the murder. Why were you with Brock?'

'While Dev was asleep, I went to the pub. My mother was driving me mad. She kept asking me questions about Billie that I didn't know the answers to and then she started fussing. Being stuck in the house with her was making me claustrophobic. I needed some space, so I arranged to meet a friend at the pub. That's when I saw Shaun.'

'Was that friend Shaun Brock?'

'No, my friend couldn't make it. I don't know Shaun Brock, that's the first time I ever met the man. He came up to me and said he'd seen me with Billie by her house and at the school, and that he was Kayden's father. He kept telling me that Billie stopped him from seeing his son, but I know the truth. I've even seen the messages to back up Billie's side. She tried everything she could to get him interested in being a father but then she got fed up and said he'd blown his chances. I thought Shaun was a bit creepy as he must have been watching us to know where we lived.'

Gina watched as Jacob made a note. She almost shivered as she imagined Shaun hanging around Billie's house and watching her. 'Did he mention her murder?'

'No, I told him and at first, he said he didn't believe me, but I don't know, he didn't seem as shocked as I thought he might be. I was choked up, but he almost looked smug. I told him I was leaving, and he followed me out into the car park. He tried to grab me and started asking things about Kayden. He knew where Kayden went to school, the after-school clubs he attended. He...' She shook her head. 'It doesn't matter.' She took a deep breath. 'I pulled his hands off me, got into my car and drove out of the car park. After that, I went back to my mother's. I think I got home about midnight.'

'Why didn't you tell me about your encounter with Mr Brock when we spoke?'

She bit her bottom lip. 'He said, if I mentioned seeing him to anyone, he knew where I lived, and he knew where my son went to school.' She paused. 'I live alone, sometimes I get scared. There's no way I could put my son at risk. I should have told you, I'm sorry but I didn't know what I should or shouldn't say. I was scared.'

Brock was still missing, and Meera hadn't called them to report seeing Kayden's father. Gina had to question where she had been all night. Jacob leaned against the wall as he waited with his pen and pad. 'Where were you last night?'

'I don't want to answer that.'

'Meera, your friend has been murdered. The man we're looking for threatened you and your son. All we want to do is get justice for her and for Kayden. It would really help us if you answered the question. You won't be judged, I promise, but we do need you to be honest with us.'

She sighed and looked down. 'I spent the night with Ed, Ed Anderson, but you can't tell Nadia, his wife.'

The plot thickened. Meera spent the night with the man who was booked in to be interviewed next and he'd told them he was in Derby, working. The lies were getting them nowhere and causing her team more work.

'Who were you meant to be meeting at the Angel Arms when you saw Shaun Brock?'

'It was Ed, but he couldn't get away. I wasn't going to stay there, I just wanted somewhere to go while I waited to find out where we could meet. That's until he cancelled on me.'

'You and Mr Anderson, what is your relationship?'

She sniffed and turned away. 'I love him. I know Nadia is my friend but since my husband died, I haven't been myself. Recently Ed has been there for me, and I know that he and Nadia aren't close any more. I shouldn't have gone there and I'm not proud of myself. You can't choose who you love. I don't know what to do.' She burst into tears.

'Did Billie know about your affair? Did she threaten to tell Nadia?'

'No, there's no way she could know. She had no idea. No one knows. We've been discreet.' Gina wondered if that was true. Meera had failed to tell them about meeting Shaun Brock and that was crucial to the investigation.

'Were you with Edward Anderson on Tuesday the fourteenth?'

She nodded. 'He came over that evening when Dev had gone to sleep. He wanted to see me.'

Gina wondered if he could have been the man in Billie's back garden that night. 'What time did he stay until?'

'One or two in the morning. He parked in another street as he didn't want Billie to see his car and he knocked when it was dark.'

'Where did he park?'

'He didn't say.'

'Did he come through the back or front door?'

'Front.'

'What time did he arrive?'

'About ten, maybe ten thirty.' The times Meera was giving didn't match up to that of Billie's caller, but he may have popped out of Meera's house. She only lived next door.

'Where was he around midnight?'

She bowed her head. 'In my bed. Please don't tell Nadia. Ed should be the one to tell her.'

Gina doubted that Ed had any intention of ever telling his wife. 'How did he seem?'

She shrugged. 'Happy to see me.'

'Did you hear from Billie that evening?'

'No, not at all. Kayden plays with Dev a lot but not every day, so she had no reason to come over. Look, I'm sorry. I didn't think my relationship with Ed would come into all this. He's the sweetest guy and he'd have no reason to hurt Billie.'

Meera's mother pushed the door open. 'What's going on in here? I hope you haven't disturbed my work.'

'Sorry, Mum. The police just wanted to have a word with me about Billie. Maybe I can come into the station later if that would help.' Meera pressed her lips together in a forced smile and stared at Gina.

'Yes, if you could come in and make a formal statement that would help.' From what Gina could tell, Meera had hidden her affair and her meeting with Brock. She thought about Briggs hiding his and Rosemary's relationship for a week or two before telling her. Did he feel as guilty as the woman in front of her? She hoped so. From what Meera was saying, Edward Anderson could not be the man who went to Billie's on the evening before her murder but then again, Meera was smitten. Would she lie for him? 'Eleven, this morning. Is that okay?'

Meera nodded enthusiastically.

'We'll expect you then.'

'Meera, why are you wearing a dress under my jumper?' Her mother scratched her messy bed hair.

'I spilled something on my nightie so had to wear this.'

'It's too good for wearing in bed.' She shook her head and left them to it. Dev bounded down the stairs carrying a Buzz Lightyear toy.

'I'll have a shower, get my son to school and then I'll come to the station.' She stood and peered around the door as Dev passed and asked his grandmother what was for breakfast. 'There's something else... about Shaun.'

Gina stood.

She spoke in a hushed tone. 'While he was angry, he called me a slut and said I was just like Billie. I don't like the man and I pity Kayden if he ends up with him. It shook me up a bit. With that and the threat, I didn't know what to think.'

The writing on Billie's wall had not been part of the information released to the public. Gina couldn't be surer that their main suspect was Brock. They just needed to find him. Officers had been posted at the entrance of his road and outside his mother's flat. The man had no recent connections, which was making their job harder. They had nowhere to look. She pressed her lips together as she thought. 'Given that you've received some threats, we'll organise for an officer to stay outside your mother's house until we find him.'

'Do you think he might come here? He doesn't know where my mum lives.'

'He didn't know where you lived or which school Kayden and your son went to, but he found out. I don't want to scare you, but I'd rather play it safe. If he comes here, we will pick him up.'

She thought back to her talk with Brock. The man also said he didn't know that Billie had been murdered and had put on a great act to back his words up. Meera said that he knew. The man was a good liar. Gina's phone beeped. It was a message from Wyre.

> *Background on Edward Anderson. He was charged with kerb crawling when he was nineteen.*

So, Edward Anderson had a history of trying to engage a sex worker. The leads were getting more tangled by the minute.

TWENTY-NINE

Gina grabbed a glass of water from the fridge in the station kitchen and drank it down in one go.

'It's another scorcher, guv.' O'Connor put a batch of cinnamon buns in the fridge. 'Thought I'd put them in here or the icing will probably be like goo if I leave them in the incident room. That sun is beating through the window this morning. Mrs O sends her regards by the way, and she hopes everyone enjoys the cakes. Help yourself.' He leaned over and put his head in front of the open fridge. 'If only I could stay here all day. I hate this heat.'

'Are you heading to the post-mortem soon?' She checked her watch.

'Yes, I best be off. I'll report back later.'

He closed the fridge door and left. She leaned against the worktop, aware that Edward Anderson had arrived, but she needed five minutes to process everything. Briggs walked in and stood at the door. 'Sorry, I didn't know you were in here.'

She shrugged. 'I'm not any more.' She went to walk past him.

'Gina, please.'

'What?' she snapped.

He pushed the kitchen door closed. 'I'm sorry for how I went about everything. I screwed up and I should have been more sensitive to how you'd feel. Please don't hate me.'

She shook her head. 'I don't hate you.' She turned to face him. 'I hate that I'm so screwed up and I couldn't be what you wanted. Don't you see? I hate myself. About what I said last night. I was just a bit emotional and it's no secret, a bit menopausal and, no, I'm not embarrassed, it's a fact of life. What I said, forget it. I'm sorry I went on about Rosemary, too. I misread a situation and I'm an idiot.' She knew what she'd seen Rosemary doing but this atmosphere between them had to end. Briggs would find out in his own time. 'I'm okay now.' A burning sensation prickled up her neck. *Not now, please.* She opened the fridge and leaned into it, just like O'Connor had and she took a few deep breaths. The pricking subsided. Saved by the fridge.

'So, are we friends?'

She caught a whiff of cinnamon bun and felt her mouth watering up at the thought of sugar swilling around her mouth. 'One step at a time, hey.' She slammed the fridge door.

'I err, spoke to Rosemary, about what you said you saw. She was pretty upset and thinks you're spying on her like some crazy person. She went on and on at me for even listening to you. I guess I had to ask the question but now, I wish I hadn't. It's all so hard as I know you're not those things.'

'You're finding it hard?' She wanted to yell at him. Gina knew what she saw, and she was trying to bite her tongue.

'I said I'm sorry. I did a shitty thing.'

'Stuff this. I don't care what your girlfriend said. That man was not her brother. Take from that what you will but I'm sick of pleasing everyone.'

She left, hurrying to the interview room where Anderson would be patiently waiting. She had it up to the brim with

Briggs and Rosemary. From now on, she was going to put her feelings first. She stopped in the corridor, fanning herself with her paperwork as heat began to climb up her neck. What had she done? That total loss of control was out of character. She couldn't go in and interview Anderson with shaking hands and a quivering voice.

As she approached the door, she listened to the man moaning from outside. 'I've got a business to run. I call in and we arrange an appointment, and you aren't ready to interview me. That's not my fault. I'm giving it five minutes then I swear, if we haven't started, I'm leaving. You'll have to contact my secretary to rebook, and I tell you something, my diary is full for the next few weeks, so it'll be your loss.'

What she wanted to do was to barge in, tell him to shut the hell up and to stop lying. Billie had been murdered and it was as if no one cared. If they all cared, they'd tell the truth and they'd find the culprit. With clenched fists, she banged the door open.

THIRTY

Gina watched as Jacob leaned back in his chair, sighing as the man went on at him. She went to open her mouth, then stopped. *Calm down, Gina*, she kept repeating in her head as she unclenched her fists. 'Apologies for keeping you waiting, Mr Anderson. Something came up and we needed to speak to Meera Gupta first. As you can appreciate, we have a lot to get through so let's get started.' She exhaled. The rage she felt was almost all consuming, but it wouldn't get her anywhere in the interview room. She knew that.

The vein on the side of his neck pulsed as he ground his teeth. 'What's Meera got to do with all this?'

'Let's save that for the tape.'

Jacob introduced them all before beginning.

'Why is this being taped?' He rubbed his unshaven chin.

'It's standard. This is a murder investigation, and we are interviewing people who knew Billie.'

'Am I a suspect?'

Gina leaned in. 'Mr Anderson, we just need to ask you a few questions. You are here on a voluntary basis.'

'Which means I can just walk out, right now?'

Gina nodded. 'A woman has been murdered and we need to catch whoever did this. We would appreciate your cooperation.'

'Okay. Just get this over with so I can get back to running my business.'

'Let's begin with Tuesday the fourteenth of June, that's this Tuesday. Can you talk me through your evening?'

'Shit.'

'What is it?'

'Shit. I was with Meera on Tuesday evening until the early hours.'

'And why were you there?'

He raised his eyebrows. 'We're all adults here. I'm not going into detail.' He paused. 'Meera and I have a thing.'

'A thing?'

'An affair, okay? You need me to say it. I turned up at her place close to ten. I know it was that time as I put my son to bed before leaving my house and he wouldn't go to sleep. I told Nadia that I had to go back to the office for a while, but I went to Meera's house.' He exhaled.

'What time did you leave?'

His shoulders dropped. 'About one thirty in the morning. I went straight home.'

'Did you leave Ms Gupta's house between nine and one thirty in the morning for any reason?'

He shook his head and loosened his collar. 'No, we stayed in her bed all that time until I got out to dress around one.'

'Where did you park?'

'Charles Street.' Gina knew that street was in the opposite direction to the library, so he'd have no reason to walk past it.

'Did you use your phone while walking from your car to Ms Gupta's house?'

He glanced between Jacob and Gina as if he might be caught out. 'No, you can check my call log if you like.' He passed his phone over. Gina scrolled through but could see that no calls had been made around the time that their witness had heard a man passing the library.

'Do you have another phone?'

He nodded. 'I don't have it on me, but I have a company mobile phone. Everyone who works for me has one. I'll bring that in later and you can see that I didn't make a call then either. I do only use it for work, though.'

'Thank you. Where were you on Wednesday from one p.m. to five p.m.?'

He took a huge breath and let it out slowly. 'That's easy, I was buying a hot tub and I have the receipt. I was in the shop at that time organising the purchase and the delivery. It was also on my route between the Derby office and the Cleevesford office.'

That would rule Anderson out as a suspect. 'Do you have the invoice?'

'Yes, and it's got a payment receipt attached to it showing the time too.' He pulled the folded-up invoice from his trouser pocket and handed it to Gina like he'd prepared for that question.

She read all the information. 'Thank you for that. We need to take a copy before you leave.'

'Knock yourself out.'

She also knew that they needed to know if it was actually Anderson himself in the shop making the purchase at the time he said he was. She passed it to Jacob, and he made a note of the name. Jimbo's Hot Tubs.

'Last night, where were you? You said you couldn't come in for this interview yesterday as you were staying in Derby all night.'

He ran his fingers through his hair. 'I was with Meera. I'm sorry I lied but that's what I was going to tell my wife, so I stuck with it. I thought it didn't matter as I didn't hurt Billie. I am a prize arsehole for what I've done to Nadia and if my affair gets

out I'm right in the shit, but I didn't hurt Billie. I had no reason
to. I barely knew her. She was my wife's best friend.'

'On May the fifteenth, there was a birthday party at your
house for Kayden.'

'So? My wife is generous like that. She let Billie use our
garden so that Kayden could have a lovely party with all his
friends. Her garden was too small. Kayden is a popular lad.'

'Did you say anything to Billie that day?'

He shook his head. 'I doubt it. I can barely remember. I'd
had a few beers with the other parents while I manned the
barbeque.'

'We have a witness that claims you were watching Billie in a
manner that they described as weird or uncomfortable.'

He shrugged. 'I'd just found out from my wife about what
Billie had been doing for money. I guess I couldn't believe it. I
found myself trying to weigh up why she would do a thing like
that when Nadia had offered to help her out. I didn't mean to
watch her. I didn't speak to her or ask her about it. By the way, I
wasn't the only one giving Billie weird looks. Gossip was rife by
then and just about everyone at that party knew what Billie was
doing, but we all knew not to say it out loud or in front of her.
Whoever hurt her was probably visiting her for sex. You should
be looking into those pervs, the type that can't get any and have
to pay for it. I'm not one of those.'

'But you are.'

He leaned back in his chair as Gina opened her file on
Anderson.

'You got caught kerb crawling when you were nineteen.'

He shook his head and huffed out a breath. 'I'd just passed
my driving test and I was lost. I was asking for directions.'

'You were charged.'

'Whatever. I have my story and just because you lot falsely
charged me; I'm sticking to it. You were wrong. Are you
arresting me?'

'No, Mr Anderson, but please stay close by. We might need to interview you again.'

'That's all I've got to say. Can I have my invoice back? I need it for my records in case the hot tub doesn't arrive next week.'

Frustrated, Gina clenched her hands together under the table as Jacob concluded the interview for the tape. Everything was still pointing towards Brock being the murderer. As Edward Anderson stood, he straightened his shirt and brushed his trousers down. The man was a liar; that was certain, but a murderer? Unless he was working with someone else, it was looking unlikely. She stared at him for a few moments wondering if he had any reason to hate Billie enough to hide the truth from them. It was convenient how he had such a tight alibi during the murder. Maybe he'd planned it that way. For now, that was a theory but one she couldn't dismiss. Until she got confirmation from the hot tub company, he was still a suspect and Meera could still be lying about the times he was with her.

'Well?' He held his hand out.

'Mr Anderson, like I said, stay close and as a word of advice, don't go asking for any more directions.' She emphasised the word directions. 'You've already lost your way one too many times.' The man seemed to care more about his hot tub than he did about his wife's best friend.

'What does that mean?'

She grabbed her things and left the room, allowing the door to slam behind her.

THIRTY-ONE
NADIA

'Shake those ropes,' Nadia called to her client, while the woman panted and held her side. 'Come on. Just one more minute to go. You've got this!' Her mind wandered for a few seconds to the evening before. Still fuming from Ed's game, she couldn't let it go. She'd called him several times. He had to have been involved and scaring her half to death, which wasn't on. No more sneaking around and trying to discreetly check messages. She had evidence he couldn't deny. She'd taken a photo of his message to Billie on the day she'd died and as for him trying to make her lose it, it wasn't going to work. She was onto him. He poured that wine and he had to have sent Meera upstairs to stage the doll's house. Maybe he drove out while sending Meera back in her car. They were in on it together, they had to be. She shivered at the thought of someone in her house and William, he thought he saw Ed. Maybe Meera had borrowed his jacket. Her son would have been half asleep. She huffed under her breath. She expected this of Ed, but not Meera.

The young woman bent over on the empty tennis court while she got her breath back. 'I'm done.' She waved a hand in front of her face and ran a hand through her hair.

'Okay. For a first session, you did really well, and I can definitely recommend some areas that we can work on. What did you say you were training for?'

'I didn't.'

That's odd. Nadia was sure her new client had mentioned a half marathon or a triathlon. 'Shall I book you in again next week?' She could do without the work but given that Ed had insulted her with the hobby remark, she was going to prove him wrong and build her business up until she had personal trainers working for her. Billie had reminded her how short life was.

The woman shook her head, her dark blonde hairline damp with perspiration. 'No.'

'Are you okay?' The woman swigged from her water bottle but didn't take her gaze from Nadia.

'How long was my sister shagging my boyfriend for?'

'Sorry?' Was Nadia meant to know the woman in front of her? They'd only met an hour ago. 'Do we know each other?'

'I'm Serena. Billie mentioned you and Meera a lot, but we were never introduced.' A tear drizzled down her cheek. 'I'm so angry at her and I can't do anything about it because she's dead. Then, I hate myself for being angry with her. She did the unthinkable to me. To her own sister and then I find out from the police about everything else she was in to.'

Nadia could relate to Serena's anger and hurt; she was feeling bad after seeing Meera with Ed. The others didn't hurt so much, they felt less personal, but Meera was her friend. She didn't know if she'd be able to trust anyone ever again.

Nadia placed a comforting hand on the woman's shoulders as she cried. 'Is that why you came?'

'I needed to find someone who knew her, someone who could tell me what she'd really been like recently. I don't know why she'd do something so awful. I can only think that she wasn't in her right mind.' Serena wiped her eyes.

'I think Billie had a lot going on and I'm not sure any of us really knew her as well as we thought. Maybe she wasn't in her right mind. She loved you, though. She was so proud, telling me of her sister who was going to become a dentist. She made one bad decision, don't let that tar all your lovely memories.'

Serena began to sob. 'Why are you being so kind to her?'

'Because we were best friends and I know she was going through some tough times. People don't do what Billie did if they're not. I'm upset that I didn't do more—' Nadia felt herself getting choked up.

'Did you know about Nathan?'

Nadia nodded. 'Yes, and no. She mentioned she was seeing someone in passing but she didn't tell me much about him. She had a lot of short-term relationships, so I rarely got introduced to her boyfriends. Do you want to get a drink at the leisure centre?' Nadia was well aware that her hour on the court was up, and she'd have to make way for the tennis players that were loitering on the other side of the fence. The attendant was grimacing while staring at his watch, obviously wanting her to hurry.

'No. I'm okay.'

'I'm really sorry for your loss. Please pass on my thoughts to your family and little Kayden. And tell Kayden that William is missing him.'

'Don't be sorry. Maybe she had it coming. Whatever Billie had turned in to, I certainly didn't know her any more.' She cleared her throat and grabbed her gym bag. 'I have to go.'

As Serena ran off the court, Nadia called after her but, in a flash, the woman was gone. Serena's words stuck in her thoughts. To say that Billie had it coming was unforgivable but then again, so was Nadia's spreading of Billie's secrets. Billie had been let down by everyone. Billie had also let Serena down. Ed had let her down. Nadia pondered about how imperfect humans were and she placed herself at the top of the list.

She tried to call Ed again. He should have been out of the

police station by now or even home. She called the home phone and his other mobile and there was no answer. Swallowing, she wondered if he'd gone to see Meera, where they'd be cooking up more plans to ruin Nadia's life. She opened the tracking app on her phone, but it was showing that the last place he'd been was Meera's mother's road, then the tracker went offline. Her tablet had finally run out of charge. She checked her fitness tracking watch. She could go home, take a long shower and have a rest until she had to pick William up. In the meantime, she'd keep trying Ed. At the very least, she'd annoy him into answering. He was meant to call her to tell her how he got on at the police station. She should have known better than expect him to do anything he said he would. Her phone beeped.

I know your secret!

'We need the court,' the leisure centre attendant called out.

Panic rising in her throat, she gasped for breath as she hurried off it. She needed to get home, now.

'You okay?' one of the tennis players asked as she passed.

She ignored him and continued to run. There was only one secret she didn't want to come out and the messenger knew what it was. Face red in the burning sun, she leaned over and fought for breath. She had a feeling something horrible was going to happen, but she couldn't work out what or when. Only two people knew that secret, her and Ed. This pretending had to stop. This game had to stop. It was killing her.

She had to get home and find that bloodied knife, the one that screamed *guilty*. That was her only way out of this huge mess. If she didn't find it, the consequences were unthinkable. She had blood on her hands, there was no denying that fact. Ed knew and Ed was making her pay. Holding her hand over her mouth, she heaved slightly as she relived the moment when the tip of the knife pierced into soft flesh. Gasping, she ran towards her car as she tried to rid her mind of the bloody image that was haunting her. *Blood on your hands, blood on your hands.* Her inner voice wouldn't shut up. It was right and Ed was making sure she knew it.

THIRTY-TWO

NADIA

She slammed the front door and headed straight to the garage. Nadia had searched it repeatedly for the knife, but she'd spotted a little bit of loose plaster against one of the walls. As for the house, she'd searched every nook and cranny. Checking her phone, she could see that Ed hadn't tried to call her but that didn't mean he wouldn't be back any minute.

She flapped her arms, trying to prise her T-shirt from her damp underarms. The coolness of the house made them feel stickier. Right now, having a shower and a change of clothes wasn't on her immediate agenda. Time was of the essence. Ed had piled a whole stack of boxes against the back wall. She pushed William's little bike out of the way, then Ed's racer. Peering into the box on the top, she could see that it was full of his corporate brochures. As she slid it off the box underneath, it crashed to the concrete floor, catalogues splaying everywhere. Next box, she slid it off and placed it to the side, dumping it on the catalogues.

The boxes weren't worth her time. What she needed to do was to expose that wall. Three more boxes later and with several piled up, she stared at the grey wall. Its stone paint as cold looking as what was probably secreted in the wall. If she could get hold of the knife, she could clean her prints off it and dump it somewhere far away. Maybe she'd drive to another county and bury it in the woods. Had Ed left the photos with the knife, the evidence he'd so proudly dangled under her nose?

She began to pick at the plaster, but her nails weren't strong enough to dig much out. She'd be there all day. A droplet of perspiration dripped from her nose. Grabbing a screwdriver from the workbench, she began to stab at the wall and a chunk of plaster flew out. Squinting, she leaned in close to try and see what was buried in the hole. There was only one way to find out what was there and that was to slip a couple of fingers in, see if she could feel the cold metal tip of a knife. As she pressed her soft flesh against the jagged plaster, a slight cut began to trickle down her wrist and she grimaced. All she could feel was paper.

Damn, it wasn't paper she was after. Slipping it out, she unrolled the scroll. Shaking, she stared at the emoji, placed the note on a box and cried. A laughing emoji with the words 'Got you' written underneath. He'd played her again. She kicked the empty boxes and trod on them with everything she had, pounding on the cardboard in her trainers as she screamed with rage. 'I hate you, I hate you, I hate you,' she yelled.

One of the doors in the house creaked. She held her sobs. 'Ed?'

Creeping out of the garage she entered the utility room and went back into the kitchen. Another creak, but this time it was coming from the snug.

'Ed, I'm not laughing.' She was distraught and his game playing had to stop. If it was his intention to drive her insane, it was working. Maybe she should turn herself in, tell the police and admit her wrongs. Maybe they'd actually believe her side of the story. Billie had been such a good friend and Nadia knew she had been awful to the woman. How had things gone so wrong between them? 'Ed?'

She wiped her tears away with the back of her hand, then placed her hand on the wall outside the snug, smearing it with a drizzle of blood. As she opened the snug door, Fluffball darted out with a meow, heading straight for the cat flap. It was no one. The cat had been trapped all day in the snug. She pushed the door open and checked the floor for little accidents. That's when she spotted the mess in the corner of the room.

There was nothing she could do now but get ready to collect William from school. Ed would have to come home eventually. First, she needed to clean up before the snug began to really smell in the heat. She jogged back to the utility to grab a bucket and some disinfectant, that's when she spotted that the garage light was off. Had she turned it off? Slowly, she leaned in and peered around the dark room. Hands trembling, she leaned further and reached for the light switch. As the room lit up, she could see that the brochures were still strewn all over the floor and the boxes were as she left them, all crushed and stomped on. It felt as if the hole in the wall was an all-seeing eye that was watching her intently, telling her that it knew what she'd done.

Her breath came in short bursts as she stepped in and gazed around. 'Ed, you're scaring me.' The light went off and the door to the utility slammed closed. Before her eyes could adjust to the tiny strip of light that came from the bottom of the garage, she felt a puff of warm breath on her neck, then a flash of white-hot pain hit her head.

As she fell to the concrete floor, open-mouthed in the plaster that she'd dug out, she tried to crawl along the ground. Grabbing anything she could reach. Her attacker sat on her back, splaying her flat as her head pounded. Her aggressor leaned over and moved the stray hairs away from her ears and whispered, 'Nadia, you know that secrets have to come out, right? Billie's have and now it's your turn.' Her attacker had to mean the knife. The one she'd failed to find.

'Please, don't hurt me.' She knew exactly who that voice

belonged to, but her strength had gone with that hard blow. She knew she needed to get up and try anything to stop what was happening, but she had no fight in her. That blow had taken her completely off guard. All she could do was think of William as another sickening blow came. The light of the doorway faded to black, and she wept as she thought of her little boy. They came for Billie, now they'd come for her.

THIRTY-THREE

Gina stood at the head of the incident room in front of the boards as she tied up their afternoon briefing. 'I've heard back from O'Connor who is still in attendance at the post-mortem. Nothing further to add that will help our case. Nothing good has come of the CCTV footage outside the library but it barely covered the one path. We know we are still looking for the murder weapon and no searches have turned it up yet, which means it's still out there. All units are still on the lookout for Shaun Brock. He is currently our prime suspect and there is a warrant out for his arrest. Anything else?'

A hum of no filled the air. Gina could see that the team were a bit despondent, as they'd reached what felt like a dead end in the investigation.

'We have officers stationed on Meera Gupta's mother's street and the same with Shaun Brock's mother's place. The poor woman is beside herself. Did Mr Anderson come back with his work mobile?'

Wyre cleared her throat. 'Not yet.'

'How about Jimbo's Hot Tubs? Have we managed to ascertain that it was definitely him purchasing the hot tub?'

'No. I called the company and spoke to an account manager. She said the owner of the business is out for a couple of days and no one else there has access to the CCTV. She said as soon as he – a man named Jim Bowler – comes back she'll get him to email it over. She did, however, give us a vague description that could be Anderson. It was too vague to be certain.'

'But so far, it looks like he's telling the truth?'

Wyre nodded.

'Can we match the blood found on the items in Brock's car to Billie's? Do we have the results yet?'

'Not yet.' Jacob peeled open a pack of pasta salad and prodded his fork in a cherry tomato, which burst up his shirt.

Gina pulled her ponytail tight. 'We need to go over everything Meera Gupta has said. I don't know why but I don't trust her. It feels like she's still holding something back and it might be just the information we need. What about her other friends? Nadia Anderson – Mr Anderson's wife?'

Jacob swallowed a mouthful and turned a page in his notebook. 'No record, guv.'

'And Candice Brent? What do we know about her?'

'Friend of Billie's. Married. Daughter of the same age as Billie's son. Works as a dog groomer. It appears that she, Nadia, Billie and Meera were all close friends. They spent time in each other's houses. Their children played together.'

Gina stared at the floor in thought. 'Yes. Meera is having an affair with Nadia's husband and all of them were involved in gossiping about Billie. They don't all seem to be as friendly as they appear. There is so much going on under the surface. We just need to scratch a bit harder. We do have some forensics results back from Billie's house.'

Wyre scraped her chair a little closer to the table.

'There were at least fifteen sets of fingerprints obtained throughout the house suggesting that she'd had a fair few visitors. We have Anderson's prints on file because of his previous conviction and not one of them matches his. We need to start requesting elimination prints from everyone we question. Given that some of the prints will be from men visiting Billie for sex, I'm surprised that more haven't shown up on the system. As for other evidence, there is nothing more as yet. The words written on the wall and on the note are in capital letters. We can look at handwriting but I'm not sure how far that will get us. The note has been analysed and we got no prints from that either. For now, go through everything again. Any CCTV that has been pulled, I want you to blow it up, look at reflections in windows. Check the registration of every vehicle that passes. The answers are out there, we merely have to uncover them.'

Gina's heart sank as Briggs entered and stood at the head of the room. She stepped aside, giving him centre stage. He didn't acknowledge her at all. 'There's been a reported incident at Mr and Mrs Reeves's house. Mrs Reeves has locked the door and Shaun Brock is threatening to smash it down. Uniform are on their way now.' Briggs's phone rang. He made a few noises and ended the call before looking at Gina. 'You have to meet uniform. Brock has taken the boy. He's on foot so he can't have got far. He's also hit Mr Reeves by slamming the front door in his face and an ambulance has been called.'

'Jacob, let's go.' Before her sergeant had a chance to finish his food, they were out the door. There was no way they were going to lose Brock, not now. They were this close to arresting him. Her heart pounded. She couldn't let him escape with Kayden. The poor child would be terrified. He didn't even know his father.

THIRTY-FOUR

Jacob pulled up behind the police car and Gina opened the door before he put the handbrake on. The ambulance had already arrived, and a paramedic had led Mr Reeves to the van. Blood meandered down his head as he staggered along. A uniformed officer called out to her. 'He went that way. Two officers are tailing him.'

Face hot and body starting to go clammy from the sticky heat, Gina waved to Jacob. 'Follow me.' She ran as fast as her legs would take her past a row of large houses and down a small path that led to a woodland trail. As she jumped down a step, she caught her ankle in a string of stingers. She trod them away and continued.

'I'm right behind you, guv.'

At least she had someone to continue forward if she keeled over. Running in temperatures close to thirty degrees was never fun but, she remembered, a child had been taken. Getting Kayden from their absconding murder suspect was her priority. She stopped and panted, trying to listen out for the officers or Kayden, but she could hear nothing except for a couple of frisky pigeons cooing above her.

She spotted a police hat in the distance. 'That way,' she called out. As she got closer, she could see the officer was walking back. 'Where is the suspect?' she called out to him.

'We got here too late. He had too much of a head start.' The officer scrunched his nose. 'I lost him.'

'How long by?' Gina got her breath back as Jacob jogged to her side.

'Only a couple of minutes.'

She shook her head. 'He can't have got much further in this heat, and he has a little boy with him. What's close by?' She placed a hand on her sweltering head and turned around on the spot.

'The woodland comes out at the lake. Another officer has headed in that direction.' The PC's radio hissed as it came into life. 'Found them. They're in a rowing boat in the middle of the lake. Brock won't come in.'

Gina began running through the trees until she reached the path. Several minutes later, she felt as though she might collapse on the pavement from heat exhaustion, but she pushed through in her drenched clothes.

'There, guv.' Jacob pointed at the boathouse where the club kept their boats and equipment. Another PC stood by the shore trying to wave the man back.

Gina forced her leaden legs that bit farther, and she stopped by the PC.

The young woman removed her police hat and used it to fan herself. 'He stole the boat from that family over there.' A man with two children sat on a mound of grass, the youngest crying against his chest.

Gina walked to the shore, her feet almost in the lake water. 'Shaun, please bring Kayden back. All this must be very confusing for him, and I know you don't want to upset him.'

Brock stood in the rowing boat. Gina watched as it wobbled

from side to side. 'I just want to explain things to him. He's alright, aren't you, champ?'

Gina's heartstrings pulled as she watched the sobbing boy nod. He'd lost his mother and witnessed his grandfather being assaulted, just before being taken by a man he doesn't know. 'Shaun, he's crying. He's upset. Please bring him in. No father would want to see their child like that.'

He ran his hands over his head. 'Just leave us alone. He's crying because of you lot, chasing us. I have rights, you know.'

'Shaun, this can all be sorted out but not in the way you're going about it. You need to bring Kayden back to shore.' She turned to Jacob. 'Can you get a boat out there? I don't like the way he's rocking that boat and Kayden isn't wearing a life jacket.'

He nodded and headed towards the boat club.

'Shaun, you've got nowhere to go.'

The man glanced around. He was surrounded by officers who were now in place. 'Why are you doing this to me? I only want to talk to him. I went to the house to talk to him, and that bastard said no. He's my son. I have rights.'

It saddened Gina that Kayden was hearing all this. The man on the boat had left him, he had denied his existence and now he'd taken him in a way that might traumatise Kayden for life. There were ways to move forward in building a relationship with his son, but this wasn't one of them. 'Yes, you do, but so does Kayden and he's scared. Please, Shaun, bring him in.'

'Stand up,' Brock shouted at the boy.

'I want Granddad,' Kayden cried, his little lungs bawling out. The boy squirmed away from Brock, remaining on the seat.

Gina wanted to reach out into the distance, take him out of the situation and hug him closely but all she could do was watch and hope that he didn't fall into the lake.

Brock dragged the boy up and the boat rocked again. Kayden let out a shrill scream. Gina's heart was in her mouth as the boy almost fell. Without a life jacket, he was in danger. Just as someone rowed Jacob towards the commotion, Brock shouted at the boy, 'Stop moving about.' Brock's arms windmilled, and the man fell into the water with an almighty crash. The boy crouched down and curled up in a ball, his arms hugging his legs as he remained low in the rocking boat. The skipper hopped over to the boy and safely began rowing him towards Gina. Jacob pulled Brock into the other boat and Gina watched, knowing that her colleague was reading Brock his rights. They now had him in their custody and the list of charges was growing.

As the skipper got out of the boat and pulled it onto the dried-up muddy beach, Gina reached in and took Kayden's hand. 'Hello, sweetie. I'm Gina and I'm with the police. Let's get you away from the water.'

He sobbed and threw himself into her arms. 'I want Nanny and Granddad.'

'It's okay.' She felt herself welling up at what this dot of a boy had been through in a few short days.

'Come on, let's get you back.' She thought again of Ms Brock, and the fact that she didn't even know she was a grandmother. Gina couldn't imagine being in her position. She missed Gracie, a lot. As soon as the case was over, she was going to visit her daughter and give her granddaughter a huge hug, but first, she wanted to get Brock in the interview room.

THIRTY-FIVE
CANDICE

Candice watched as the last of the children left with their parents while Poppy's teacher, Mrs Hallam, kept checking her phone. With a beaming smile, she waved at the teacher. Poppy ran over, flinging herself into Candice's arms. 'Hello, sweetheart. Have you had a lovely day?' She held her daughter close and inhaled her strawberry shampoo. Billie's murder had made her realise how suddenly everything could end. She couldn't bear to never see Poppy again. Candice glanced at William as he gripped his book bag. The little boy gazed around the playground searching for his mother.

'Mrs Hallam said my reading is super, Mummy. I made you a picture.' Her daughter thrust the piece of yellow sugar paper at her.

Candice turned it over and held it upright. 'That is beautiful. Is that Mummy and Daddy?'

She nodded, her red bunches bobbing. 'And that's me.' Poppy pointed at the blob of red in front of them. A happy family of paint blobs.

'It's beautiful. You're such a clever girl. As soon as we get home, we are going to put it on the wall. Daddy will love this.'

Mrs Hallam ended her unanswered call and ambled over in her flat, wide shoes. Candice wondered if the woman had ever worn make-up in her life. That would never be her. 'Mrs Brent, could I have a word? It won't take long.'

She snapped out of her thoughts and glanced back at William. 'Poppy, can you play with William for five minutes while Mummy talks to Mrs Hallam.'

The girl giggled and ran over to William, leaving Candice with the teacher. 'Is everything okay?'

'Yes, Poppy is fine, in fact, she's doing so well, I'm having to give her more challenging books to read. She's such a delightful child to teach.'

Candice beamed with pride, knowing that all the extra time spent reading and doing basic counting and sums had paid off. 'Is that what you want to speak to me about?'

The teacher shook her head and began glancing back at the school gates, her eyebrows furrowing. 'William's mum isn't here yet and that's strange as she's usually on time. I've just tried to call her but there's no answer. I know that you're authorised to collect William and you've often taken him home.'

'So, you wondered if I'd drop him back?'

The woman checked her watch. 'I'd be able to wait longer on a normal day, but I have an urgent dentist appointment.' She rubbed her cheek and grimaced. 'I need a filling and I don't want to miss it. Can't bear to spend another minute in this pain.'

'Of course. I pass Nadia's on my way home. In fact, I was going to her house after school so it would be a pleasure to drop him off.' She wasn't intending to go anywhere near Nadia's but that didn't matter. She wasn't about to leave William waiting and she wanted to check on Nadia.

'Thank you. In the meantime, I'll leave Mrs Anderson a message telling her that William has left with you. We're all really sorry about Billie, and poor Kayden losing his mum like that,' the woman said.

Candice felt herself choking up. 'I still can't take it in. We all miss her so much.'

Mrs Hallam pressed her lips together in a sympathetic smile. 'If you see Kayden, please tell him that we are all thinking about him. The children are making him some cards, which I hope to send to his grandparents soon. So sad. Anyway, I must head to my appointment.' The teacher flinched and held her cheek again before walking off in pain.

Candice wiped her watery eyes before turning back to the children. She couldn't let them see her like this. The last thing she wanted was for them to be upset. 'William, Poppy, let's go.' The boy and Poppy hurried over. Candice ruffled his hair and smiled. 'Your mum is running a bit late, so we'll drop you home.'

'Yay,' he yelled as the two children ran to the car.

Several minutes later, Candice pulled up on Nadia's drive. Her car was parked up at the side of the garage, but Ed's car wasn't there. She stepped out and unclipped the children. William ran to the door and immediately knocked. There was no answer. He lifted the letter box and yelled, 'Mummy,' at the top of his voice. His bottom lip came over his top lip as they all waited.

Candice stepped in front of the snug window and peered through the glass, flinching as Fluffball jumped onto the ledge. That's when she spotted the pile of cat mess on the carpet. She stepped in front of William and knocked again. 'Kids, can you wait in the car?'

'Where's Mummy?'

'I'm sure she's just popped out or maybe she's in the garden. Can you both wait in the car while I check?'

'Race you to the car,' Poppy shouted as she sprinted. Candice watched as they both got back in. She walked around the huge house, peering in through the hall window and the dining room window. No sign of Nadia or Ed.

The garden gate was open like it quite often was. She

pushed it and followed the side of the house until she reached the garden. Slowly creeping to the side door that led to the utility room behind the garage, Candice grabbed the door handle and exhaled. She hated just walking in. 'Hello,' she called out. 'Nadia? Ed?' Fluffball darted towards her and hissed before running out of the house. Candice flung herself back and gasped as her back hit the wall. The cat had scared the life out of her. It wasn't normally that unfriendly.

Her footsteps echoed on the kitchen floor. 'Hello.' The garage door was wide open. Glancing back and forth, she remained still, listening for anything or anyone but all she could hear was the hum of the fridge. With a trembling hand, Candice pressed the light switch and stared open-mouthed at the writing in red on the back wall. BITCH had been scrawled in capital letters and there was blood smeared underneath and droplets on the catalogues that were strewn everywhere. Sprinting as fast as she could out of the front door, she leaned over the bonnet of her car and tried not to look at Poppy and William. The last thing she wanted was for them to see the alarm in her eyes. With a sick feeling churning in her stomach, she called the police. 'I need to speak to someone, now. It's my friend and there's blood everywhere.'

THIRTY-SIX

Gina sighed as she watched the minutes ticking away. It was getting ever nearer to teatime and still Brock was pleading 'No comment' all the way. The suspect's solicitor cleared his throat and whispered to Brock.

A damp patch had formed under each of the solicitor's armpits, spreading outwards on his baby-pink shirt. 'My client wishes to make a statement, and that's all he's going to do today. I'm requesting a short break so that I can discuss this with him.'

Jacob pressed the stop button on the tape after announcing the time. Gina and Jacob walked the solicitor and Brock to a private room, while they loitered further down the corridor. She waved a handful of paper under her chin, but it gave barely any relief from the intense heat and still air. 'I guessed he was going to go no comment all the way. We've arrested him on suspicion of murder, kidnap of his son, assault of Mr Reeves and perverting the course of justice. We need to get to the bottom of Billie's murder. Did you see his eyes when I mentioned that he had opportunity and motive? He's been caught lying about so many things. When he saw the CCTV from the pub, he looked defeated. I wish we had forensics back from that bloodied toy in his car. It would solve a lot right now. Everything seems to take so long.' Gina clenched her fist. Waiting was one of the most frustrating parts of the job.

'Given his charges, guv, he's not going anywhere for the time being.'

'True. His solicitor can make a plea for bail, but all Brock will get is cosy in a cell tonight and until his case is heard. Fingers crossed that we get the blood results through soon.'

Jacob leaned against the wall. 'I'll check again with Bernard when we finish with Brock. See if I can bump it to the top of his list, along with everything else that needs doing urgently.'

The solicitor stepped out of the room; lips pressed together while he took confident strides towards them. Brock followed with his chin down as he dragged his feet towards the interview room. He pulled up his shirt and began to nervously scratch at the burn scarring on his stomach.

'Let's find out what he has to say.' Gina took her seat in the corner opposite Brock and his solicitor, and Jacob sat beside her and picked up a pen from the table. Gina threw the batch of paper on the table, knowing that the heat was about to get turned up. She pressed the fan on while Jacob introduced them all for the tape, along with the time and date. The papers flapped every time the fan rotated. Gina grabbed her bottle of water and placed it on top of them.

The solicitor loosened his grey tie and twitched his bulbous nose. 'My client has given me a statement to read out.'

Gina raised her eyebrows and stared at Brock, but the man was still looking down, trying his hardest not to give anything away.

'Okay, go ahead.' Gina leaned forward.

'My client has insisted that I use his exact words.' The man puffed out a breath before picking up the piece of paper to read. 'I'm sorry for all the trouble I've caused. I didn't want to scare my son, but I knew how everything looked. I wanted to explain to him that I didn't hurt his mother. She was a good mother and I regret not being there for my son. I admit I hurt Mr Reeves earlier, but it wasn't my intention. He went to close the door on me and as I pushed it back open the edge of the door caught his face and he fell backwards into the hall. I did not intend to injure or harm him in any way, it was merely an accident. It happened so fast, he may have thought that I hit him, but I didn't. I'd like to send him a full apology.' Brock leaned in and whispered to his solicitor again. The man turned over the sheet of paper.

'Is there more?' Gina asked.

The solicitor nodded. 'Just continuing with the statement.' He paused. 'My intention was not to deceive you when I didn't tell you that I already knew about Billie's murder.' The solicitor took a sip of water. 'I felt that because I'd been trying to contact her about seeing Kayden and things were becoming heated, I'd get the blame. The blood on the toy in my mother's car is my own blood and now that you have taken a swab, you'll be able to check. I suffer with nosebleeds. I admit going to the pub and seeing Billie's neighbour. Yes, I tried to ask her about Kayden, what he was like now and how he was doing at school. That's when she told me about what had happened to Billie. I think at that point, she too saw me as a potential suspect and things got heated. I followed her to the car park, and I shouldn't have but I didn't mean to make her uneasy her. She drove off and that's the last I saw of her. I did not murder Billie. I was nowhere near Billie's house that day. I spent some time on my own, trying to get my head around everything. I bought myself a new top from the charity shop on Cleevesford High Street, then I went to the gym to see if I could join. They will provide me with an alibi. I do not have anything else to say except I want to make it up to my son. I've been a bad father, but I want the opportunity to show that I've changed.'

Jacob made a note to follow up at the gym and the charity

shop. Gina bit her bottom lip. If his alibis came through that would take Brock off their suspect list and with it looking more unlikely that it was Edward Anderson, they were once again in a corner. She leaned back.

'Can I speak to my mother?' Brock looked up. 'She'll be worried and none of this is her fault.'

Given that he'd lied, and he had injured Mr Reeves and taken Kayden, the man was asking for too much. 'You will be taken back to the cell while we process your charges.'

'Wait, I told you the truth. I haven't done anything. All I wanted was to see my son. I'm guilty of being a father. I need to tell my mother where I am. She'll be worried about getting her car back. She has a bad heart.'

Gina shook her head. The man in front of her had left it too many years and he'd gone about everything in the wrong way. But her heart and sympathy went out to his poor mother. She couldn't leave the woman in the dark. 'I'll let your mother know where you are.'

Jacob finished speaking into the tape, ending with the time. 'Seventeen hundred hours.'

Someone tapped at the door and O'Connor peered through the glass. 'Excuse me.' Gina stood and opened it, before following him from earshot of the door. 'Please tell me you have the blood results back?' She didn't trust anything Brock said. The man was a habitual liar and only irrefutable evidence would help at this stage.

'No, sorry, guv, but there has been a development.'

'Okay. What do we have?'

'It looks like there has been a struggle at Nadia Anderson's house. There's blood in the garage and in red pen, on the wall, someone has written the word "Bitch".'

A fluttering sensation stopped in her throat. 'Is she dead?'

He shook his head and patted his shiny head with a handkerchief. 'No, she's missing and there's not that much blood. Bernard's team is already on the way to the scene.'

'Will you deal with Brock and let his mother know where he is and that he's okay? The woman is in bad health and seemed lovely, so please treat her delicately.'

'As always it's the families that suffer.'

Gina darted back to the interview room and caught Jacob's attention. 'We have to go, now.' She knew full well that Brock had been otherwise disposed all afternoon and the writing on the wall suggested that the person who had murdered Billie had now taken Nadia. One thing was for certain, she knew where Brock had been for the last few hours so the timeline would be crucial to the investigation. She had to find the woman before it was too late.

THIRTY-SEVEN

As Gina pulled up behind Jacob, she turned off the engine and stepped out of the air-conditioned car into the wall of evening heat. The tarmac on the road shimmered, adding to the misery. Magpies cawed in the trees at the side of the house and a blackbird hopped on the front lawn. The red-haired woman was trying to placate her bored daughter at the roadside, choosing not to bake in her car. Her oversized sunglasses masked any expression she might be harbouring, but Gina heard her sniff before she wiped her nose delicately with a tissue.

PC Smith clumsily hurried over and checked her in on the crime scene log. 'Where are we with it all?' Gina asked, holding her hands above her eyes to shield them from the sun before it disappeared over the rooftop.

'We've just got the cordons in place. That should keep any passers-by away from the scene. The husband, Edward Anderson, has just arrived back, and he showed Bernard into the garage. Mrs Anderson's friend, Candice Brent, said that Nadia hadn't been there to pick up her son from school, so she brought him home. That's when she found the scene in the garage. She's already given elimination prints as she did enter the scene. I asked what she touched but she was in shock and couldn't really remember. Her husband is on his way to collect their daughter just in case she needs to go to the station. Bernard has said that anyone entering must suit and boot cover up. Mr Anderson has tried to call his wife repeatedly, but her phone keeps going straight to voicemail.' Smith used his hat to fan himself as he blew out a puff of breath. 'This heat is a killer.'

'Who's knocking on doors around here?'

'Kapoor has already started, and she's enlisted a small team to help.' Gina glanced down the road and watched the young officer's ponytail swish as she turned into another house. 'The main problem being, most people were out at work and, as you can see, it seems like a quiet road. There are no people about or children playing. So far, she hasn't managed to find anyone who saw a thing. It's like a ghost came in and took Mrs Anderson. We live in hope that someone might have CCTV. But the cameras we have found only point towards where cars would be parked on drives.'

Gina sighed. 'The houses are so spaced out as well.' Each one had a long drive, most of them separated by hedges that appeared to reach the clouds. The beginnings of a pink sky began to form above, reminding them all that night was slowly approaching. The sun was finally vanishing for the day. In one sense, Gina was grateful that it was summer. Daylight would last longer, and they could continue searching the property and the garden with ease. There would be no need to set up portable lights for a while. 'Have we found the entry point?'

'The utility door was unlocked, and the side gate was too. Unless the perp left them unlocked when they left, there are no other clues. There's no damage to any windows or doors.'

'Do the Andersons have CCTV?'

'They do but it's not connected. Mr Anderson said he had a few problems with it and was meant to call someone to fix it, but he hadn't got around to it.'

Gina glanced through the snug window and watched Edward Anderson pressing his phone to his ear. Had he intentionally not got the CCTV fixed? Given that he was having what seemed like an intense relationship with Meera, was that motive enough to want to get his wife off the scene? The words on the wall had linked Billie's murder with Nadia's disappearance. The same red writing in capital letters, both misogynistic in nature. Due to the blood at the scene and the fact that Mrs Anderson was missing, they had all they needed to search the property. The man still hadn't given them his other phone to look at and they couldn't verify that he was at Jimbo's Hot Tubs in person on the day of Billie's murder. His history of approaching a sex worker in the past kept him in the suspect limelight. He glanced out of the window and sharply turned his back to Gina. She hurried to the front door that was ajar. 'Mr Anderson.'

He ambled to the door. 'Sorry, I was just calling my mother to check on my son. As you can appreciate, he is wondering why he couldn't go in his house and why his mother wasn't home.'

'I know this is hard,' – Gina swallowed, remembering to treat the man as a victim for now – 'but would you mind stepping out of the house so that any evidence won't be disturbed? Please stand outside until forensics have finished, and I'll come and speak to you in a moment.'

Firstly, she needed to see the crime scene. She wanted to compare the letters on the wall to those that she'd seen at Billie Reeves's house, and she wanted Bernard's initial take on what had happened. Deep down, panic was rising for the young missing woman.

'Of course not. I want my wife found. Please find her.' He nervously scratched his chin.

Gina wished the man's response seemed genuine but something in his eyes told her that everything coming out of his mouth was because of expectation. He had to act like the worried husband.

'Are forensics just swabbing things and looking for fingerprints?'

Gina nodded, knowing there was a lot more to it.

'They won't go through all my drawers and cupboards, like on the TV. It won't be left in a mess. And my son's bedroom, nothing will be disturbed?'

'We'll be as respectful as possible. I'll make sure of that.' She tilted her head and bowed her head slightly.

Gina put on her crime scene suit and boot covers before proceeding through the house. Although thin, the extra layer made her feel like she was a boil in the bag meal. 'I'll come and speak to you in a few minutes.'

He grunted a response and stepped onto the drive.

Gina heard Bernard's voice coming from the garage. Stepping plates had been arranged from the kitchen to the utility and to the garage. She carefully used them until she reached the internal garage door, leaving a tinny echo with each step she took. A welcomed coolness hit her as she cleared her throat to get his attention.

'Ah, DI Harte. If you could stay by the door, that would be great.'

'Sure. Bernard, can you tell me anything? I know you haven't had much time to process the scene yet.' A crime scene officer completely covered in a white suit nudged past her with a camera. The other one was bagging up a brochure that was dotted with blood and various numbered markers had been placed.

'Yes. The spatter tells us that the victim was struck about here.' He stood by the wall.

'And all the brochures?'

'There are specks of blood on them which means they'd

already been scattered all over the floor before the victim had been injured.'

'So, there may have been a struggle?'

'It looks that way. There is also a trail of blood on the floor. It's not too heavy which is why you can't see much but it runs from here, to here.' He pointed. 'It's consistent with the victim trying to crawl away. The garage door is also slightly open. We couldn't tell from the outside on arrival, but it hadn't clicked back into its locked position.'

'Looking like the perp may have taken our victim through the garage door and into a car?'

He nodded. 'Yes, because look here.' She gazed at the grey concrete floor. 'There are more specks of blood and a scuff mark from a shoe that is consistent with the victim being dragged on her back and it disappears at the edge of the garage.'

'Do you have the victim's phone?'

'There is no phone in the garage, the kitchen or the utility room.'

Again, the phone had gone. Billie's had also been taken. 'The writing on the wall, is it the same pen as the writing at Billie Reeves's house.'

'It's a definite match. We have logged the exact colour and make from the previous crime scene which made it easier to match this time.'

'How common is the pen?'

'It's sold everywhere. It's a basic permanent marker that can be bought anywhere from supermarkets to pound shops. It's cheap and there are millions of them out there.'

'Have you found anything else?'

'A red hair but again, we're thinking it will be a match from the friend who discovered the scene. There is still so much to do. We should have more in a short while.'

'Is it okay for us to look around the house or do you need more time?'

'The attack took place here but if you remain suited and go with care, the other rooms should be okay to search. Mr Anderson came in through the front door and he only went in the snug. Your officer managed to keep him away from the corridor, the kitchen and the garage.'

'Great. I'll form a team and speak to the husband and the friend first.'

He tucked a bit of stray beard into his beard cover. 'Just keep the team small. Not too many people traipsing around. The attack was contained here but it may be that the attacker went into other rooms first. Stick to the stepping plates and keep to the edge of the stairs if you go up.'

She tilted her head and smiled under her face covering. 'No problem.' She glanced one last time at the wall and that horrible word. Her brows furrowed as her line of sight reached the hole in the wall. 'What's that?' She pointed. 'The hole?'

'We don't know. It looks like the plaster came away. There are chunks of it on the floor and speckles of plaster dust.'

'I wonder if she found something in there, or maybe she was hiding something. It's possible that the attacker was after it.'

'I'm just here doing the science but that might be a possibility.'

'Have you found anything around that seems out of place?'

'Oh yes, one thing. There was a small piece of paper on the floor with the words "Got you" on it, along with a laughing emoji.' He reached into an evidence box and passed the bagged item to Gina. She glanced through the plastic and saw that it had been typed up on A4 printer paper that had been folded up.

'Any prints on it?'

'A partial. It's latent so you can't see it with the naked eye. We'll get it back to the lab and follow up with a clear copy so that it can be run against the database.'

'Thank you.'

Jacob peered around the corner. 'Guv, Mr Anderson is kicking up a bit of a stink and Mrs Brent is asking when she can leave.'

She thanked Bernard and his team before heading out of the garage. She tried to picture Nadia in her mind. After a potential tussle that caused the catalogues and boxes to fall over, she was struck. She fell on her front, leaving a few drops of blood on the floor. The smear on the wall suggests that she may have reached out and tried to use it to steady herself. Had she almost given up by this point? Maybe her attacker struck her again and rolled her onto her back before dragging her towards the garage door and bundling her into a car. Was there a bloody car out there somewhere, or had the attack been more calculated? If her assailant premeditated the attack, had they lined the car with polythene and since disposed of everything, or was Mrs Anderson still in the car, cooking alive in this heat? She pictured the terrified woman fighting for her life, thinking of her son and wondering after Billie's murder, if she was next. She needed to speak to Edward Anderson now. She wanted his work phone and no more lies. Time was against them.

As she passed the snug, her attention was on the tiniest of smears on the snug wall. She bent over and peered at it. 'Bernard. Blood on the wall here.'

He hurried through the house. 'No one else is to go near the snug.'

She backed away, leaving him to secure what she'd spotted. If Nadia was alive, the clock was ticking.

THIRTY-EIGHT

'I want to go in my house.' Mr Anderson hurried over to Gina just as she left the house.

'Mr Anderson, the team are still working the scene.' She removed her forensics gear at the doorstep.

'How long are they going to be and why aren't you out there looking for my wife? Instead, you're here, keeping me out of my house. My son needs some things and so do I.'

'If you speak to one of the officers after we've spoken, I'm sure they'll be able to get everything you need for now. I need to ask you a few questions.' She walked away from the front door and beckoned him over onto the grassy front garden.

'Hey,' the woman with the red hair called out. 'My daughter is getting scared. Will I have to wait here long?' Candice Brent pulled her little girl close and swallowed. All the waiting was a lot for such a young child. Gina could appreciate that but she needed the woman to stay put.

'Mrs Brent, please bear with me a little longer. I'll come over to you in a moment.'

'Okay, sorry to interrupt you. I'll be by my car.' The woman grabbed her daughter's hand and headed back towards her car.

At least the sun was going down so the heat wasn't as intense as earlier. Gina watched on as an officer gave the woman and child a bottle of water each.

Mr Anderson folded his arms and stood in the shade. 'What am I meant to do? I need to pick my son up and he'll want to come home.'

'We're trying to make this as quick as possible. Mr Anderson, where were you this afternoon?'

'At the Cleevesford office.'

'Was anyone with you?'

'No, everyone else was on site or out quoting for jobs.'

'Do you have CCTV at the office?'

He sighed. 'I do but it's the same as here, it needs fixing. I've just been so busy lately; I haven't sorted it.'

'Did you speak to anyone at the office or on your way to or from the office?'

'No.'

So far, the man couldn't provide an alibi for his movements. 'We found a note at the scene and there is a fingerprint on it. Did you print up a note that says, "Got you" on it, followed by a laughing emoji?'

He let out a frustrated roar and gripped his hair with one of his hands. 'Yes. It was a joke. Nadia and I are like that. We leave little gifts for each other hidden in the house. Some are fun things, like earrings. She's left me a cigar before, and jokey notes like the one you found. I know it sounds silly, but we've always done it and it's a laugh, that's all.'

'Did you make the hole in the plaster?'

'Yes, I put the silly note in the hole, and she must have found it. It was my turn to hide something. If you don't believe me, there's also a gift hidden under our bed in a little box, it's a fancy diamanté hair clip that she had her eye on. Now I have some questions. I sneaked a look at the garage. I had to see it. Who wrote that word on our wall?'

'That's what we're trying to find out.'

'How dare someone come into our house and...' He clenched his fist and stared at Gina, the intensity making her stiffen. 'You're not trying hard enough. My wife is out there and she's bleeding.' He jabbed the air with his pointed index finger. 'She's scared and William is missing his mother. She's hurt and...' He began to gasp for breath.

'Mr Anderson, are you okay?'

He nodded and placed a hand on his chest. 'I might look brash, like I don't care much about anything, but I do. This has knocked me sideways.'

Something screamed to Gina that he might just be telling the truth, but she needed to press him more. 'You didn't bring your other phone in for us to analyse.'

'Really, you're going on about my work phone after all that's happening. I didn't think it was important because Billie's murder has nothing to do with me. I have an alibi. I was at Jimbo's Hot Tubs. You need to take your focus off me and catch this maniac. Here, have the bloody phone. Do what you like with it.' He pulled it from his pocket and thrust it into her arms.

She took it off him and called Jacob over. Her colleague left PCs Kapoor and Smith and hurried over. 'Mr Anderson's company phone, the one he said he was bringing in. Do you have any more phones?'

'No.'

She walked across the grass away from Mr Anderson and spoke in a hushed tone. 'Can we pull the records just in case there has been any deleting going on? We need to get into his bin folders.'

Jacob nodded as he took the phone to record the details. Edward Anderson had given it to them and said to do what they wanted with it. She hurried back to the man. 'Thank you. We really appreciate your help. A family liaison officer is on the way.'

'I don't want one.'

'The person who has your wife may call. We need to put a trace on your phone and be there if they try to make contact.'

'Dammit. I best not bring William back home tonight. This will be too much for him. He can stay with my mother. I don't want him to see all this.'

'I know this is hard, but we are doing everything we can.'

'Whatever.' He pulled his personal phone from his pocket. 'Do you mind if I make a couple of calls? I need to call my sales manager, get him to hold the fort for the time being and I need to see if my son's okay. The poor boy is as confused as hell.'

'Of course not. I'll come back in a few minutes, then I'll send an officer over to take a statement.' That was perfectly timed for her to speak to Candice who was now leaning against her car, listening to someone speak through her phone. Her hair that was tidy when Gina had arrived on the scene was now a bit unruly at the sides, where she'd been twisting it around her index finger. Her little girl tugged on the hem of her dress, moaning about having to stand around. She listened as the woman spoke. 'How long are you going to be? I need you here. Poppy needs you.' She paused and shook her head as she wiped the trail of tears from her cheeks. 'Just tell them you have to leave. It's an emergency.' The woman flinched as Gina got closer, then she ended the call without another word and the little girl cried and once again began tugging at the hem of her dress.

THIRTY-NINE

CANDICE

'Mrs Brent. I'm DI Harte.' The detective smiled at Poppy. 'You can call me Gina.'

Candice put her phone back into her bag. 'Sorry, that was my husband. He said he'd come here asap and that was ages ago. He's just left work but should be here soon.' She'd already told the first officer on the scene everything she knew but still, they'd insisted that she stay and tell it all again to the detective in front of her. She wiped her eyes again, leaving another streak of mascara on the white tissue.

'Mummy, I want to go home,' her daughter bawled.

The detective kneeled on the pavement. 'I'm really sorry as I know it's hot and you've been so patient, waiting all this time. How would you like to help that lovely police officer over there to collect everyone's names as they arrive? He's very funny and knows some good jokes.'

Poppy gripped Candice's hand and gave a few more hiccupped sobs before stopping.

'It'll be okay, sweetie. Mummy will be here and Daddy's on his way.'

Her daughter nodded and allowed the detective to take her

hand and lead her to the uniformed officer with the clipboard. Candice watched as he smiled and spoke in an animated voice. Poppy was soon giggling. Whatever he said had made her laugh. As the detective headed back, Candice sat on the bonnet of her car, her legs feeling a little wobbly. She'd already told everyone everything she knew and said she'd go to the station later to make a statement. Right now, she wanted to take Poppy home and lock the door on the scary outside world.

'I'm sorry to have kept you waiting, Mrs Brent.'

The detective seemed nice and caring. 'Please, call me Candice.' She kicked her sandals off, releasing her sore feet and stood on a shady part of the pavement.

DI Harte nodded. 'Can you just talk me through what happened this afternoon?'

'I've already told the officer everything.'

'I know, and I'm sorry to have to ask you again, but your friend is missing and all we want to do is find her and bring her home safely.'

Candice closed her eyes and pictured the scene and the blood. The thought of it was sickening. Only after standing around had she been toiling with all that had happened and no matter how hard she tried not to overthink things, she could still smell the hot metallic blood that seemed to coat her nostrils. And where was Gavin? She felt like he'd abandoned her in her hour of need. It was easy to convey the perfect marriage and the perfect family. All that happy family stuff she posted on Instagram was nothing more than fake news. She had as many problems as the next person. Poppy had as many whiny moments as the next child, and she didn't wake up looking as perfect as she made out when she posted photos of her perfect breakfast-in-bed moments. She and Nadia were alike in that way, but neither would admit it. Nadia was gone. She let out a small sob.

'Candice...'

'Sorry. What I saw, it keeps going through my head. When I

went into the garage, I felt as though I couldn't breathe and...'
She choked out another sob and shook her head.

'Would you find it easier to come down the station now
where it might be cooler?'

'No, I'm okay. I need to wait for my husband to collect
Poppy. I don't want to take her to a police station.' She swallowed and shook her head. The last thing she wanted to do was
go into a police station at all. She wanted to go home. She also
wanted to forget that Billie's younger sister, Serena, had kept
leaving her messages. She didn't even know the woman. It was
all getting too much. She wished they could all go back a few
days when they all felt so safe and life was simpler. All she
wanted was to sip wine in Nadia's back garden and watch while
their children played, but those days were gone forever. Tears
flooded her face. She pulled another tissue from her bag and
blew her nose hard.

'Do you need a few moments?'

'No, I need to do this, for Nadia.' She wiped the sore deli-
cate skin under her nose and flinched at the stinging sensation
from too much rubbing.

'In your own time.' The detective pulled a tiny notepad
from her pocket and a pen from another.

'The day seemed like any other. I was at home tidying my
salon.'

'Salon?'

With a shaky voice, she continued, 'I'm a dog groomer. My
garage is a dog salon.' Candice opened the bottle of water and
took a sip of its warm contents. 'Then I had to pick Poppy up
from school. They finish at three fifteen. I was rushing as usual.
Nadia and I usually joke that I'm always rushing and she's
normally early. Today, she wasn't there and the kids' teacher,
Mrs Hallam, said that she'd tried to call Nadia but there had
been no answer. I've picked up William on lots of occasions, so
I'm authorised to collect him from school. I said I'd drop him

home...' Candice shook away her inner thoughts that were threatening to overwhelm her. She gripped her trembling hands behind her back.

'And after that?'

'I put the kids in the car and drove straight here to drop William off. At first, I was worried. I thought Nadia might be ill or an emergency might have cropped up. It's unlike her to not turn up. If something had happened, she'd have called me and asked if I could collect William for her. I even checked my phone and there were no missed calls. We got out of the car, that's me, William and Poppy. Then we went to the front door and knocked, but there was no answer. I knew there was something wrong, it was like I could sense it. That's when I told the kids to get back in the car.' Candice felt her chest tightening.

'I know this is hard but you're doing really well.'

'I looked through the window and saw the cat in the snug. There was also a pile of cat mess up the far end and that seemed strange too. I know Nadia has a cat flap and a litter tray. Fluffball is a well-trained cat so I guessed he must have been accidentally shut in the room at some point.'

The detective made a few notes. 'Where did you go next?'

'I thought I'd try the back gate. Although I felt something wasn't right, I hoped that Nadia was in the back garden. I thought maybe she'd fallen over or hurt herself. The back gate was open, which wasn't a huge surprise because she quite often forgets to lock it. I checked the garden and couldn't see her, so I tried the utility room door and that was open. I went in and the air felt strange.'

'In what way?'

'Not as in smell or sound, it was silent. I'd never heard Nadia's house in silence. She loves a bit of music or the radio, or William is always running around. I called out to Ed and Nadia but there was no answer. As I walked through the utility room, the cat darted past me, hissing. It looked scared. I was quite startled by that, and I remember thinking that my sense of worry was stupid. I kept telling myself that Nadia had just gone out somewhere with Ed, as her car is parked over there, and maybe they were caught in traffic. But Fluffball never hisses at me. He's normally a friendly cat.' Candice stopped and thought about that moment.

'What happened then?'

'Sorry. I went through the kitchen; I checked the snug, walked around calling them, then I saw that the garage door was open. When I reached the garage, I turned on the light and stepped in. At first, I didn't see that word on the wall. All I saw was the mess. There were boxes and brochures everywhere and a hole in the wall. I stepped in and walked around, that's when I spotted the blood smeared on the wall and that word almost took my breath away. I knew something bad had happened. I ran out of the front door, opening it from the inside and I hurried straight back to the children. That's when I called the police. A uniformed officer arrived quite quickly, and I've been standing on the kerb since.'

The detective undid one of her shirt buttons. Candice watched as the skin on her neck reddened before spreading to her chin, leaving a cherry-bright shine on it. 'Excuse me, I can't bear this heat.' She exhaled and continued, 'Do you know of anyone who would want to hurt Nadia? Has she had any disagreements with anyone lately?'

Candice knew this question was coming and it was important to tell the police everything. 'Nadia and Billie had a bit of a falling out. Nadia let Billie's secret slip. Billie told her in confidence about what she was doing, for money. I assume you know.'

'We do but can you tell me again?'

'Billie was sleeping with men for money. She found these men online and she told Nadia in confidence. Nadia told a couple of other people and gossip spreads. She didn't mean it nastily when she told, she was concerned. By the time Billie held Kayden's party back in May, everyone knew. No one said much to each other or to Billie's face, but you could cut the atmosphere with a knife. Nadia spotted Ed staring at Billie and their marriage was going down the pan at the time. That man has never been faithful to her. When Billie and the other parents had left, she went mad at him. She didn't know I could hear them arguing. I was downstairs with the children, but I thought I'd help to tidy up a bit. I left William's toys on the landing to be put away and I could hear them in the bedroom. Nadia was shouting at Ed, saying that half of the parents at the school had fallen out with her because they felt she could have helped Billie instead of gossiping, but the other half were mean to Billie. Nadia was crying, saying it was all her fault. Ed then piped up, shouting that everything was her fault as she couldn't keep her big mouth shut and she should keep out of other people's business. He's not a nice person. It was like he was getting off on her crying.' Candice glanced over and saw Ed watching her from right outside the front door. He was too far away to hear but she knew that he was aware it was him she was talking about. Her heart began to pound so she sipped more water. 'They weren't happy.'

'Did you hear anything else?'

'Yes, Nadia accused Ed of sleeping with Billie. She knew that he'd been seeing someone else. I heard Ed call Billie a slut, which I thought was a revolting thing to say. He said he'd never even look at her twice. That's when I heard the bedroom door open, so I ran back downstairs. I didn't want them to know I'd been listening. I still don't want them to know.'

'You mentioned the other parents. Did anyone else have a problem with Nadia or want to hurt her?'

'No. As I say, she had a few issues with some of the parents, but I can't think why anyone would want to harm her over a bit of gossip.'

'Anyone else you can think of who might want to harm either Nadia or Billie?'

'I know Billie didn't always get on with her sister, Serena. They argued a lot, but I don't really know why.' She paused, biting the end of her red nail off. 'I can't keep this to myself, and I don't know what it means.' She was totally betraying Nadia, and it didn't feel good, but she needed to be truthful.

'It might be the information that helps us find your friend.' The detective placed her notebook by her side and looked into Candice's eyes.

She felt her insides churning. 'When they were arguing, Nadia kept begging Ed to tell her where the knife was hidden.'

The male detective hurried over. 'Guv, I need an urgent word. We have a development.'

'Excuse me a moment.' DI Harte walked away with the man and Candice could feel the tension as they spoke.

'Hey, I got here as fast as I could.' Gavin looked flustered as he hurried to her side. His creased shirt hung out of his trousers and his tousled hair gleamed with perspiration. 'Work was a nightmare.'

'Daddy.' Poppy left PC Smith and ran as fast as she could to her dad while Candice snubbed him.

'You took forever. I needed you and...' She burst into tears, the enormity of the day finally getting on top of her.

Gavin gripped her tightly and pulled her into his arms. 'I'm so sorry, love. I couldn't get away, but I came straight here. What's going on?'

Candice wiped her eyes and looked back at the scene. 'It looks like they're arresting Ed.' She watched as the man shouted and raised his arms. Within moments he was in a police car being driven away. 'It was him all along.' Candice shook her head. 'He killed Billie and he's done something to Nadia.'

FORTY

'Right, team. I know it's late, but we have a breakthrough. I want to get everyone caught up while we give Edward Anderson's solicitor a chance to turn up. He has exercised his right to have someone present and he's contacted his family solicitor.' Gina pointed to the new additions to the board. She watched as Jacob typed out a message on his phone, probably to tell Jennifer that he was running late. O'Connor began munching on a cinnamon bun and he passed one to PC Kapoor. Wyre leaned back in her creaky plastic chair and stretched her hands above her head.

Gina glanced at the photos of Billie and the new board headed up with a photo of Nadia that they'd pulled off her social media. In it, Nadia looked radiant in a glowing post-workout way as she tried to promote her personal training business. 'Fill us in with what happened with the hot tub lead, Wyre.' While Wyre spoke, Gina pulled out her packet sandwich and took a few bites.

Wyre flicked through a few pages in her notebook. 'On finding out that we couldn't get the CCTV from Jimbo's Hot Tubs for a few days, I called them back and the administrator had managed to speak to the owner. He agreed that if we could send an officer who was able to navigate the system, we could go and look at the CCTV. I managed to contact a police officer at Derby who was more than willing to head over and check this for us. He managed to find the time stipulated on the receipt and he took a still of the frame that showed the man paying. The man who bought the hot tub was not Ed Anderson. He's shorter and has jet-black hair. We haven't yet verified the identity of this man.'

Gina turned to Jacob. 'Tell us about the message on Anderson's phone.' She loved it when a case was coming together. Whether Anderson spoke or not that evening, she was going to sleep well. They had evidence stacking up against him.

Jacob placed his phone down and Gina watched as it constantly lit up. Ignoring it, he spoke. 'There was a message in Anderson's bin folder, and it was from Billie Reeves's phone number. He'd obviously tried to delete it and then thought that we wouldn't be able to retrieve it. On the afternoon she was murdered, Billie sent him a message saying, "Stop harassing me or I'll call the police." We don't yet know how long he'd been harassing her or what this harassment involved, but it was bad enough for her to threaten him with the police.'

Gina stepped back. 'Lastly, we have a partial print on the inside sliding lock on Billie's back gate and it is a definite match to Edward Anderson. He's been to her house, and he locked the gate from the inside. The circumstantial evidence is plentiful and right now, he's our prime suspect. There is one other thing. After speaking to Candice Brent, the woman who discovered the scene in the Andersons' garage, we now know we are looking for a knife that may have been used in another crime and possibly in Billie's murder, too. Mrs Brent claims that she overheard Nadia begging Anderson to tell her where the knife was hidden. To be able to match the knife with Billie's wound, we need to find the knife and we need to find out why he was hiding a knife from Nadia. One more thing, Candice Brent claims to have heard Anderson calling Billie a slut, the exact word that was written on Billie's wall. We should have the search warrant soon. We already have access to the house, but we want to be able to search Mr Anderson's car, his company vans and his offices. There are four in total and they're not all local, but we can't leave anything out. O'Connor, can I task you to chase the warrant up?'

He chomped on the last bit of cinnamon bun and swallowed. 'Yes, guv. I'll get onto it now.'

'One last thing, Wyre, can you investigate Serena Reeves, Billie's younger sister? They weren't getting along, and I want to know why. I know the evidence is stacking up against Anderson, but I'm not ready to put all our eggs in one basket. Also, check Nadia's work schedule. Her social media tells us she uses Cleevesford Leisure Centre to provide training for her clients. We need to check if she had any bookings on that day. It would help if we found the last person she met or spoke to.'

'Of course, guv.'

'I'd like to interview Serena tomorrow, depending on how the interview with Mr Anderson goes. If he confesses and the case is closed, then we can all go home and have a good night's sleep. But for now, I hope you'll all help in getting through the huge mound of work and leads that have come in. I know you've put in a long couple of days, and I know you're hot and tired, but I fear for Mrs Anderson. She's out there. She's hurt and time is against us. O'Connor, could you please catch up with the tech team? See if anyone has come across Billie on any of the websites that we know offer escort services online. Not having any of her tech is making this case harder than it needs to be. Also, have them sifting through Nadia's social media.'

'I know they've been looking at the escort websites, guv, but they haven't come across Billie yet. There are so many profiles to go through. No one uses their real names so they're having to look at the photos.'

Gina swallowed and checked her watch. Her throat was bone dry. 'When I get home tonight, I'll keep looking, also. Can we check to see if Anderson's solicitor has arrived?' Wherever Nadia Anderson was, she needed them to do everything they could to help her before it was too late.

Briggs entered. 'A solicitor has just arrived and he's asking for our suspect on the Billie and Nadia case.'

Gina turned back to the team. 'Jacob, could you take him to Anderson and everyone else, you know what you need to do.' The group dispersed and Gina followed Briggs out into the hallway and through to the kitchen. 'Sir, wait.'

'What is it, Gina? Come to sabotage my relationship again with more accusations?'

'I'm sorry. I should have minded my own business, but I still care, and I don't want to see you get hurt.'

He shrugged. 'The only one hurting me is you. I trust Rosemary, I really do. She wants to be with me. We've moved in together and everything's going well.' He really was in denial and Gina couldn't do anything about it. She shouldn't have spoken to him so sharply but there was no way of getting through to him. 'Haven't you got a missing woman to find?'

He stormed out, leaving her with an emptiness that she knew would be hard to fill. A lump formed in her throat. It really was over. Gina knew what she'd seen. Briggs was right though. She shouldn't be in the kitchen talking to him about his personal life when Nadia Anderson was missing. She'd do her job, go home and trawl the net for escort services. But right now, she had a suspect to interview.

FORTY-ONE

Edward Anderson remained tight-lipped as his designer-suited solicitor had recommended. Gina had asked all the questions, but none had been responded to.

'Where were you on the afternoon of Billie's murder?'

'Where were you this afternoon, between two and three fifteen?'

'Who purchased the hot tub on your behalf?'

'Why are your fingerprints on Billie Reeves's gate lock?'

'Where is your wife?'

'Where is the knife?'

The questioning went on and on, but Anderson ignored her. All he could do was stare at the wooden table that divided him and his solicitor and Gina and Jacob.

'Mr Anderson, you've been arrested on suspicion of Billie Reeves's murder and the kidnapping and assault of your wife. You have nothing to say at all?'

He cleared his throat. 'Find my wife.'

'Why don't you tell us where your wife is?'

He slammed his fist on the table, the recorder jumping, and

everyone stared in silence. 'Because I don't know where she is. I did not murder Billie Reeves.'

'But you won't tell us where you were on the day of her murder.'

'I didn't do it.' He shook his head.

His solicitor whispered in his ear. The suave man pushed his glasses up his nose and removed his pocket square. He took a moment to dab his brow before speaking on his client's behalf. 'Mr Anderson has nothing further to say. The onus is on you to make sure your case will stand up in court and it must be proven beyond reasonable doubt, but you have doubt.' The man leaned back. 'You have doubt because you cannot prove my client was anywhere near Miss Reeves on the day of her murder.' The solicitor re-folded the pocket square and placed it neatly back in his top pocket.

Gina slapped the pages of her notebook closed. They weren't getting anywhere. Maybe a search of his house, businesses and car would get the ball rolling.

Jacob turned to the recorder. 'Interview terminated at twenty forty-five on Friday the seventeenth of June.'

Feeling her fingers itch with frustration, Gina needed to get out of the room. They had so much evidence. Either Anderson was refusing to confess, and he did it, or he was hampering their case by not telling the truth of what he had been up to. She stood and left the room, hurrying along the corridor and to her office. As she entered, the stale smell and sticky heat hit her. All day, her window had been shut, the blinds had been open, and the sun had been beating in. She fell into her chair and took a few deep breaths in her sauna of a room. She dug her nails into her arm until she felt a trickle of blood. Numb – that's how she felt. She couldn't even feel pain. A person with no feelings was nothing but an empty shell. Her shell was so thin, one tap and she'd crack into nothing but dust.

'Guv.' Jacob tapped on her door.

She sat up straight with one swift movement and forced a smile. The smile wasn't reaching her eyes and she could see that even Jacob knew she was a fraud, a fake person with no substance. 'I'll be ready in a moment.'

'Great.' He sheepishly took a couple of steps into her office and sat down opposite her.

'You okay?' she asked.

Jacob placed his hands on her desk. 'I'm hunky-dory. I know you'll be mad if I say something. We've been colleagues for a long time, and I don't want you to be angry with me... I'll just say it. I know you're not okay, guv, and it's okay to feel the pressure sometimes. You're so strong for all of us, all the time. Look how you supported me and Jennifer.'

She'd pushed her colleagues away. They could tell she wasn't right. As soon as she got a moment, she'd go to the doctors and try to sort her hormones out. They could see her burning up every five minutes and maybe they sensed her sadness. Losing Briggs had hit her hard. 'I think this case is just getting to me. With what we do, you see the world in a whole new light. Other people see the good in folk, I can only see the bad. I see a world full of greed, hate, violence and anger and I know the bad outweighs the good. No one cares about anyone but themselves—'

'You do, we do. I get where you're coming from, but I'm lucky. I have Jennifer to talk to, you have no one. When things get bad, we sound off at each other and put the world to rights. We know that we must keep fighting for our victims and we know that once we've crawled out of one hole, another ten will appear, but we keep going.'

'You're right. Thanks, Jacob.' She stood and grabbed her car keys. 'I need to buck up and get to the Andersons' house while Bernard is still there. Let's go and search the place. We have a knife to find.' She hoped that would be the end of it. Her views on the world hadn't changed but Jacob had warmed her heart with his concern.

'That's more like it. Let's go and find ourselves a knife.' Jacob stepped towards the door.

That knife might seal their case against Anderson but first they needed to find it, that's if he hadn't disposed of it.

FORTY-TWO

CANDICE

Candice cleaned the table on which she groomed the dogs and threw the cloth into the laundry bin. It had been easier once darkness had fallen but it hadn't taken her mind off Nadia. Nothing would take her mind off her friend. She thought about her business and the new premises. Now, she didn't want any of it, but she wasn't going to tell Gavin yet. As she went to turn, she trod on his foot and let out a scream. He held his hands up. 'I didn't mean to make you jump. Are you okay? Are we okay?' How long had he been watching her clean?

She nudged past him and headed out of the house and into their garden where she sat on the bench that she'd lovingly positioned in the rose bed. 'Is Poppy in bed?'

He nodded. 'She's fast asleep. I think the drama of the day tired her out.' He sat beside her and placed an arm around her shoulders. 'I really am sorry it took me so long to get to you when you needed me.'

She shrugged. 'Why did you take so long?'

'I had a meeting with the app developer, and I had things to sign off on. When you said the police had arrived, I knew you were safe. I'm an insensitive prick. Please forgive me.' He leaned in closer like he always did and stroked her cheek. 'Have you heard anything about Nadia, yet?'

She shook her head. 'I told them.'

'Who and what?'

'The police. I told them about the knife, the one I heard Nadia and Ed arguing about.'

'But you weren't sure what you heard, you said it yourself. Was that wise?'

She nudged him away and leaned forward. 'Billie was stabbed.' In her mind Ed needed blaming for that along with Nadia's disappearance. He was a lying cheat. Everyone knew he was having an affair, or even affairs, even Nadia, but she put up with him, which always annoyed Candice. Nadia had spilled her fears out about Ed after a few glasses of wine one evening. Once again, Nadia had said too much and she couldn't even remember, just like at Kayden's birthday party. A flutter in her chest made her expel a slight gasp.

'You do know he could get into real trouble for something you're not sure you heard right?'

'He did it. You only have to look at him to tell. You saw him tonight. He harboured the look of a guilty man.' He was guilty of plenty, and he was a liar. She felt her bottom lip begin to tremble. She couldn't cry, not again, not now. Candice had told Nadia that she and Gavin had been going through a bad patch, Nadia had told Meera and Billie, along with a few mums at the school gate. Candice wished that she'd never said anything now. Her life felt as though it was spiralling downhill and there was no going back. She knew that she too had been party to some of the gossip, especially when she found out about Billie. It had been so easy to join in with the aim of fitting in but not any more. She wanted to be a better person, for Poppy's sake. From now on, she vowed to be the mother Poppy deserved. 'Did you see the look on his face as they arrested him?'

'What I saw was a man who had something to hide, but

murder and kidnap? Really? How long have we known Ed for? I'll answer that, years.'

She folded her arms. 'Have you ever cheated on me?'

'Where did that come from?'

'Everyone is cheating on everyone lately. I want to know if you've cheated on me, and I'll know if you're lying.'

He gripped her hand. 'Look at you, look at Poppy and all that we've built together. I would never cheat on you. You're the best thing in my life. I'm not Ed.'

She turned to face him, and he leaned in to kiss her, his lips delicately reaching for hers. She pulled away. 'I'm sorry. It's been a long day and I think I just need some sleep.' She didn't know who she could trust any more.

'How was work?'

She pursed her lips and sighed. 'Quiet. I think I need to rethink how I get more dogs to groom, especially if I'll be running a bigger place soon.'

'Great, maybe I can help you this weekend. We'll sort something. We still need to look at your website.' He stood and smiled. He'd been promising to help her with her business for ages but as usual, his promises were empty. The weekend would come, and he'd conveniently forget, besides, everything that had happened made it seem so insignificant. 'I have a couple of calls to make. Will you be okay?'

The story of her life. Gavin always had work to attend to. She needed him yet still, in a minute, she'd be sitting alone on the bench not enjoying the cloying perfume of the roses. She'd once loved that smell, but everything eventually turned to rot. She watched as her husband hurried back into the house, then she heard his office door closing. Always closed, that's the way he liked it. Always locked, but he wasn't careful all the time. She knew all his secrets. Each and every one of them. She glanced at her phone and reread the message from Serena, then she replied. Maybe she could meet the woman for a coffee, after all, she'd just lost her sister in a horrific attack. She glanced up and watched as Gavin walked across his office and sat at his desk, the light from the small room spilling out onto the patio.

Her nails dug into her palm as she envisaged barging through his office door, grabbing his computer and bashing it on the tiled floor. How dare he leave her upset like this? She thought of Poppy lying in bed fast asleep and a tear rolled down her face. Everything was hopeless and unless she did something, her whole world was going to come crashing down. But first, she needed sleep. She knew she'd lie in bed for hours thinking of Nadia and all that happened in the garage. She couldn't get the word bitch out of her head and the red pen it was written in. It was going to be a long night and there was no way she'd be able to rest. From where she was sitting, she could hear her husband pushing his office window open and then he continued tapping away. The piercing sound of a scream filled the air. Foxes always sounded like people being attacked. It was as if Billie and Nadia were in her head. She placed her fingers in her ears, pressing her eyes closed. *Go away.*

She wanted the screaming to stop.

She wanted Gavin to stop.

Her loud sobs joined in with the distant foxes; sobs she had no control of. It was as if something evil was closing in on her. Coming to take all that she was and all that she had.

FORTY-THREE

Darkness had fallen and before Bernard left, he'd set up some portable lights throughout the garden. Gina got out of the car and the officer guarding the scene opened the cordon so that they could go through. She stepped into the hallway, Jacob following closely. Before getting started, she took out her phone and called O'Connor who was searching Anderson's Cleevesford office with Kapoor and Smith. 'If you find that knife, call me straight away.' He'd acknowledged her request and ended the call. The coordinated searches had started. All of Anderson's offices were now flooded with officers looking for that knife or any other evidence that tied him in with Billie's murder or his wife's abduction.

Four uniformed officers awaited Gina's instruction. She called Wyre over. 'Firstly, the two officers in the kitchen will remain. There is a trace on the home phone should anyone call. In an ideal world, we'd have Mr Anderson here to answer but he is our main suspect. This is just to cover us. A call is not anticipated.' The two men waved. 'I know Bernard and his team have been through everything in the garage so, Wyre, could you and a couple of officers take the kitchen, the snug, the office and the utility room? There's a lot to cover but with so many scenes to search, we're thin on the ground.'

'Of course, guv. Is Bernard coming back?'

'He said they have what they need so, no. Before we go, can we make sure the cat has food and we'll need to find out if one of Anderson's friends or relatives can take it in for now. There is a cat flap so if it has food and water, it will be okay for a short while. Bernard said that the cat hasn't been back all day. I think all the commotion has scared the poor thing.'

Wyre nodded and called two of the officers over and they began searching the snug and the hallway.

Gina smiled at the remaining officers and Jacob. 'We'll head upstairs and once done in the house, we'll look at the garden and shed.' She took a few strides along the hallway and entered the huge open plan kitchen and living area before taking to the stairs. Turning the light on, she took one step after another until she reached another long corridor with doors coming off it and a central picture window that framed the road. She pushed open the first door and turned on the light. Above the bed was a beautiful plaque with William's name on it. His large bed was covered in stuffed toys at the bottom end and the bed sheets were ruffled, just as they'd been left that morning. The room was huge, giving him a seating area with a TV at the one end. She gestured to the PCs. 'Can you take the spare rooms and the bathroom? Jacob, can you take the master bedroom. Check under the bed to see if there is a fancy hair clip in a box?' They all nodded. 'Remember, we're looking for a knife. Billie's tech is still missing, and Nadia's phone is missing, so if you find any laptops, tablets or phones, bag them up. They will need to be sent to tech for analysis.'

'Okay, let's get on with it,' Jacob said as he ushered the officers forward.

Once they'd gone, Gina stepped into William's room. For several minutes, she checked drawers and the wardrobe; under his bed, in all the nooks and crannies of the room. There were toys galore and boxed games. After sifting through everything, she turned her attention to the doll's house and tilted her head. Walking over, she reached in and flicked a switch. All the lights in the little house came on, illuminating every room. She released the metal catch and opened the house up, displaying the eight large rooms.

Miniature plastic and wooden children sat on the lounge floor, playing with little wooden toys. A woman doll was sitting at the kitchen table with a bottle of wine. A man doll was sitting on the toilet with a tiny dog at his feet. Gina smiled, loving entering William's world. Then, her smile turned into a sad biting of her lips. Poor William's world had been turned upside down. His mother was missing, and they'd arrested his father. His friend's mother had just been killed.

Gina's gaze fell on the kitchen where the miniature plastic crocodile that she'd seen the other day had been leaned against the worktop. She began to open the tiny, hinged cupboards, which revealed a collection of pots and pans.

A loud crash came from one of the other rooms. 'Dammit!'

'You okay,' she called out.

'Just dropped a pile of books on my foot,' Jacob shouted back.

Attention back on the doll's house, Gina's gaze followed the stairs up to the landing that led to three bedrooms and a large bathroom. She began opening all the wardrobes and doors. As she opened the last one, she stopped. It was guarded by a paper monster that had been drawn by a child. Loosely scribbled in, Gina couldn't mistake its scary spiky teeth and its elongated claws. She shivered as she opened the wardrobe. There was a little boy doll made of plastic. The doll's arms and knees had been bent so that it could be pushed into the corner of the wardrobe. She pulled her phone out and took a photograph. Had William feared something? Was he acting his own fear out with the dolls? She took another look at the scene.

The crocodile was Billie. Gina had seen the costume, and the boy had to be Kayden. Kayden must have either shared his fears with William or created the scene when they were playing together. She shook away a pang of sadness. Whatever was going on with all the adults in their life, the children had known something, and it was affecting them.

'Guv, you have to come here.'

She followed Jacob's voice to the master suite. As she entered, he held a photo out to her. The woman's side was covered in a huge blue bruise, but the photo was cut off at the shoulders and only reached her abdomen. A hand covered the breast in view. 'Where did you find this?'

'It fell out of the old dictionary, over there. When I dropped the pile of books, it must have fallen out.'

'Check the rest in case there are more.' Gina fell to her knees and began flicking through all the books, tipping them up and fanning them out in the hope that there were more. That photo had knocked her sick as it could have been of her, back when her abusive ex-husband Terry had given her a beating. Her letting him die at the bottom of their stairs had been the saving of her. She swallowed. Only Briggs knew about that incident, and he now hated her. She slammed the books on the floor in turn, but nothing else came out of them. She grabbed the photo again and squinted at the bruising. In the middle, the skin had broken, and a vein of blood had clotted into a fine scab.

'It looks like Anderson needs to answer a load more questions.' Jacob began to neatly pile the discarded books up.

'He'll deny it's Nadia and he'll say he knows nothing about it. Or it could be a photo of an accident. It will just be another circumstantial piece of evidence to go with the rest. The only thing that is going to truly nail him right now is that knife. Wait... there is a tiny birthmark just under her armpit. At least we have the means to positively identity the woman in the photo.' Gina looked away from the photo. 'Where the hell is Nadia?'

Jacob exhaled and rubbed his eyes. Midnight was fast approaching. He shook his head. 'I'm exhausted, sorry, guv.'

She patted him on the shoulder. 'Get this photo bagged. When everyone's finished, we'll head home. We're no use to anyone with no fuel in the tank and I can already tell that tomorrow is going to be full on.'

'Agreed. I need to check on Jennifer, see if she's okay. She's been messaging me. I keep telling her she'll be okay tomorrow. A part of her is dying to get back to working on Bernard's team, but the other half of her is saying that she won't make the day. I keep saying that it doesn't matter, to just build up to full time in her own time and do her best.'

'You're a good man, Jacob. I know Bernard will appreciate any time she can manage, even if it's only a few hours. Let me show you what I found?' She pulled her phone out and held up the photo she'd taken.

'Creepy.'

'Along with that photo you're holding, we're onto something. I don't think the knife will be in the house and I think that Nadia was looking for it when she dug the plaster out of the wall. Did you find the fancy hair clip?'

'No. There's no sign of any fancy boxed hair clip under that bed or anywhere in this room.'

'I don't even think there's a hair clip. That man is a seasoned liar.'

A short while later, Gina stretched and yawned in the hallway as she declared the end of their search. Various items were bagged but only the photo and the doll's house were significant. Her phone rang. 'O'Connor?'

Jacob and Wyre stood in silence, waiting for their colleague to blurt out what he had to say.

Gina ended the call. 'They have a knife. It was found hidden under the carpet in Anderson's office. It's also got some crusting on it that looks to be dried up blood and it's on its way to the lab as we speak.'

'Yes,' Jacob shouted as he clenched a fist.

'You've done a great job, all. Go home, get some sleep, and I'll see you first thing for the briefing.' She turned to Jacob. 'We'll need to speak to Serena Reeves while we wait for the lab to work the knife. We only need the blood matched to Billie's and we'll have the evidence we need. Before we get too victorious, Nadia is still missing. Anderson hid that knife, and all the evidence is pointing to him being the murderer. We have him in custody which means, if he took his wife, she has been left alone somewhere or she's...' She paused, not wanting to face the alternative. 'Or she's already dead. We're working on the hope and assumption that she's still alive and she's in danger. The weather is fatal when it's this hot. If alive, she might not have access to water or food. We know she's hurt. We must find Nadia.'

Gina got into her car and stared out of the window for several minutes as everyone left. One uniformed officer remained outside the door, remaining in place at the crime scene. She waved to him as she pulled off.

Even though it was still sticky hot, Gina shivered. *Where are you, Nadia?* She thought of William and how he needed his mother. The image of that huge bruise in the photo turned Gina's stomach. She pulled over and stepped out of the car gasping for breath. It's easy when people tell victims of domestic violence that they need to move on, forget it and live their life once they're out of danger, but they know nothing. The nightmares never leave. She gasped as thoughts of what Nadia had been through pulsed through her mind. The woman in the photo had to be Nadia. If Anderson had caused her bruising and he'd hurt his wife... she'd what? She clenched her fist and kicked her car. She couldn't even find Nadia. The word failure repeated in her mind.

Failure, failure, failure. She couldn't remember a time when she hated herself more.

She walked around to the back of her car and opened her boot. Nadia's garage door was left open. She pictured the perpetrator straining to place their victim in the boot of the car. Was Nadia bound and gagged or was she unconscious from her injuries? Had that car been parked up in the beating sun all day, leaving Nadia to cook? With trembling fingers, Gina slammed the boot shut.

FORTY-FOUR

Saturday, 18 June

Gina jolted up, her hair stuck to her forehead and her body burning like a furnace. She wrestled with her laptop and the leads as she fought with the bedcovers, flinging them off rapidly. Hot, so hot. The creeping and crawling around her neck as the heat radiated sent panic rising, and the itching was unbearable.

Reaching out, she flicked the switch on her lamp, illuminating her messy bedroom. Sitting up from the dampness on the sheets underneath provided no relief at all. Another night sweat. She stumbled up and an empty pop bottle crunched underfoot as she trod on it. She threw the sheets on the floor and grabbed a creased but clean set from the wardrobe. It was four in the morning; she'd only been asleep about an hour and her head was thick with a tiredness that had no chance of being satiated. Nadia's Facebook and Instagram feeds hadn't helped, and the woman had only been on TikTok for about a month and hadn't uploaded any videos.

After reassembling her bed, she lay on top of the sheet like a snow angel in only her underpants and waited for her humming heart to calm down. It was over, for now. Sitting up, she lifted her laptop onto the bed and hit the button. As it whirred into life, she went back to the escort website she'd just opened before nodding off. The 'Hi There Horny' site stared her in the face, along with a woman's wobbly boobs jiggling about in a bra that looked like it was made of string. She clicked into the escorts page, browsing down rows of them. Each one promising to relieve any horny person in no time. She flicked to another page and several trans women popped up. Billie was nowhere to be seen. Gina glanced at the lists of people all advertising their wears, then she came to a page of men, mostly young. So many people choosing a life of sex work, some in dire need of money just like Billie was. She tutted angrily as she continued clicking and scrolling. The cost of living crisis was getting worse, and she could see more people entering worlds in which they never thought they'd be party to. To the browsers, the people on the website were no more than a plethora of body parts. That's all they'd been reduced to. Gina knew better. They were siblings, parents, cousins and friends. At least, she hoped they all had someone.

She held her breath as she stared at the woman at the top of the last page. It could be Billie in a wig. Half of her hair covered her face as she looked down. Golden locks fell over bare shoulders and the headshot stopped at the lace top of a pink bra. Gina clicked on the details. The woman was local to Cleevesford and had a contact button. She offered satisfaction, discretion and a service that a person would want to keep coming back for. Her name – Princess Kitty. There was a button underneath – more photos. Clicking, Gina was faced with a heavily filtered photo of a woman in a tiara wearing nothing but a white lace ball mask and a frilly white tutu. Positioned on a bed, knees digging into the mattress, hands pushing breasts up, the woman's pink candy-coloured lips formed a high-gloss smile for the camera. Gina zoomed in. She recognised the wardrobes in the background. The photo was taken in Billie's bedroom. She scrolled down to the reviews and comments section. Some were lewd, others were more enquiring in nature, but one thing was for sure, none of the people commenting had used their real name.

She picked up her phone, called the station and asked to be put through to the digital forensics team. 'It's DI Harte. I've found Billie Reeves's profile online. I need you to contact the website and get everything you can. We need her personal messages, information on their users, the lot... I know it's not going to be easy, but they won't want to be dragged through the media.'

As Gina lay on her bed she wished she could call Briggs and share the joy with him, but he'd be in bed with Rosemary. They'd be snuggled up now that she'd moved in with him and her little boy would be sound asleep in the next room. A pang of jealousy flashed through her as she rolled over. There's no way she'd sleep now. Instead, she started reading more of the messages and wondered if Edward Anderson had left one of the lewd ones. Billie's murder had been more personal than some random punter from an escort site and Nadia had been taken too. Nadia was not a sex worker and Anderson had to be the link. One message stood out more than the others. Her stomach churned as she read it.

USER – BenedictCarnY
Sluts will get what they deserve!

FORTY-FIVE

CANDICE

'Serena, hi. Are you going to be long, because I'm busy today? If you're not coming, could you let me know?' She ended the call after leaving the message, hoping that Serena hadn't answered because she was driving. She didn't even know if she'd recognise the woman.

Candice checked her watch; it was already nine thirty. She'd told Gavin that she was just popping to the supermarket while he made Poppy's breakfast. She'd even poured all their milk down the sink, saying that it had soured to give her the excuse she needed to leave. Waiting to meet Serena felt weird. She barely knew of Billie's little sister, but the woman obviously couldn't say what she needed to say in a message and Candice was intrigued.

A woman with a pushchair struggled to get through the door. Serena didn't have a baby so it couldn't be her. Jumping up, Candice ran over and opened it. 'There you go, hun.' She smiled at the cute baby. The woman thanked her and lumbered over to the counter.

Sitting back down, Candice swirled the filter coffee around in the chipped mug. The café on Cleevesford High Street wasn't a café she'd normally go anywhere near with its cheap plastic chairs and smeared tables. The smell of burned sausages had entered her nostrils and stuck at the back of her throat. Normally she'd meet friends at garden centres, or maybe even a wine bar, where the surroundings were a bit classier but Serena being a student probably used places like this, as they were cheaper. Candice had never experienced student life, but she'd heard that it was tough financially and she could sympathise. She swallowed. What was she meant to say to the woman who had just lost her sister? Her own upset couldn't compare to that of Serena's.

The café door pinged, snapping her out of her thoughts. Serena caught her breath as she hurried in. The woman walked a little stiffly as she pulled her black T-shirt down over her pale torn-at-the-knee jeans. Her hair hung over her shoulders in slightly tangled clumps, like she'd either just rolled out of bed or been in a brawl. 'Sorry, I'm late. Everyone seems to be off work today and I couldn't find anywhere to park outside the houses. I had to park miles away.' She hurried up to the counter. 'Can I get you a drink?'

One of those hideous coffees was enough. Candice shook her head. 'No, I'm good thanks. My husband's cooking breakfast so I haven't got long.' There was something she recognised about the young woman, but she couldn't think what.

After being served, Serena hurried to the table. The other woman's baby began to cry. 'Can we sit outside?'

'Yes, of course.' Candice followed Serena out, leaving the rest of her drink on the table. It was bugging her now. Where had she seen Serena before?

'Sorry, I thought it would be more private and quieter out here.' Serena slammed her drink down and the liquid sloshed over the top. 'I know we don't really know each other but I feel like I'm going insane with my parents right now.' She paused. 'Did Billie ever talk about me?'

Straight to the point. There were no cries of how much she was missing her sister or how terrible her murder was. Billie had barely spoken about Serena, but she'd mentioned her in passing. She knew that Billie's parents saw Serena as the golden child and Billie felt that she didn't match up. 'She said you were studying to be a dentist, that's all. I'm really sorry for your loss. I can't imagine what your family is going through. Billie was a special person and we all thought the world of her.' Candice fidgeted in the seat. She wanted to go home, to cuddle Poppy and to think about Nadia. There was too much going on in her head to concentrate. She shook her head and stifled a little cry. 'Sorry, my friend has gone missing, and I need to be at home in case anyone calls.'

'That's partly why I wanted to see you, in person. I found out my so-called boyfriend was sleeping with my sister, and I was livid. A part of me needed someone to sound off at. My sister has been murdered and all I feel is angry with her. I'm so angry with Billie and I can't shake that anger away. I should be distraught but...' She shook her head. 'Then I heard that Nadia was missing.'

'You know Nadia?' Candice wasn't aware that the two were friends or acquaintances.

The young woman fiddled with the wooden stick that she'd used to stir her coffee with, twiddling it and pulling shreds of wood away before depositing them on the table in wispy curls. 'No, but I saw her yesterday and an appeal went out this morning. It was on the news. I was scrolling Facebook and people are gossiping, saying that her husband did it. That he killed Billie and took his own wife.'

Candice went to speak but stopped and cleared her throat. 'I was at the house yesterday afternoon. They arrested him. Is that what you wanted to know?'

Serena shook her head. 'They haven't charged him yet. I know that much. My parents keep calling the station.' Serena hugged herself. 'I think I might have been one of the last people to see Nadia alive and I don't know what to do. What should I do?' She sniffed back a sob.

Shrugging, Candice leaned forwards and tucked Serena's hair behind her ear in a motherly fashion. 'It'll all be okay. Start at the beginning. You said you saw Nadia yesterday?'

The young woman's shoulders curled. 'Yes.' She paused. 'I did something stupid. Nathan pushed me to my limits and in my stupid head I began to blame you, Meera and Nadia for their affair. It kept going through my mind that you all knew my sister was shagging my boyfriend, that you were all laughing at me.'

'Serena, we didn't know that he was your boyfriend. Billie hadn't even introduced us to Nathan.'

'I know that now.' Serena sipped her coffee. 'Other people saw me yesterday and I looked upset when I left Nadia because I'd been speaking to her about Billie and Nathan. She didn't know who I was to start with.' Swallowing, Serena continued, 'I booked a personal training session with her and all through it, I couldn't speak but once I started, I couldn't stop. This sense of pressure had built up and I know other people were waiting to use the tennis court while we were talking, but I didn't care that I was keeping them waiting. They saw me throwing my arms in the air, looking upset.' She paused. 'I just want people to know, however much I argued with my sister, I'd never hurt her and as for Nadia, I'd have no reason.'

Candice leaned in. 'What was it that you and Billie argued about?'

Tears streamed down the woman's cheeks. 'I lied about not knowing about Billie and Nathan. I came home for a visit; it was a bit of a surprise. Mum and Dad weren't in, and I heard noises coming from one of the bedrooms. That's when I saw them, Billie and Nathan. That vision I have of their naked bodies coiled together as they moaned wouldn't leave my head. I wanted to shout at them, hit them even, but I was dumbstruck. All I managed to do was sneak back down the stairs and out of the house. Instead of saying anything, I got into my car and drove away. It reeled and reeled inside me until I couldn't hold back. I called Billie up and told her that I hated her. I'm not proud of the names I called her, but I blamed her. I know that Nathan was to blame also but I couldn't lose him, and it was easier to blame Billie. She said she'd dump him. I thought she'd tell him straight away, but the call never came. I couldn't talk to him about it, I just couldn't.'

'So, Nathan has no idea that you knew he was sleeping with Billie?'

'No. I'm ashamed to say that I wholly blamed her and now I know it was him too and I hate him. I hate myself for being such an idiot. And... our last words were horrible and now Billie's dead.'

Candice sighed. She could see why Serena was upset but she needed to get home. Gavin would wonder why she was taking so long. There might be some news about Nadia, and she had to be there. If she told Gavin where she was, he'd probably moan that she was interfering but then again, he was happily lying so what did it matter if she had her secrets too? 'So, you feel bad about arguing with Billie before she was killed?'

'No, I wish that was all I felt bad about. I lied to the police, and I don't know what to do. I needed to speak to someone, and my mum is falling apart. Kayden's dad took him yesterday and then the man hit my dad. I feel as though my family is falling apart and I don't have anyone to talk to.' Sobbing, Serena pulled out a line of crumpled toilet roll from her bag and blew her nose.

Heart pounding, Candice couldn't hold back. 'What did you lie about?'

'I wasn't at uni when Billie was murdered. I moved into a bedsit in Redditch a couple of weeks ago. I dropped out.'

Candice stared at the woman. 'And you knew that Billie was sleeping with Nathan?'

Nodding, Serena couldn't stop crying. 'I hated her so much. I hated Nadia too. I hated you. I hated you all and I hated the world.' She rubbed her eyes and stood, almost knocking the light chair onto the floor. She fought with her tangled bag strap before turning to go.

'Serena, wait.'

'I've got to go.'

That's when the recognition clicked. 'Serena, why were you standing outside Nadia's back fence on the day of Kayden's birthday party?' That's who Candice had seen loitering, watching them all. The woman turned and a look of horror filled her face before she ran down the path.

Candice watched as Serena ran into the distance and turned the corner. Ed was a suspect, now Serena would be too. The man who served them came out for the cup. Candice pulled her diamanté hairgrip out and repositioned it, clipping the one side of her hair back. Gavin had given it to her that morning, saying that he'd bought her a gift. It would take a lot more than a hair clip to make things better. She flung her bag over her shoulder and hurried to the supermarket across the road, head spinning with all that she knew. Should she tell Gavin or call the police? She pulled her phone out and stopped at the bus stop. Serena didn't seem right and nothing about their conversation felt right either. There's no way she could keep what she'd heard to herself. It would be wrong. 'I'd like to speak to DI Harte, please.'

FORTY-SIX

Gina paced in front of the boards, staring at Nadia and Billie's photos. 'There are no updates yet on Billie or whoever left that message under her profile. Hi There Horny are being cooperative but they are saying it will take a while to get an IP address for the user that we're interested in.' Gina pointed to the screen grab photo. 'Sluts get what they deserve! By user Benedict-CarnY. We have a match on the word used at the scene of Billie's murder. This message was left the night before the murder and it's threatening in nature. Who is Benedict?'

Jacob shook his head. 'We don't have anyone named Ben, Benedict, Benjamin or anything similar involved in this case. The same with Carny.'

'How about anyone else here? Have you come across any name like Benedict while investigating?'

Wyre shook her head and O'Connor said no while eating a bacon sandwich.

'BenedictCarnY is a mystery. This user could unlock a lot about the case. Tech is currently working through all Edward Anderson's devices and word this morning was, he has no links to the Hi There Horny website. What we still have is the knife but as yet we don't have any results. We can't yet confirm that the blood belongs to Billie or whether its dimensions match the knife used to kill her. We know the measurements are close.' Gina glanced at the photo that Jacob found in the dictionary and pointed. 'This photo was hidden in a book. Could it be that Nadia was trying to build a case against her husband and this photo was a part of the evidence? There is a birthmark under the woman's arm so we can rule out that this photo is of Billie. Anderson is refusing to talk so it's all down to us to build this case and I know we're getting close, so stay on it.'

'We still don't have any more news on Nadia,' Wyre said.

'Sadly, that's true. An appeal went out this morning. She is still out there so we have to treat everything as urgent. I want her brought back safely.' Gina bit her bottom lip, flinching as she tore a tiny piece of skin. 'We need to find her.'

It was easy to say but Gina knew they had nothing when it came to Nadia's current location. No one in Nadia's street saw her or saw anything unusual that day. No one had any useful CCTV that pointed in the direction of the Andersons' house, which meant they had nothing useful from the neighbours. As hard as she tried, Gina could not relax any of her muscles and an ache was setting in. 'We do have a match on the partial print that was on the emoji note, found at Nadia's house. It belongs to Mr Anderson, but he did tell us he wrote that note so it doesn't help us really.'

'What's the plan, guv?' O'Connor rolled up his foil and threw it into the bin.

'I need to speak to Billie's sister, Serena. They had an argument and I want to know what that was about. It would be easy to sit here, saying we have our murderer, but we don't have conclusive evidence against Anderson. We don't stop until we have what we need, and we look wherever the investigation takes us. We also need to head to the leisure centre. Nadia used it for her work. She might have a locker, or she might have spoken to someone. Wyre and O'Connor, could you please contact Meera Gupta again. She was having an affair with Nadia Anderson's husband while claiming to be a close friend to Nadia. She is also the likeliest person to crack if she knows something. Jacob, we'll head to the leisure centre and Serena's parents' house.'

A member of despatch poked her head around the door. 'Guv, I've just had a call and I thought you'd need to know what was said. I tried to put it through to your office, but I see you're here.'

'Thank you. Who was it?'

'A woman called Mrs Brent. She wanted to report that she'd met up with Serena Reeves this morning and she asked me to tell you that Serena said that she'd argued with Billie and that she had left university and had been living in Redditch.'

Gina placed both hands on the desk at the head of the large table. 'So, Serena lives in Redditch, nice and close to Cleevesford. She had opportunity and the argument might mean she had a motive. We need to speak to her now. Wyre, can you call Serena Reeves and ask her to come here to discuss her sister's case, not mentioning what Mrs Brent has said? I think it's best she comes in.'

'Yep.'

'And we'll head over to speak to Mrs Brent now.' She grabbed her bag and looked at Jacob. 'We'll take your car.' There was no time to waste. Gina needed to know all that Mrs Brent knew before speaking to Serena. They were close, so close.

FORTY-SEVEN

Aisling gave her white ferret, Kooky, a little tug as he tried to lead her deep into the undergrowth. No doubt Kooky had found a hole he wanted to explore but she wasn't up for that today. She had a shift at the coffee shop in an hour and she couldn't afford to miss it. If she did, her dad would have a go at her, like he always did. That's why she came out. Kooky didn't need a walk but it saved her from hearing her dad's latest lecture of what she should do with her life.

The Mutt Trail was one of the best trails for dog walking in the area. The mud path weaved up through the woodland and over the stream. She smiled as she passed all the clearings she used to hang around when she drank with friends, only a few short years ago.

A man with four dogs on leads was approaching ahead. The two boxers barked, and the collie cross pulled on his lead. The old terrier sat panting in the pink dog pushchair. She spotted the man's T-shirt. Matt's Dog Walking Services. There were always people walking the dogs of others along this track, which is why she felt safe.

'Kooky, stop it. It's okay, they're on leads.'

Suddenly the boxer broke loose, and the panicked man began shouting for Rufus. As it bounded forwards, she went to grab the dog's lead, but as she did, she accidentally dropped Kooky's. She knew she'd done it instantly but as she turned to pick up his lead, it was gone. The barking dog wrenched her hard through the undergrowth, dragging her violently while chasing Kooky. She had to hold on to the dog. If she didn't, he might hurt her best friend. She glanced back to the man for help, but he was too busy tying the other two dogs up while the terrier tried to jump out of the pushchair.

'No, stop,' she called as the dog continued to drag her lithe frame through a jungle of stingers. Then prickles on her arms and ankles hit instantly. That's when she spotted Kooky's lead, caught on the branch of a fallen tree. She hauled the heavy dog back and avoided the huge trail of slobber coming from its mouth as she tied it to a branch, its deep barking, relentless.

Kooky flexed and bent his neck as he tried to escape the lead and the dog barked, but it wasn't barking at Kooky. It was barking at the hair splayed out on the hard muddy ground. The animals had known. They weren't trying to escape, they could tell. Aisling's hands began to tremble as she pulled back the straggle of long grass to reveal the pale-faced head of a woman. A trail of ants crawled alongside her, carrying bits of leaf.

'Bad dog,' the man said as he came for the boxer. 'I am so sorry, is your ferret okay?'

She couldn't speak. She couldn't say a word. All she could do was stare at the word 'Bitch' written in red on the woman's forehead.

'Oh, my goodness.' The man stared at the dead woman as he pulled out his phone.

Aisling picked Kooky up and held his wriggling body close to her and stepped back.

'Police. We need the police. We've found a body on the Mutt Trail. A woman, maybe late twenties, early thirties... From the look of her, she's dead.' As he finished the call, Aisling felt his hand on her arm.

'Don't touch me,' she yelled as she ran back to the trail. 'Someone killed that woman.' She glanced around until she was dizzy. Where were all the people who were normally walking? It was just her and dog guy. The trees seemed to be spinning around her and she couldn't breathe properly. The heat, it was filling her up, like a kettle of water had been poured down her throat. As her vision prickled, she felt herself going, then she thudded to the ground.

FORTY-EIGHT

CANDICE

'Gavin, when I went to the shops earlier, I saw Serena, Billie's sister. She told me something and I had to call the police so they're coming over. Can you please take Poppy to your mum's? She's seen enough. I don't want her here when they arrive. Please ask her if Poppy can stay the night. Tell her we have an emergency but don't tell her about Nadia. I don't want her calling every five minutes and fussing.'

'Okay.' He stopped wiping crumbs off the worktop and threw the dishcloth into a bowl of soapy water. 'Yes, I think that's for the best. You've been home half an hour. Why have you only just told me?'

'I, err, I don't know. I thought I'd just report what I knew and that would be it. I didn't think they'd want to come here.'

'And what do you know?' He stepped closer to her. She felt his breath on her shoulder and a few goosebumps formed. There was something overbearing about him and his hefty presence.

'Serena wasn't at university on the day Billie was murdered. She's moved back and not told anyone. She was going on about this big argument she had with Billie. She walked in on Billie having sex with her boyfriend and yesterday, it sounds like she was the last person to see Nadia alive. I couldn't hold it back. I had to tell the police.' She stared into space.

'Is there something else?'

'Only that Serena was at Kayden's birthday party, back in May.'

'I don't remember Billie saying that her sister was there.'

'I saw her peering over the fence, watching Billie. She's weird.'

'And you went to meet her on your own? Come here.' He pulled her close as he comforted her. She tried to feel a spark for him, anything, but there was nothing at all. As he stroked her back, she wished he'd just stop. That's what happens when the trust has gone. She'd been silently smug when she'd heard about Nadia's marriage troubles, never thinking she could be going through the same at any time. 'Just tell them what you know, and everything will be okay. It sounds like Serena has a lot of explaining to do.' He pulled away and kissed her before calling Poppy. 'I see you're wearing the hair clip.' He ran his fingers along her head until they stopped on the hair clip. 'It suits you.' Turning to the stairs, he hurried up, calling for Poppy to put a few things in a bag. She listened as her little girl happily ran back and forth upstairs, eager to get to her grandmother's house.

Several minutes later, the front door slammed, and Gavin's car pulled away. She hurried to the window and waved at Poppy. His office – she had very little time and she needed to get into it. Hurrying through to the utility, she took the door to the extension at the front of the house and she almost gasped. Gavin had left his office door open. She ran straight to his computer. It was turned off. She turned it on and waited for the login to appear and when it did, she typed his password in. It was wrong. She tried another, followed by Poppy's date of birth, his mother's maiden name. All of them – rejected. In a fit of rage, she hit the keys. It took ten minutes to drive to Gavin's mum's house, so she'd already lost five, maybe more. He didn't often stop for a drink or chat so he could be back before she knew it. She rooted through the desk drawers, which were full of stationery he'd never used.

She felt underneath his desk, what for? She had no idea. What she really wanted was to look at his computer again. She'd seen the website he'd been using, and his history had led her to the Hi There Horny website. He must have known that she'd been snooping, otherwise why would he have changed his password? What she really wanted was something concrete to confront him with, but that was proving difficult.

She almost slipped in her ballet pumps as she ran over to the sideboard, again it was full of junk. As she rooted through the top drawer, all she came across was work-related paperwork, mouse mats, old bits of tech. That's when she spotted the mauve coloured box that was wedged against the wall, down the side of the cabinet. She crouched and reached through the cobwebs until her fingers felt the box. Whacking it, she moved as it flew past her feet. She grabbed it and stood. She'd never seen this box before.

Gently, she lifted the lid and noticed that whatever had been sitting on the pillow was no longer there. The slight ingress in the material and the shape of the box led her to believe it was something long and thin. It didn't have the grooves for a necklace or earrings. She slipped the hair clip from her hair and placed it in the box. It was a perfect fit.

As the car door slammed, she dropped it and a card fell out onto the floor. She grabbed the clip and slid it back in her hair. Heart banging, she knew she needed to get out. Snatching the card, she almost fell into the wall as she read it. She thrust the message into her bra before placing the lid on the box and throwing it back into the corner.

His key was in the door. Just as she skidded out of his office, she noticed the dead flies leading to the box, all disturbed when she plunged her hand into the cobweb. She fought with the sticky spider twine on her wrist as she closed his office door and hurried out. 'How was Poppy when you dropped her off?'

He popped his keys on the table and took a moment to stare at her. 'Is everything okay?'

He took a couple of steps closer, and she felt like she needed to run.

Slowly, his hand reached her head, and he adjusted the hair clip. 'There.'

She forced a smile, hoping that the jitter running through her body wouldn't reveal itself. 'I'm going to clean the dog grooming parlour. It's getting into a bit of a mess.' That was the truth.

'I thought it was already clean.'

'I saved a few jobs for today.'

'Oh, I signed the lease on the new place. You'll soon have a proper parlour and a shop. We must celebrate.'

The last thing she felt like doing was breaking out the champagne with all that was happening. 'Okay, that sounds good.'

'Right, I'll make you a drink and bring it in.'

'I've just had one.' She needed to be alone with her thoughts until the police came.

He scrutinised her further before reaching down to her arm and pulling a clump of spider web from her. 'I thought the police were coming.'

'They are.'

'So, finish cleaning it later. I'll put the kettle on. They'll no doubt want a drink.' He paused and furrowed his brows. 'You look like you've seen a ghost.'

'It's Nadia and Billie – what happened to them. I'm scared.' That was a lie. She was mostly scared of what would happen next.

He pulled her close and kissed her head. 'Don't be. Nadia is probably just having some time out from Ed and as for Billie, it had to be one of her clients. It's sad, I know it is, but you don't have to worry about anything. Go and wash those cobwebs away and I'll open a packet of biscuits.'

She didn't need telling twice. Running up the stairs, she hurried into the bathroom and locked the door. Head against it, she waited for her heart to stop pounding as she fought the urge to smash something up. She pictured herself pulling the sink from the wall and slamming it onto the cold slate tiles but instead, she calmly walked over to the mirror where she cleaned her arm, flattened the frizz in her hair and rammed the note into her make-up drawer. No one need ever know about the note from Ed to Nadia, telling her how sorry he was. Sorry for what, she had no idea, but that hair clip didn't belong to her. Gavin had taken it and that worried her more than anything. Keeping her family out of all that was happening was proving to be getting harder by the second. Her mind focused on Poppy. She would not mention anything. Her daughter's future depended on it, and her little girl needed her parents, and she needed them to stay together and at least pretend to be happy.

She flinched as someone knocked on the door. The police had arrived. Wiping the smear of mascara away, she stared at her reflection and smiled. That's how she wanted to be seen. If the mask slipped, it was game over and that couldn't happen. She only had one thing to say, and that message would come with relaying the truth of what she'd been told. Serena did it. She killed her sister because she was jealous, and she's done something to Nadia because the woman was her sister's best friend. She mouthed the words to herself. 'Gavin did not hurt Billie. Gavin did not hurt Nadia.'

Voices filled the hallway downstairs. There was no avoiding facing the police.

FORTY-NINE
CANDICE

She calmly walked down the stairs to see Gavin pouring coffee for the detectives. They were sitting at the kitchen table, the man writing in a notebook. 'Here you go,' Gavin said as he placed the steaming hot drinks on the table. 'I'll leave you to it. If you need me, I'll be in my office.' Gavin did a half nod and turned to leave.

'Thank you for coming.' Candice smiled, but not too much of a smile. Just enough to put them at ease. She knew the name of the female detective. It was DI Harte, but she couldn't remember the man's name. A sudden urge to cough came from nowhere. As she gave in to the nervous tickle, she felt the hair clip slipping ever nearer to her shoulder as it drew her red hair straight. She wanted to wrench it out and sling it across the room into Gavin's lying face, but he'd left, and she needed to calm down. She should have snatched it out in the bathroom, but her mind had been on everything except the damn hair clip. It was too late now. Then again, only she knew that the grip was a gift from Ed to Nadia. The police knew nothing about it and why would they care. It's just a hair clip. *Calm down*, she kept repeating in her head, in the hope that her body would stop humming as blood pumped through her veins. She pictured the fine veins on her pale skin, bulging blue on the sides of her face, and her teeth clenched.

'Mrs Brent. We're following up on the call you made about your conversation with Serena Reeves. When did you see her?'

Candice gently slid out a chair and sat at the table opposite DI Harte. 'I spoke to her this morning. We met at the café on Cleevesford High Street. There's only one café, I can't remember the name.'

The DI shuffled in her chair. 'I know the one. Who arranged to meet who?'

'It was Serena. She kept messaging me, asking if we could talk so I met up with her. I thought she just wanted someone to chat to, given what happened to Billie, but then she went on to tell me that she moved to Redditch a while ago and that she saw Nadia yesterday. I felt a bit worried, maybe even scared at this point. What if it's her and she was out to get me next? She went on to say that she'd argued with Billie after finding Billie and Nathan, that's Serena's boyfriend, in bed together.' Candice realised she was speaking at lightning speed. She took a breath and continued. 'She knew that her boyfriend was cheating on her with her sister.' Candice shook her head and scrunched her nose. 'Something else she said set me on edge.'

'What was that?'

'She lied to Nadia, pretending that she wanted a personal training session yesterday but really, she wanted to question Nadia about Billie and Nathan. She told me she blamed us. By us, I mean Nadia, Meera and me. At this point, I felt she could easily have hurt her sister and Nadia. She looked at me funny, got up and ran off. She scared me.' The detective's gaze fell on her hair clip. She brushed her fingers over it, sliding it off into her hand in the hope that nothing was thought of the gesture.

'That's a lovely hair clip.'

Knees trembling, Candice prised her hand open to reveal

the glistening gems embedded onto a silver stick. It was too late to hide it, and something told her the detective knew it was relevant. She glanced out of the window, her mouth filling up with saliva as nausea threatened to overpower her. 'Thank you,' she muttered. 'It was a gift from my husband.' The room went silent, the type of silent that is purposely inflicted to make a person squirm and Candice was doing exactly that. She pushed the plate of biscuits towards the male detective. 'Would you like a biscuit?'

'No, thanks.' His smile reached his eyes. He was classically handsome, his hair neatly combed. He looked down and scrawled a few notes. Candice tried to read them upside down, but they were too squiggly. She had no chance of reading anything he'd written, then he flicked the page over.

DI Harte's face reddened, and she took a deep breath. 'Well, thank you for calling us and if you hear or remember anything else that might help, please do call again. I'd like to speak to your husband before we leave.'

'Gavin?'

'Yes, please.' DI Harte took a biscuit and bit into it. A dusting of crumbs landed on the table.

'I'll just go and get him.' They both watched intently as she left the room. Hurrying out of sight, she ran to his office and almost bumped into the door as she went to push it open. It was locked. She rapped on the wood a few times. 'Gavin, the police want to speak to you.' She used her loveliest of voices, just in case the detectives could hear but she doubted they could. Peering through the kitchen, she checked that one of them hadn't followed her through and was listening at the door. She was safe, they hadn't.

Gavin pulled the door open, and the air nearly sucked her into the room as he dragged her in. He snatched the gift box from his desk and held it up. 'Have you been going through my things?' he asked in a hushed tone, a speck of spittle escaping.

She shook her head. 'I came here looking for some paper and I spotted the box. It's lovely, is it for me?'

He threw the box down. 'You know this room is off limits.'

Shaking, she took a step back. It wasn't like Gavin to grab her like that. She could still feel the imprint of his fingers on her shoulder. He was desperate, that much she could see. How could she have kept the perfect marriage pretence up for so long? 'The police are waiting.'

He took a deep breath and ushered her out before locking the door. As they turned back into the kitchen, Gavin stood against the wall. 'Candice said you wanted to speak to me. How can I help you?'

DI Harte stood. 'How well did you know Billie Reeves and Nadia Anderson?'

Candice could see her husband's hands clenching. 'I don't know Billie and my wife is always at Nadia's house. I really haven't had much to do with them.' His face had that genuine warm look that most people fell for which was a complete transformation of the one she'd just seen. 'I really wish I could help as what happened to Billie was awful. My wife has been so worried, haven't you, babe?'

Candice nodded and a tear fell from one of her eyes. 'It's just so—' Bursting into tears, she sat back at the table.

'It's okay.' Gavin pulled her close and held her and all she wanted to do was run as fast and as far away as she could. She wanted to get Poppy and never come back. Soon she would but for now, Poppy was in the safest place. 'As you can see, all this is upsetting Candice. It's been a hard week. First Billie's murder and now Nadia is missing. Then this morning she got upset again by Billie's sister. I mean the woman lied about being at uni and then she lied to get an appointment with Nadia, then Nadia goes missing. As far as we see it, my wife had a lucky escape. I don't trust that woman.'

'Have you ever met Serena Reeves?'

Gavin scrunched his brows. 'No and I don't want to, not after she scared Candice.'

'Where were you on the evening of Tuesday at around eleven thirty?'

He scrunched his brows. 'I was here, in bed.'

Candice wiped her eyes. That was the night before Billie was murdered. Why were they asking Gavin that question? He was in his office, that's what she thought.

'Mrs Brent. Can you confirm that?'

Candice nodded. 'Yes, we were definitely in bed, together. I was reading and Gavin was half asleep. Poppy had been a bit fussy that night, so we hadn't been in bed long. She sometimes struggles to get to sleep. It's one long round of reading stories, waiting for her to nod off and sneaking out of her room.' Had she offered up too much information? They wouldn't question Poppy, would they? No, they couldn't. Not without her say so and there was no way she would allow them to ask Poppy anything. She was only five. Candice tapped her feet on the floor. She stopped it, immediately.

That deafening silence – again. Candice felt her fingers entwining under the table with Gavin's, then he gripped her hard. A piercing ringtone made her flinch.

'Sorry, I have to take this.' The DI stood and walked to the front door where she left and took the call. Breath held; Candice waited until Harte returned, while the male detective remained seated in his chair. DI Harte burst back in. 'We have to go. Please stay close by, we may need to speak to you again later.' She exhaled before she went red.

Within moments, the two detectives were standing by their car on the roadside, hand gestures galore as they spoke. Candice pushed the window open and listened as best she could. She heard the words Nadia and body. They had found Nadia. Stomach churning, she fought the urge to run to the bathroom and allow the panic inside to overwhelm her. Breathe in and out. She had to stay on top of this.

She almost jumped as Gavin came from nowhere and placed a hand on her shoulder. 'Now we need to talk.' She didn't want to talk; she wanted all this to be over. He reached her face with his finger and moved a curl behind her ear. He led her to the office and slammed the door. She couldn't control the shaking of her legs or the quivering in her voice.

'We weren't in bed together on the Tuesday night.'

He grabbed the gift box and held it between them. 'You want the truth, about this and about where I was?'

She nodded. She deserved every bit of the truth, and she was going to get it, but at what cost?

FIFTY

Gina got into the car as Jacob turned the key in the engine.
'Nadia is alive. She's sedated and will be having surgery soon.
It's touch and go as to whether she'll survive, given the amount
of blood she's lost. They're working on her as we speak, and
Wyre and O'Connor have abandoned everything else to head
over to the scene where they'll meet with Bernard.'

'Shall we head there, guv?'

'No, we'll continue to the leisure centre. The best thing we
can do right now is to keep looking for evidence and hope that
Nadia wakes up soon. We won't get any immediate information
from forensics.' She continued to relay what she'd been told.
'The perpetrator wrote the word "Bitch" on her head and that's
consistent with what was written on her garage wall.' Gina
shook her head. 'She was left to die at the edge of the woods.
One stab wound – just like Billie's. She was literally dumped
close to the road. Tyre flattened grass shows that a car must
have backed up to the bushes. Problem is that the ambulance
also parked there too when it arrived.' She paused as her phone
rang again. 'O'Connor? Please tell me you have something we
can work with.'

The man blurted out everything at speed, to the point Gina couldn't make out what he was saying. 'Slow down.' She ended the call when he'd finally finished.

'What did he say?' Jacob indicated and took a corner.

'We have two witnesses who heard some commotion going on where Nadia was found. A car engine was running outside the witness's cottage at around three in the morning. This was followed by a few thumping sounds. She didn't look out of the window, but she is certain about the time and what she heard. Her daughter was staying too, and she heard it also and has confirmed the time. You know what that means?'

Jacob nodded as he went over a speed bump. 'Edward Anderson didn't take his wife and leave her at the edge of the woods.'

'Yep. We still have a bloody knife but who knows what that will show us. I wish everything worked faster.' Gina pressed her lips together as Jacob pulled into the leisure centre. She was sticking with her plan. Leisure centre; then speak to Serena.

They still had Anderson. Everything pointed at the man, but they had him in custody at the time one of the crimes was committed. He was guilty of something, but he wasn't guilty of leaving his wife to die in the woods. She hadn't forgotten that he'd lied about being in a hot tub shop. They also still had the photo of what could be Nadia's bruised ribs. Jacob pulled into a space at the back of the leisure centre.

She let her mind whirr over the facts before speaking. 'When Billie was killed, her death happened almost instantly. With Nadia, the killer missed the mark. They didn't leave a trace of themselves at the scenes which means, to a certain degree, they're forensically aware, but who isn't these days? You only have to watch a few true-life crime programmes and you know it all. They failed the second time. Are there two perpetrators or is one person winging it and hoping for the best? We need a press release, and everyone needs to know that we have found Nadia Anderson and that she's alive. With that, we need an officer to guard her room. I'll call Briggs so we can get this out to the press. If the killer knows that they've slipped up, they're going to panic. Nadia would have seen or heard them. She might know who they are, and she will tell all. It's time to flush the killer out.'

FIFTY-ONE

'I'll just get the manager,' said the girl who was manning the leisure centre reception. Gina leaned on the counter as Jacob checked his messages.

'Is Jennifer on site today?' Gina asked.

He nodded. 'Yes, I was just checking to see how she was. She turned down desk work and managed to wangle being at the scene.'

'Good for her.' Gina was genuinely pleased that Jennifer was making such a good recovery.

The girl came back. 'Follow me.' As they headed past a busy gym, she knocked on the door marked 'Manager' and entered. 'DI Harte and DS Driscoll here to see you.' She smiled and left them with the stout man in grey trousers and a polo top with the leisure centre logo printed on the breast.

'I'm Cole, the manager. Take a seat. I heard the news this morning, about Nadia going missing. I hope she turns up soon.'

'We've found her. She's getting treatment as we speak.'

'Is she okay?'

Gina watched the man, analysing every muscle movement. He was the first outsider to the station to know that Nadia had been found and was still alive. Gina nodded, not wanting to give any more away.

'Yesterday, she booked a court for one of her private sessions. She always seems pleasant and friendly. I'd hate for anything to be seriously wrong, but I did hear about the other woman, the one who was murdered. You can't believe things like that go on around us. No one's safe any more, I keep telling my wife that.'

'Can you tell me more about her booking yesterday, or did you see her?'

He clicked on a couple of buttons. 'It's in the diary and I anticipated you'd ask so I pulled the CCTV which we do have on the court. As silly as it sounds, we get teenagers breaking in at night and they drink there. We like to monitor what's going on.' He scrunched up his wide nose as he concentrated on the screen. 'I personally didn't see her yesterday. I don't have the name of the person she was with, but you can see from the image that it's a young woman with light-coloured hair, maybe blonde.' He turned the computer screen around.

Gina squinted a little at the poor-quality image. It was Serena. She looked a lot like Billie but was a little more voluptuous. 'Can you press play?'

He nodded and pressed the button. She watched as Serena's hands flew up in the air. The woman looked upset before running off and there were other people waiting. 'Who are these people?' She pointed.

'Those two guys had the tennis courts booked after Nadia and the other chap works for us. He clears the place up ready for the next person.'

'Does Nadia have a locker here?'

'We have public lockers and staff lockers. Nadia only rents space from us so she's not staff. If she used any locker, it would be a public one. Thankfully, we have CCTV on those too. It makes everyone feel safer knowing their belongings are being monitored.' He clicked then began watching. 'Ah, here.' He pointed to the screen. 'That's Nadia using locker ten.' He continued scrolling forward. 'She goes back and grabs her bag after the session, but she doesn't take everything. She locked it up and took the key with her.'

'Did she come back?'

'No. We keep digital records of who comes and goes and, in Nadia's case, if they have a plus one with them. I guess the other woman's name would be on the sign-in list and the information is uploaded there and then. I should have checked. It's down to the fire regulations that we keep it. Hold on one moment.' He switched screens and tapped again. 'Serena, that's the name the woman signed in with. No surname.'

Gina had already identified her, and she really wanted to move on. 'Nadia's things will still be in the locker, then?'

He nodded. 'I guess so. People don't usually use them overnight, but it looks like she did. She comes here a lot, so it does at least make sense.'

'We need to take a look. Would that be okay?'

'Of course. Follow me.' He stood and led them out, past the swimming pool and along another corridor. The humidity hit Gina instantly, that and the smell of chlorine. 'Here it is.'

'How do we open it?'

'I have a skeleton key. People are forever losing them and panicking.' He turned the key in the lock.

Gina stepped forward and inhaled the smell of washing powder. She lifted the folded hoodie up and shifted the tennis shoes aside. Several energy bars and drinks littered the back of the locker and a few business cards lay scattered on the metal base. There appeared to be nothing personal. She pulled a shoe out and pressed her fingers into the end. Nothing. She did the same with the next one and her fingers gripped the cold stick that was tucked into the toe of the shoe. Pulling it out, she held it up and passed the memory stick to Jacob. 'We need to get this back to the station.' For some reason, Nadia had left the stick here and not left it at home. She was hiding it and Gina wanted to know why. Her phone rang. She left the manager and Jacob while she walked away to take the call. 'Sir.'

Briggs cleared his throat before speaking. 'Just to let you know, I'm up in fifteen minutes. I'll be announcing that we have found Nadia Anderson and that she's alive. PC Kapoor will remain outside the hospital room when she's in recovery. Her situation is still bad. It's touch and go at the moment. Nadia isn't quite stable enough for the surgery, but it should go ahead. Also, her family have been informed and her mother is on her way over now.'

'Sir.'

'Yes.'

'We've found a memory stick in Nadia's locker at the leisure centre, but she isn't here to give us permission to read it. Can you deal with that for us? We're on our way back and we'll pass it straight to digital forensics.'

'Yes, I'll sort it. There is something else. You need to hurry back.'

'What is it?'

'Serena Anderson is coming in around lunchtime but firstly, Edward Anderson has asked to talk to you, and he won't talk to anyone else. We need you back here, now.'

FIFTY-TWO

Gina barged past the desk sergeant and hurried through to the incident room with Jacob on her tail. The tech team had opened the stick and she knew they'd forward the information on it to her immediately. 'Can you turn that computer on?' With all other detectives out and Briggs handling the press, it was just her and Jacob.

He pressed a button and they both stared at the computer as it whirred away. 'It's on, guv.'

She opened the file from tech. 'Untitled files.' She clicked onto the first one and gasped as she opened the four photos. 'The date is the same as the birthday party for Billie's son. The one held in Nadia's garden. What monster could do this to her?' Gina swallowed as her gaze flitted between them. Bruises to the woman's chest and arms. Gina spotted the birthmark. It was Nadia in the other photo. She flicked to the next. A cut to her thigh and an awkwardly taken photo facing away from a mirror, where Nadia had managed to capture the scratch on her back.

'Bloody hell.'

Gina opened the other files, all dated earlier and stopped on a video. She tensed up as she hit play. A teary Nadia began to speak. 'If you find this, something terrible has happened to me. My husband has been hurting me for years and he plays these sick games...' She bursts into tears, mascara running down her face. Gina looked away and took a deep breath, trying to ease the nausea running up her gullet. 'I've learned to not keep things in one place. He always finds everything. This is for Billie. I'm sorry, Billie. When you left Kayden playing with your iPad, I emailed you a video message, saved it, then deleted the email. Check your documents. Please?' The video ended.

Standing, Gina kicked a chair over. 'The one thing we need right now, we haven't got. Anderson had every reason to hurt Billie and take her tablet, but he didn't take his wife.' She clenched her fists as she closed her eyes, reliving Terry's fists pummelling her, him forcing her to do repulsive things when he was drunk; the cuts, the broken ribs, the bruises and the pressure in her head felt as though it was about to explode. Itching coming from her core, needing to flex out and hit something, even hit herself.

'Guv... take a seat.'

'I don't need a seat.' Yes, Jacob knew about her past abuse and so did the whole station. It had come up in a previous case. He knew the pain and angst she was suffering from at this precise moment. She turned away and allowed the tension to ease. 'I'm okay now. Just seeing these injuries.'

'The guy's an animal. We can arrest him with this new evidence. He won't get away with it and as soon as Nadia comes around, we can also ask her about this memory stick.'

'If she comes around. It's touch and go. This memory stick might be all we have.' She held her hands up in the air before bringing them to the top of her head and pacing. 'We need Billie's tablet. Right.' She headed towards the interview rooms. 'Anderson is waiting in interview room one and I'm the only one he will speak to. I hate him.'

They hurried along the corridor and stopped outside the room. 'Let's do this, guv. You can do it.'

'Thank you. Jacob?'

'Yes?'

'Do you ever buy Jennifer jewellery?'

'Yes, earrings mostly. I bought her a necklace with a pendant on it but mostly earrings.'

'Never a hair clip or slide? You know, something fancy, maybe silver and sparkly?'

He pressed his lips together and shook his head. 'No, I'd have never thought of buying something like that.'

'Hmm, a grip like that would be quite a unique gift then?'

'Very unique. I think I know where this is going.'

She pushed the door open and calmly took a seat next to the wall. Jacob took the seat next to her. A smug expression filled the solicitor's face. He thought Edward Anderson might be leaving the station. He thought wrong. Anderson had a lot of explaining to do.

Several minutes later, introductions over and tape rolling, Gina leaned in. 'You said you had something to tell me. What is it?'

The solicitor smiled. 'I've been informed that Mr Anderson's wife was found this morning and that Mr Anderson's wife was left there at the same time he was in your custody. My client needs to be released.'

A niggle at the back of her mind wouldn't leave and before things got a little more heated when she pulled out the photos and video from Nadia's locker, she had to ask, 'We couldn't find a fancy hair clip under your bed. You mentioned that you and your wife play these games, where you hide presents and notes.'

'My client—' Anderson held a hand up and hushed the man.

'I left it there ages ago. Maybe she moved it?'

'Can you describe it?'

'Long, silver, thin with diamantés along it. It sparkles under the light. I don't know much about hair clips. It was in a box, maybe purple, pink or blue. I can't remember.'

'It wasn't there. We found no hair clip.'

He shrugged. 'Well, I don't know where it is. Why would I lie about something like that?'

Gina wanted to throw all his lies back in his face, but she thought better of it. He was talking. The hair clip that Candice was wearing when she arrived looked to be the same as Anderson was describing and she said that her husband gave it to her. Maybe this once, Anderson wasn't lying.

'Maybe Nadia found it and took it to work or wore it out and lost it. That happens. This isn't relevant. I have nothing more to say about hair clips. How is my wife? I want to see her.'

The solicitor placed an open hand, shielding his whispers and Anderson whispered back. 'There is something important my client wishes for me to tell you and he doesn't wish to say anything else.' The man pulled out a legal pad, covered in the neatest cursive handwriting Gina had ever seen. 'The blood on the knife that you have in evidence. My client knows who it belongs to and he's willing to provide any samples you need to prove that.'

Gina furrowed her brows. 'Whose blood is it?'

'It's mine.' Anderson ran his fingers through his hair. 'I want to report a case of domestic abuse. My wife lost her temper one night and stabbed me with that knife. Her fingerprints are on it also.' He stood and began pulling his T-shirt over his head. Amongst his ripped muscles, he pointed to a jagged scar on his upper arm. 'This scar will match that knife, if there's any way of telling. I didn't go to hospital, so you won't find any records. I bandaged it up and hoped for the best. It took forever to heal and at one point, I thought it was infected.' He licked his lips. 'Despite everything, I love Nadia and I'm concerned about her. I've been told she's in hospital and is in a critical condition. I need to leave here. I need to be with my son, and I need to be out for when Nadia comes home.'

That had confused the case and without being able to speak to Nadia, things were getting ever more complicated. Gina placed the memory stick in a laptop. 'For the tape, I'm playing Mr Anderson a video of Nadia Anderson speaking, and I'm showing him a selection of photos showing bruising and cuts to Nadia's body. The video contains audio.' She watched him as she played the video, followed by the photos. 'We found a memory stick amongst your wife's belongings in a locker at the leisure centre and it contained this video and these photos. She's scared.'

'It's all an act and those bruises, she does them to herself.' The solicitor's eyes widened as he whispered into Anderson's ear. 'I have nothing more to say.'

'Did you take Billie Reeves's tablet?'

The man stared directly into Gina's eyes and remained tight-lipped, then he whispered to his solicitor. 'My client doesn't know anything about a tablet.'

'Why are your fingerprints on the lock of Billie Reeves's garden gate?'

'Okay, I just went over one day and she was all agitated so I locked the gate. I told her to keep away from Nadia, that's all. I did not hurt Billie then or at any other time.'

'When was this?'

The solicitor stared at Mr Anderson before whispering in his ear. 'My client has nothing more to say.'

Gina glanced at the last photo and on Nadia's back was what appeared to be the curve of a nail dug into her flesh so hard there was a trickle of blood. There was no way her own hand could have got into that position, which meant at the very least Anderson was lying about that injury. 'Edward Anderson, I'm arresting you on suspicion of assault on Nadia Anderson. You do not have to say anything. But it may harm your defence if you do not mention when questioned something which you later rely on in court. Anything you do say may be given in evidence.' The knife and Anderson's claims had thrown her but for now, she'd bought them more time to investigate. They needed Nadia to make a recovery, wake up and tell them who tried to kill her. She also needed to get the blood sample checked against Anderson so she could deal with his accusation. She checked her watch. Serena Reeves would be waiting.

FIFTY-THREE

CANDICE

'You soon called the police about Serena,' Gavin gripped her arm.

'But this is different. I'd never do anything to break our family up.'

He dropped her arm and began to pace. She should have left his office, ran as fast as she could and removed herself from the situation, but she couldn't. It was as if her pumps were made of lead and her bones were stiff. She had to do everything she could to fix things. That's what she always did. She fixed things. She fixed people, problems and herself when the situation called for it. She tried to tell Nadia that breaking confidences was a bad thing to do but half the time, Nadia didn't even seem aware she was doing it. Even Candice had pleaded with Billie to stop selling herself, but it was to no avail and then Billie stopped answering her calls and sitting at the furthest end of the table when they met as a group. It was inevitable that something bad would happen and her husband had been right in the middle of it. Right now, she needed to plead with him to calm down. 'Gavin,' she shouted. 'Can you keep still for just a minute? You're driving me insane.'

'Keep still. Really. Those detectives will be back any minute, you know that. You heard them. They have found Nadia's body. I'm sorry about the hair clip, I really am. Stupid prick! I don't know what came over me. I saw it in their house when I got Poppy from William's bedroom, and I took it.' He hit his forehead with an open palm with an angry grunt.

They were really in a bad place, and it was set to get worse, fast. Her vision wavered like she was standing on a turbulent plane and the walls felt as though they were closing in, walls expanding and contracting with her heavy pulse. If she had to stay in his office a moment longer, she'd faint. 'We need to get out of here. I need to get out of this house.' She ran out of his office, gasping as she grabbed her bag.

'Where are you going?' He chased after her, just missing out on grabbing the back of her top.

'Anywhere. Away from this house.' Where were the car keys? She fumbled in her jacket pocket and in the bowl of junk by the front door where her nail pierced an overripe peach. She held her hands up and pummelled his chest as she burst into tears, letting everything out. It was his fault and she hated him.

He held her tightly. 'I stuffed up. I'm sorry and I'll do anything to keep our family together. Anything. I'll spend the rest of my life making it up to you. Yes, I wasn't home on Tuesday night and yes, I was at Billie's. I won't lie to you.'

Too late. He'd already lied too many times.

'Why did you have to go looking, why?'

'Because the truth matters.' She sobbed into his T-shirt. 'You're a liar.'

He leaned back. 'I am and I hate myself right now, but I'm not a murderer. I did not hurt Billie, ever. You know me. You know I couldn't do that.'

'Do I?' She held her hands up and dropped them to her sides. 'Why did you go with her?'

'Don't ask me to answer that.'

'I deserve the fucking truth, all of it.'

He leaned up against the front door. 'I...' He shook his head and started again. 'I was losing you. I missed the closeness. We haven't had sex for nearly a year. Every time I come near you; you look at me like I'm disgusting.'

'Don't give me that shit and don't blame me. Every day of our marriage I've done everything I can to please you, everything. You've been distancing from me, and this is an excuse. Blame the wife for lack of sex. That's a good one. Original – not.'

'I know I'm asking a lot and you can hate me all you like, but I need you on my side right now. Look at me.' He held her chin and lifted it until her gaze met his.

She didn't recognise him any more. On Tuesday, he'd called up that evening when Poppy couldn't sleep, and he'd read their little girl a story over the phone. He was working, that was all. Working as he couldn't sleep. Working as he had a tight deadline. Working – always working. He hadn't been doing any work, he'd been paying their hard-earned money over to Billie for sex. She stared at him, his resolve crumbling in front of her. He'd never looked so small, pathetic and weak. She imagined him seeing that hair clip at Nadia's and sniping it like some sad kleptomaniac, unable to keep his hands off the shiny prize. Yes, he was drunk, and he thought it was a good idea at the time, but she could have worn it in front of Nadia. Was he capable of really bad things? His petty theft was the least of her problems. 'I don't know you. I don't know you at all.'

They both looked out of the window as a car drove past and he exhaled. 'I thought that was them. Can we get out of here? I need some space to think. The police can't come back and see us like this.'

'I'm not coming.' Candice headed back to the living room. 'If the police come back, then so be it. I haven't done anything.' Maybe she couldn't keep everything to herself any longer.

Maybe it was time to tell them that Gavin had stolen the hair clip from Nadia and Ed and that he'd also been paying Billie for sex. The situation had passed the point of no return. The very thought of the truth coming out made her wince as if she'd sucked on a lemon. Everyone would know that she was an inadequate wife, that she couldn't satisfy her husband or keep him happy. The humiliation would kill her. She could move, maybe go and stop with her grandmother in her Spanish villa for a while until things died down. Leaving the country would be the best option. Poppy could go to school there.

'I need you.' He spun her around. 'Please.'

'Let go of me.'

He began clenching his teeth and staring at her. 'Get in the car.' His grip tightened and she pulled back, knocking an ornament off the window ledge. As he dragged her, all the coats came off the coat rack and she got tangled in trainer laces. Outside, she grabbed the door knocker so hard it pulled away and all she heard was metal jangling on the drive as it fell. Gavin kicked the tangled trainer against the wall.

'No.'

Before she could get his hands off her, he dragged her across the pavement. He threw her into the passenger seat. As he went to walk around to the driver's side, she opened the door and ran. Within seconds he was on her, pulling her back. She yelled but it was no good. The neighbours were at work. That didn't stop their dog from barking at the commotion. 'I'm sorry, really sorry.'

What was he sorry for, making her get into a car? Manhandling her? What he did with Billie? For the lies? 'No, please. I can't go in there.' He popped the boot.

'Just get in.'

'No.'

He pushed her in fighting and yelling. His strength won. Her handbag had tangled around her neck and the button had popped on her shirt. She thudded face first into the bloodied plastic sheet in the boot of the car and all she could see was the manic look of horror on Gavin's face. For the first time in their marriage, she knew at this moment in time, he was capable of killing her. She listened as he turned the radio up so loud, she felt it booming underneath. Then a newsflash came on.

Nadia was alive and it was only a matter of time before Nadia spoke.

FIFTY-FOUR

Serena leaned over the table, her lank hair falling over her face. 'How could she do this? I laid my heart on a plate. I told her everything as I needed a shoulder, someone to talk to and she goes and reports me to the police. I did not kill my sister.'

Gina was trying to take everything in. Anderson's claims that Nadia was abusing him. The photos of Nadia's abuse that Anderson said she did to herself. The finger impressions on Nadia's back that proved that statement to be false. And now, Serena.

'Serena, you failed to tell us that you live in Redditch now, that you had opportunity, and you don't have an alibi for the time that Billie was murdered, or when Nadia was taken. You admit you were angry at both Billie and Nadia.'

She started to sob, and huge teardrops began to plop onto the wooden desk. Jacob passed her a box of tissues and she tugged at one. 'I would never kill my sister. I was angry, yes. How would you feel if the person you loved was sleeping with someone else and then triple that shock when you find out it's your sister?' Gina could well imagine how awful her ordeal of seeing Billie having sex with Nathan must have been. She only had to imagine Briggs and Rosemary together and it made her want to curl up in a ball and never leave the house again. Every time she saw him or heard his voice, it stung. As it stood, they still hadn't found the murder weapon and it had now been established that the knife with Anderson's blood on it, was not the knife used to kill Billie or stab Nadia. And, it did have his blood on it. He was telling the truth about his own stabbing. Anderson was clear of murder.

'Being cheated on hurts. Catching your partner and your sister in the act, I can't imagine the pain, the anger. Serena, did you go to Billie's that afternoon and drive a knife through her heart? Did you kill her?'

'No. If I'd have done that, I'd have requested a solicitor. I wouldn't be here talking like this. I would never have hurt my sister. I might have hated her for what she did but kill her, no.'

'Nadia knew. The others knew. You felt humiliated as you were the last to find out. What did you do with Nadia?'

'I did not hurt Nadia. Why the hell would I?'

'You said yourself, the pain of them all laughing at you was too much. That's why you went to see her. That's why you sent Mrs Brent the messages to meet you. Was she going to be next?'

Serena shook her head, smirked and blew her nose. 'That cow has a lot to answer for. I only wanted to talk to her. I thought she'd help but no, she felt the need to exaggerate everything and blame me.'

'Exaggerate? Please tell me how she exaggerated what you said.'

She shrugged as she dropped a pulled clump of hair to the floor. 'She could tell I was upset and that I felt guilty for the hate I had in me, and she made out that I murdered my sister. I said nothing to give her that impression.'

'Do you have Billie's tablet?'

'No.'

'Do you know someone called BenedictCarnY?'

She scrunched up her nose. 'No. The only Benedict I've heard of is Benedict Cumberbatch.'

'Why didn't you tell us that you lived in Redditch?'

Serena shook her head rapidly and her features tensed as if she was turning into a statue.

'Why?'

'Because I knew I'd be a suspect.'

'Serena, can we search your flat, car and have your phone.' Gina felt her heart racing in the hope that it could be that easy to either find the evidence they needed or prove Serena's innocence.

The young woman removed her keys from her pocket, along with her phone and slid them across the table. 'I gather you'll just get a warrant if I say no. Those are the keys to my apartment.'

Gina took the phone.

'What's the passcode?'

'Teeth32. Adults have thirty-two teeth.' She shrugged.

Gina unlocked the phone and began scrolling through the messages of which there were a few showing that the sisters had bickered, but nothing that suggested murder.

'I have a confession to make.'

'Go on.'

'I followed Nathan, and I took some photos around the back of Billie's house. I don't know what that makes me, but I was upset, and I wanted proof that him cheating wasn't a one-off. I did something stupid and I'm sorry. I call it investigating; you might call it stalking. My life is ruined anyway. I've lost my sister; I've left uni and my life is a complete mess and my nephew is devastated, and my parents are going to hate me.' Again, tears began to flow as the enormity of her confession sank in. 'I think I caught the back of a man in a dark coat, at least I think it was a man. I thought it was just someone coming from one of the houses. As it was me who was snooping around,

I was more nervous about me being caught out the back of her house, so I didn't give him a thought.'

Gina flicked through the photos and saw a couple of Nathan leaving Billie's house and one of Nathan in Billie's kitchen, making a drink.

She picked up the keys hoping that O'Connor and Wyre could leave the woods and head over to Serena's apartment. She had too much to work out and at this stage, only needed the most relevant of information that would help the case. She flicked through a few more photos.

'That's the one.' Serena blew her nose.

Gina pinched to enlarge the one side of a figure by the back gate. The photo had been taken in the dark and was grainy and only showed up the slightest of outlines. 'Did you hear this person talk, cough, anything?'

'No, but when he'd gone, I watched Billie through her window. She was crying. I wanted so much to knock and see if she was okay, but I shouldn't have been there and I was still angry about Nathan. A part of me was glad she was upset, although I didn't know why. I guess now she didn't want to sleep with guys for money. It must have been hard.' She shook her head. 'Everything is so messed up.'

'Why didn't you tell us all this to begin with?'

Serena raised her eyebrows. 'Durr, because of this. I didn't want any of this. Why would I want my parents to know about Nathan and Billie and to know that I'd ditched my uni course while they were still sending me money to help buy food? My mother never shuts up about how proud she is of me, telling everyone who will listen. Why would I want you to know that I'd been watching Nathan and my sister?' Serena stared into space. 'She's dead and I'm never going to see her again. It's just hit me. Billie is dead.' She lifted her feet up onto the chair and hugged herself. 'I have nothing more to give or tell you.' Staring at the wall, Serena began to rock slightly.

'Are these photos of a party?' Gina glanced at children and adults in the garden. She recognised the Andersons' house, the Brents, Meera, Billie's parents and Billie. It was as if the two photos had been taken over a fence.

'Yes, I wasn't invited to Kayden's birthday bash. Billie thought I'd be busy with uni work. My emotions were all over the place. I didn't trust Nathan and I was so mad, I wanted to ruin the party. I just felt left out of everything. Yes, I was the daughter who was going to become the dentist, but Billie brought chaos with her all the time. Mum and Dad were always consumed with her and Kayden. Billie brought the drama; they were always worried about her, and she upset Mum by not getting her life together.'

'So, you were jealous of Billie?'

'Yes. I guess I was. Everyone loved Billie...' She paused. 'I wish she was here.'

There was a knock at the door and Jacob spoke to the tape to end the interview.

Gina stood and left the room. 'Sir.'

Briggs stood there, a lovely smell of aftershave teasing her senses. She still had a pillowcase that had that smell. 'It's Nadia. She's just come out of surgery and she's stable, for now.'

Gina held a fist up. 'Yes. Is she able to talk to us?'

'They said they'd need to see how she was when she came around, but it wasn't likely. We already knew about the stab wound, but they said when they checked her more thoroughly, it looked like she'd been hit with something blunt over the back of the head. Amongst other things, she will probably be concussed.' He stood there in awkward silence.

'Chris, I'm sorry for everything. I really am.'

'And me.' He shrugged and walked off.

'Sir,' she called.

He turned back.

'We're a bit thin on the ground. This case is taking every

resource we have, and no one is here to help. Could I give you this phone? It belongs to Serena Reeves. She's just confessed to following her sister and boyfriend, and she took a few photos. One photo shows the side of a person, in the dark, at the back of Billie's house. Could you see if anyone in tech can try to sharpen or enhance it?'

He walked back, smiled and took the phone. As his little finger brushed her hand, it felt like a jolt of electric running through her. He stopped for a second too long before continuing up the corridor with the phone. Had he felt it too?

She shook thoughts of him away, for now, knowing that the only way they could even have a working relationship was for her to back off completely and to never mention Rosemary again.

Nadia was coming around and that was the best news ever. She must have seen her attacker and Gina wanted to be the first person to see her when she woke up.

Her mind went back to the hair clip. It had niggled like something rotten. Nadia would be out of it for a while yet so that would buy her a little bit of time to follow that hunch. Something was off in the Brent household. She'd spent too much time concentrating on Edward Anderson and not enough considering the others.

Jacob left the interview room. 'I've messaged Wyre and O'Connor. They're rushed off their feet but as always, Bernard will let us know as soon as they find anything so they're heading here to get Serena's keys. Then they'll take a look in her apartment. They also checked on the charity shop and the gym to see if Brock had been there on the day of Billie's murder. He had been to both, like he said.'

Brock wasn't in the clear for hurting Mr Reeves or kidnapping Kayden, but he was in the clear for Billie's murder. 'At least we can strike him off the list now. I don't know how we're keeping it together. If only the public knew how stretched we are. I want to go back to the Brent household.'

'Really?'

'I know I'm harping on about that hair clip, but I don't believe or trust what they've said. That photo on Serena's phone, it could look like many men when it comes to build, shape and size but it could also be Gavin Brent. What if he took that hair clip and he gave it to his wife? If he's killed Billie and he attempted to kill Nadia, we have a dangerous person on our hands. I don't know about you, but I felt the table humming a little with Candice's shaking when we were there. You could see the tremor she was trying to hide. The woman was a nervous wreck.'

As they followed the corridor, a girl was chasing a ferret. 'Kooky,' she called. Gina placed her hands out and caught the creature's lead before passing it to her. She took the ferret back into the waiting area.

'Oh, she's one of the people who found Nadia, here to give a statement. Uniform will take it but I think she told us everything she knew at the scene, after she came round. Poor girl passed out.'

'Right, we must go now because if I'm right, I'll never forgive myself for not going back to see if Mrs Brent is okay. I think she was terrified and now that the news is out about Nadia, the killer will be desperate.'

FIFTY-FIVE

NADIA

I don't know who I am, what I am or if this is death. I hear the bleep, bleep of machines and now they're gone. I'm running from everything I ever trusted and knew. They're all after me. What happened?

One minute, I'm there.

Where?

Where was I?

It was dark, so dark and I couldn't see or feel. It was as if my body was made of cotton wool, like now. I sank deeper and deeper into the darkness, unable to escape and then boom, the beep, beep, beeping keeps coming back.

'Mrs Anderson. Do you know where you are?'

'Hmm.' I can't talk. My lips aren't working. It's no good, all I can do is give in to the sinking feeling and fall deep into the darkness. As I enter the long, black walk, I drag myself along the floor before managing to stand. Then I see him. I see him with my friend and they're naked and close. I want to yell and shout but her name is gone. My head, it's all wrong, I can't remember anything.

Then, I'm at the school and the parents are all looking at

me. Fingers pointed, whispering. 'No,' I yell and fight, telling them to leave me alone. I know I'm to blame but I don't know why.

'Mrs Anderson? Nadia. You're safe and you're in Cleevesford General. Things might feel a little fuzzy for a while as you've had an anaesthetic and you're suffering with concussion.'

I can't stop crying. I don't know why I'm here. All I know is that everyone hates me, and someone wants to hurt me. Who wants to hurt me? Am I Mrs Anderson? A few moments pass and I manage to rally around slightly. The room is blurry.

All I can see is the eyes and they look deep into my soul. I scream and scream because I can't remember. Please make this end. Please. 'I'm losing my mind.'

'It's okay, Nadia. You're going to be fine.' A hand strokes mine. It's the lovely nurse. I'm in hospital.

'Who are you?' I need a name. It might help.

'Meera. Your friend Meera.' The voice sounds demonic and as I slip into a thought that won't leave me alone, all I see is Meera with an evil laugh. I try to move my arm but it's as if it's filled with concrete. I try to shout again but the dryness in my throat has won. 'Stop shouting, I'm here to help.'

I don't want her here. It's all coming back. She and Ed were having an affair. Billie must have known. They're trying to get rid of me and there's nothing I can do about it. I imagine poison running through my veins or a pillow over my head. I'm going to die.

FIFTY-SIX

As Gina hurried out of Jacob's car, she ran up Candice and Gavin's drive. Her heart sunk. A trainer leaned up against the brick of the porch. Jacob stood by her side. She went to grab the knocker, that's when she noticed it on the floor and there were two holes where it had been wrenched out of the door. A smeared handprint snaked down the glass panel and Gina swallowed down the sick nerves that told her she was right to be worried about Candice. 'I don't like this,' she said.

She peered through the window and coats were strewn all over the place and an ornament had been smashed. Only one car was on the drive, the other had gone. 'Guv, she might be in there.' He leaned over her and knocked hard.

Gina pushed the letter box just as the neighbours' dog barked. 'Mrs Brent,' she called. 'Please open the door.'

'I'll try the back.' Jacob began walking alongside the large semi while Gina called for backup.

'We need uniform. There's sign of a disturbance at the Brent household.'

'Guv.' She looked up. 'The back door is open.' Jacob beckoned her to follow him, and she didn't waste any time in going through the side gate and along the cluttered path. She nudged past the child's scooter and the mouldy old fence panel.

'We're going in. Candice may be in there and she may be hurt. The back door is unlocked so no forced entry needed.' She ended the call.

As she gazed up the long garden, nothing seemed out of place at the back of the house. She nearly tripped over the snaking hosepipe.

Jacob pushed the door open wide and stepped into the kitchen. 'Mrs Brent? Hello.'

Nothing but silence. Gina stepped into the kitchen and crept through to the lounge where the chipped ornament lay on the floor. She didn't disturb the coats, the shoes or the handprint. 'We need to keep this area secure for now.' Stepping back, she glanced around the lounge and back towards the kitchen before running back through the house. 'The office.' She passed the back of the kitchen until she reached the open door. A small gift box lay on the desk and a pile of paper had fallen to the floor. She put on a pair of latex gloves and opened the box. There was nothing in it. 'Mrs Brent.' Nothing. 'We need to check upstairs.'

Jacob nodded, then they went back through the lounge.

Step by step, Gina felt heat crawling up her neck and a line of perspiration under her hairline. 'Mrs Brent.' Bedroom one was clear. Bedroom two, the room with the Disney mural was clear and the playroom at the end of the landing – clear. She nudged the door to the bathroom and exhaled. 'She's not here.' The bathroom cabinet was slightly ajar. Gina leaned over and opened it. Nothing. She slid open the top drawer that was bulging with make-up. That's when she spotted the card. She reached in and pulled it out. 'There's a note from Edward to Nadia on this card saying he's sorry. It's the same colour as the gift box in the office. It had to contain the hair clip. Can I have Mrs Brent's phone number?'

Jacob scrolled through their online system and showed her the number. She punched it into her mobile and began calling but the call ended as if the phone was no longer in operation. 'We need all units on this. I want Mrs Brent found.'

'On it, guv.' He placed his phone to his ear and stepped out of the room and down the stairs.

Gina clenched the sides of her hair and let out a silent scream. It had been too obvious that Mrs Brent had been in some sort of trouble and Gina had left her with her husband. The news about Nadia had broken and he had to have taken her. One thing was certain, looking at the mess left behind, she had not left voluntarily.

'Guv, I found the keys to the garage. Isn't she a dog groomer?'

'Yes.' She ran down the stairs and through the internal garage door. Nothing seemed out of place. The stainless-steel table sat in the centre of the room and a noose hung down from a frame; one that would normally keep the dog in place while being trimmed. Right now, it looked sinister. Cupboards filled the back wall, and a deep dog bath and drying station filled the other. The whole room stank of disinfectant and light bounced off every surface. On the desk sat a pile of papers all showing vacant factory units that were local to the area. Where to start?

She ran back to the office and opened Gavin Brent's drawers and there was more paperwork. A flyer for the dog grooming business and notes for a new website but underneath it, a photocopied single page for the lease of a unit. The only problem was the page showing the address was not there. Gina scrutinised the lease and it referred to another section on page three that would list the address. She rummaged around the drawer and amongst his pens and stationery. 'This is the same colour and make.'

Jacob looked up from the sideboard. 'Huh.'

'The same brand of red pen used in Billie's house and

Nadia's garage. We need to contact the letting agent on this lease and find out which unit this relates to. He's taken her there. He must have.' She paced up and down as she pressed the numbers. 'We're too late, I know we are. Why did we leave her this morning? Why?' An answerphone kicked in for the letting agent. 'Damn, what kind of business is this? Have uniform arrived? Please tell me they're here as I want this scene secured.'

Jacob went out of the office and back through the house. 'They're just pulling up.'

'Great, quick info handover. Keep trying Halston Groves Commercial Lettings. As soon as someone answers, tell them we're on our way. In the meantime, Candice's life depends on us not screwing this up. I'm going to call PC Kapoor. We can hurry over and speak to Nadia. She's out of surgery. We can only hope that she remembers what happened.'

She felt her phone start to buzz. 'Hello,' she said as she answered.

Her heart began to speed up. 'PC Kapoor has just caught Meera sneaking into Nadia's hospital room. We need to get there, now.'

FIFTY-SEVEN

CANDICE

As Gavin sped along the roads, taking corners without any warning, Candice slid on the plastic sheeting, feeling the grit and secretions of Nadia all over her. So hot, she was almost poaching in her own sweat. He turned the radio off. 'Gavin, let me out,' she yelled, tears sliding down her face. Her racing heart felt as though it might choke her. Gasping, she fought for the next breath. Banging on the boot, she waited to hear him respond but all she could hear were the bumps in the road and the sound of the engine. Disorientated, she had no idea where he was taking her. There had been twists and turns galore. What she did know was that this was a fight for her life. It was going to be him or her.

As he took another corner, her mouth smashed into something hard behind the plastic. A drizzle of warm liquid slid down her cheek. As she clenched her teeth, an excruciating pain shot through her jaw. One of her teeth had broken. She spat out the fleck of tooth. Kicking out in all directions, she had to find a weak spot in the car. One chance was all she needed, and she'd run as fast as she could. Not before taking Gavin out. She'd seen every horror film going. When people ran, their aggressor chased them. One hit, they get back up. If she got the chance, she had to go in there as hard as possible before making her escape. It was the only way.

The car hopped over a bump and for a second, it was in flight. She knew exactly where they were. That was the hump-back bridge that went over the brook, on the outskirts of Cleevesford. He was taking the country roads to avoid anyone seeing him. She wondered if the DI had returned and seen the mess they left behind. They'd have alerts out. She'd heard of number-plate recognition, and they'd easily find out which car was missing off their drive.

With her sharp red fingernails, she fought until she managed to pierce the thick plastic. A few seconds later, she could fit a whole hand through. 'Come on,' she roared, poking and stretching away. 'Yes.' Her yell was victorious as she grabbed hold of Poppy's rounders' bat, the one they took to the park. There would be no more happy family moments like that any more. As soon as he opened that boot, he was going to have it and he was going to have it hard, straight in the face. It was her or him, and Poppy needed her, not the wide-eyed animal that had her trapped in the boot. She didn't know Gavin at all.

An image of her little girl flashed through her mind. Gavin had ruined their lives. It was all his fault, and they would ulti-mately pay the price; that's if she made it through this ordeal. She needed to hurry out of this nightmare, get Poppy and leave. She tried to hear her daughter's giggle in her mind, but it was hard over the growling engine. All she heard was rage. 'Please let me see Poppy again,' she whispered as a sob escaped her mouth. She wanted to hug her little girl's lithe frame and stroke her red hair.

Without warning, Gavin accelerated, thrusting her back again. The car skewered, snaking from side to side. They were going to crash. He was killing them both, there and then, and there was nothing at all she could do. Heart banging, she clenched her muscles and closed her eyes. *Don't let go of the bat*, she thought as her whole body crashed into the front of the boot first and was then flung back. Bones stiff, she cried out as she straightened her left arm in agony She could move it, it wasn't broken. They'd crashed in the middle of the countryside, and she couldn't hear anything. 'Gavin.' She roared as loud as she could, repeating his name. Where had he crashed them? Was he dead?

Grabbing the bat, she hit one of the tail lights, knocking it clean out, then she peered through the gap. She flinched as a glint of sunlight nearly blinded her. In the distance she could hear cars going up and down the dual carriageway that crossed this route. No one was going to find them here. It was down to her to escape. She wiped the string of blood that was seeping from her tooth and bashed at the back of the seats with all she had. That's when she heard footsteps crunching on twigs.

Gavin whispered through the tail light gap. 'Shut the hell up or I'm going to stab you in the heart, do you hear me? Then, I will take Poppy far away from all this. You had to go and ruin everything.' He slammed his hand on the boot, making her scream out.

'Gavin, please,' she cried. 'We can talk about this.'

'There's no more time for talking.' As he bent over and peered through the gap, she thrust the bat out of the hole straight into his cheek and she heard the crack.

'Bitch.' He snatched the bat, pulling it out. He now had her only weapon. She watched as he rolled the bloodied item around in his hand, as if he was warming up to bat a ball. He brought it down on the bumper and she shrieked. 'This is how it's going to play out. I'm going to reverse this car and hope to hell it still starts. If it doesn't, you best say your final prayers as I'll kill you here.' He smirked. 'Maybe not. There's not a place in heaven for people like you.' He paused. 'You will not win this one. I'm going to drive and you're going to make zero fuss. If I see that you've waved at anyone through this gap' – he hit the gap with the bat – 'I will crash us both face on into a tree. The crash I just caused; it was a warning. The next time, it will be the real thing, as right now I have nothing to lose. You caused this.' He hit the car again. 'Do you understand?'

She nodded as tears soaked her face. Mouth parched and throat like sandpaper, she needed him to drive away, out of the sun. If she had to stay in the tin box of the car any longer, she'd die of heat stroke. 'Can I have some water?'

He stared directly at her and grinned. 'No.' With that he walked away, and she hoped with all she had that the car would start. She closed her eyes, picturing the knife plunging through her soft flesh, right through her beating heart. She tried to imagine the pain along with how it would feel to gasp for those dying breaths. The car rocked as he thudded into the driver's seat.

'Please start,' she kept repeating as her bottom lip trembled. If not, it was all over. She sobbed for herself, and she sobbed for the daughter she might never see again.

FIFTY-EIGHT

Gina hurried behind Jacob as they entered Cleevesford General Hospital. She finished her phone conversation with O'Connor.

'Any updates, guv?'

'Yes, Anderson has come clean about the hot tub. His colleague, a Mr Graham Wilcox, bought it on his behalf with his card. He was having a spa treatment at a posh hotel with another one of his colleagues. Another affair with someone who was married. That's why he wouldn't speak. He said it would ruin her marriage and she begged him not to say anything.'

'It sounds to me like it's already ruined. I don't know what's up with these people.' Jacob shook his head.

They ran into the recovery ward and were buzzed in after waiting for a few seconds. Gina flashed her identification at the nurse who was manning the station. 'Where's Nadia Anderson, please?' Gina stood there, hands on hips as she tried to get her breath back. She checked her watch. The day was running away with them.

'We put her in a room at the far end. I'm really sorry.' The young female nurse gnawed on the inside of her cheek.

'Sorry?' Gina's brows furrowed. Jacob nodded to her and continued up the corridor while Gina hung back.

'About leaving Mrs Anderson.'

'What happened?'

'I told your officer we needed to do some checks on her and that it would take a few minutes. She was desperate for the loo, so I said I'd stay in the room, but I had an urgent call to tend to another patient. I thought Mrs Anderson would be okay for a couple of minutes but then that woman found her way in without permission, distressing the patient.' Gina could see that the nurse's hands were shaking.

'Please, it'll be okay.'

'Thank you. I really am sorry.' Gina smiled as she left the nurse tapping away on her computer.

Shouting echoed from outside the private room at the end. As she got closer, she could see a woman in her fifties arguing with Meera. 'How dare you even be here? She doesn't want to see you.' The woman slapped Meera across the face and Jacob intervened, restraining her before any more damage was done. PC Kapoor stepped back and remained against the door of Nadia's room, ensuring that no one else would even try to enter.

'I know and I'm sorry,' Meera blubbed, eyes red rimmed from crying. 'I wanted to tell Nadia how sorry I was. I didn't mean any of this.'

'And now you've made things worse. You saw my daughter hooked up to those beeping machines, and you chose to come here now and upset her more. You have a nerve. You and that tosser deserve each other. You're both scum.' Nadia's mother's bun had begun to loosen, and her face blushed a plum colour. She escaped Jacob and pushed Meera. 'Go away, now before I do something I might really regret. No one hurts my daughter like that.'

Meera took a few steps back and grabbed her bag off a plastic orange chair. Gina glanced up the ward that came off the corridor and several tired and ill-looking people were taking in the argument.

Jacob gently led Nadia's mother aside and Gina beckoned for Meera to follow her. 'You were not authorised to enter Mrs Anderson's room.' She was angry with the woman for upsetting their victim. She swallowed down her frustration. Now was not the time. She'd heard it all. Meera was basically begging Nadia for forgiveness. It's a shame she hadn't thought about their friendship before she slept with her friend's husband, but it wasn't Gina's place to express judgement.

'I needed to come. I still care about her.' She sniffed and placed a hand on her flushed cheek. 'I don't blame Nadia's mother for slapping me. I deserved it. I've been a horrible friend and all I want to do is to make it up to her.'

'Meera, did Nadia say anything to you about what had happened?'

Tears slid down her cheeks and bounced off her chin. 'No, it was like she was terrified of me, like I might kill her. She raised her hands and kept trying to slap me away. I would never hurt her.'

That was debatable. Meera might not have taken her and stabbed her, but the emotional hurt she had caused would be hard for Nadia to get over. 'Is there anything else we should know? I'll be straight with you. A woman's life is in danger and if you know anything, now is the time to say it.'

'I don't know anything.' She broke down.

Gina took a deep breath and walked over to PC Kapoor. The woman bit her bottom lip. 'I was only gone a few minutes, guv.'

'It's okay.'

'It's not okay. When I got back, the nurse had gone and Nadia was screaming and when I saw Mrs Gupta next to her, I ran in there, scaring Nadia even more. She kept screaming repeatedly. I'm sorry, guv. I feel like I stuffed up.'

'You were here alone. We're understaffed, and you needed the loo. There was nothing you could do. Please don't beat yourself up about this. Did she mention anyone by the name of Benedict Carny during this time?'

'No, guv. She was terrified and shouting, that was all. I'm sorry to have to tell you that they gave her something to calm her down. She is quite drowsy.'

Damn, that wasn't what Gina wanted to hear. Had Meera not turned up, Nadia wouldn't have been sedated. 'I best not waste any time then.'

PC Kapoor stepped aside, and Gina entered the room to the sound of beeping. Nadia's half-closed eyelids registered her presence. 'Nadia, it's DI Harte. May I sit?' She didn't want to alarm the dopey patient.

Nadia let out a groan.

'Can you tell me anything about your attack?'

A tear drizzled down the side of her face and she mumbled, 'Shiny.'

'Shiny. What was shiny?'

She mumbled something incoherent then forced one eye open wide, but only for a second.

'Do you know Benedict Carny?'

She shook her head.

'Please, Nadia, if there is anything at all you can tell me, it would really help. I know you've been through a lot. Your friend Candice has been taken.' She wondered if Nadia would name Gavin Brent.

A piercing yell came from Nadia's mouth, and she mumbled again as if fighting a deep sleep. 'Shiny, so shiny,' she yelled, again. Her lids were virtually closed. 'The knife.'

'Nadia, please. Stay with me.' It was no good. Nadia couldn't fight the sedative any longer.

'He'll kill me,' she murmured before drifting off to sleep.

'Who will kill you?' Gina didn't know if Nadia meant Mr

Anderson or Gavin Brent. She stormed out of the room. 'Nadia said that someone wants to kill her. Call the station and get another officer here. We can't leave her alone for a second. Not now.'

PC Kapoor picked up her radio and stepped to one side. Meera had left and Jacob was comforting Nadia's crying mother.

Gina's phone began to ring. 'O'Connor?'

The signal was muffled, then he spoke. 'Wyre has managed to contact the letting agent. They don't normally open on a Saturday, but the manager is heading in to assist us. They'll be at Halston Groves office in Cleevesford in half an hour.'

'Leaving now. Oh, do a bit more digging on the Brents. I want everything you can find.'

'Will do.'

She ended the call and looked at Jacob. 'We need to go.'

'Wait, is there any news on the animal who did this to my daughter?'

'PC Kapoor is staying here. As soon as we hear anything, we'll let you know.'

With that they hurried out of the building, back into the scorching heat. Benedict Carny kept going through her head. Who was this man to Gavin Brent? As they reached the car, her heart began to pound. If this lead didn't pay off, Candice was a dead woman. If she wasn't already.

FIFTY-NINE

CANDICE

She held her breath as she listened to Gavin turning the engine. The car chugged and then fired up. As he reversed, it clunked. *Please don't break down.* Candice closed her eyes, only opening them when they were back on the winding roads. She exhaled. The car had started, and she had to come up with a plan. Where was he taking her? Think.

There were two places. His mother had a static caravan at a local holiday park. Maybe they were going there. It would be busy, though. Especially on such a gorgeous weekend. No, it was too obvious. She had no idea. She swallowed. If he was capable of driving them into a tree, maybe he'd drive them over a bridge. It could be that he was planning on ending them both today. 'Let me out,' she sobbed. Sliding forward, she peered out of the gap and that's when it hit her. They were near the industrial estate. They were going to the new premises, the one that they were still working on.

He slowed the car down as they turned into the industrial estate and pulled up. She reached around the whole of the boot, in every crevice but there was nothing of any help. Her finger pricked. She lifted the small item up and saw that it was Nadia's earring. That wouldn't help. She threw it back down. The hair clip. It was in her pocket. After she'd slid it out of her hair, she'd popped it into the pocket of her jeans. She reached in and pulled it out. It wasn't long but it tapered, and it was all she had. Gripping it hard, she shuffled back and waited.

She listened as the shutters on the building came up. The click of a key turning in a slightly rusty lock, followed by his returning heavy footsteps. He was coming back. 'Try anything stupid and I'll snap your neck.'

'Please just let me out, Gavin. I won't try anything. We need talk about this. Poppy needs us both.'

The boot popped. He stared intensely before reaching in and dragging her out. Her body slumped to the pavement, slamming her knees into concrete. She let out a quiet moan. Anything more would give him the excuse he needed to hit her with the bat he was gripping. 'I think we're beyond talking.' For a moment, she'd thought about trying to flag someone down, but she couldn't. No one else could be involved. Besides, there was no one in the unit next door. She could see through a gap in the foliage that their shutters were down. Theirs was divided by trees and it was the last on the road. No one could see or hear them and screaming wouldn't make much difference. It would only antagonise Gavin.

'We're not,' she pleaded. 'We can get Poppy and leave, right now. We don't need to say anything about this or Nadia or Billie to anyone.' For a second, she saw the Gavin she'd fallen in love with, then she remembered what he'd done; how he'd deceived her and lied. A slight wash of confusion passing across his face told her that she had to keep him talking. 'Come on, Gavin. Poppy will suffer if we don't get through this.'

He glanced in the boot, his gaze following the plastic sheeting. 'No, there is no other way.'

'What are you going to do with me? Lock me up in the dog parlour?'

He reached down and grabbed her collar, dragging her into the unit. As he entered the main room, he flung her to the tiled floor. She glanced all over at the candy-pink walls that were waiting to be adorned by the finishing touches she was planning to add. The central island with the stainless-steel bench and noose, just like the smaller version in their garage, shone under the strip light. It was all so shiny and new. Glinting and gleaming, except for what her eye was being drawn to.

She heaved as she saw the ropes on the floor at the one end of the room. The blindfold gave her the shivers as she wondered if Gavin would use it on her. She pictured Nadia bound and lying helpless on the cold floor, vision blocked; the empty bottle of water being slowly poured into her thirsty mouth along with sleeping pills. Had Nadia screamed. Gavin liked to hear women scream, it was something he asked her to do all the time when they were having sex. He'd whisper, *scream for me*, and she would. Had Billie screamed? Had her husband, the man she chose to spend her life with, paid her friend to scream?

Gavin paced back and forth, shaking his head. 'No, no, no,' he repeated.

Now was her chance to escape her psycho of a husband. She grabbed the edge of the unit and as soon as he turned his back, she darted past him.

He reached forward and gripped her in his rock-solid arms, yanking her back. They both tumbled to the floor. It was now or never. She aimed the hair clip at his eyes and went to stab him, right in his eyeball but he turned at the last minute and she caught his cheek. It was too blunt. She couldn't drive it in deeply.

'Bitch.' He rolled on top of her, pinning her down before he aimed a punch at her face. Through dazed vision, she watched as his face contorted while he flung the diamanté clip across the room. He hit her again. She couldn't run, she couldn't even stand. She was spent and it looked like he was almost spent if the sweat dripping from his brow was anything to go by. He dragged her across the room leaving her wedged in a corner, stale, hot and bleeding. She pressed her hand to her mouth and almost cried out because of the pain in her tooth.

She tried to lift her bad arm, but it was too stiff. If she tried to fight him or scarper, he'd overpower her again. She watched as he walked over to the ropes. Reaching under the sink unit, she felt something long and cold. She glanced down at the bloodied knife. As he turned to come back with the rope, she slid it up her sleeve. She wasn't going to fight him again. If she did, she'd lose. 'Why are you doing this?'

He began to tie her feet together. 'Poppy. She will live a normal life, one without you. You are going to disappear, never to be heard of again.'

'What are you going to do with me?' Tears meandered down her face.

'I don't know,' he yelled, sending her heart racing again. 'But I won't have us dragged into a police investigation. I won't have our faces on the news. I won't have Poppy growing up with kids calling her the daughter of a murderer. I have money. I've always had money set aside. Never thought I'd need to do this.' He finished tying her feet up.

'Please don't hurt me, Gavin.'

'There's no coming back from this.' He pointed at her with the bat and then he pointed at the mess that had been left from Nadia. 'There's not much time.' He threw the bat to the floor and grabbed another length of rope before helping her to a sitting position.

He was right. Nadia was in hospital. Nadia had lived. There was no going back to their old life. 'So, let's get Poppy and leave together.'

'I don't want to leave with you. I tried to tell you to come with me when we were at home so we could sort something out, but you refused. I had to drag you here, kicking and screaming.

You smashed my face with a bat, then you stabbed me with the bloody hair clip.'

She held her hands out. It didn't matter if she was bound as long as he tied them in front of her. She'd be able to reach the knife and saw them apart. 'I'm sorry.' She hoped to gain his trust back. That was her only way out of all this. He was waiting for her to attack him and if she wasn't careful, that bat would strike her head. He didn't have a plan, she could tell. If he had a plan, he'd have executed it by now. He was pondering what to do next. He wrapped the coarse rope around her wrists, and it prickled, her skin cells mixing with Nadia's.

He took a deep breath, grabbed the bat, and threw it into the sink. Blood trickled from the stab wound to his face. 'Shit.' He wiped it with the back of his hand before heading to the back-room toilet and washbasin.

As she listened to him rummaging she pulled the knife from her sleeve and began to saw. If she hurried, she'd be able to free herself and leave without him knowing. The main door was unlocked. She sawed and sawed until the rope dropped. Feet next. Within seconds, she was free.

He was coming back. As he re-entered the room, she placed the rope back over her wrists and feet. Too late. He turned to the door, snatched the key out and locked it before coming back to sit on the grooming table, back to her. He pulled the SIM card out of his phone and snapped it. He dropped his phone to the tiled floor. As he stamped on it, it shattered.

Time was running out. She quietly stood, allowing the rope to drop as he kicked the pieces of his phone while releasing a deep guttural scream. Silently crying at the pain in her mouth and bones, she brought the knife above her head, knowing that one of them was about to die a painful death.

SIXTY

Gina pushed opened the door of Halston Groves Commercial Lettings.

'Are you police?' the woman asked.

'Yes, DI Harte and this is DS Driscoll.' She opened up the photos on her phone and placed it down in front of the woman. 'Take a look at that lease paperwork in the name of Mr Brent. What property does it relate to?'

'Just bear with me a moment. The system is still warming up. Our IT seriously needs updating.'

Gina tapped her fingers on the other side of the woman's desk as she leaned over waiting.

'You might as well take a seat. It's still whirring away. Can I get you a drink?'

'No, thanks.' Candice didn't have time for them to sit around drinking tea and smiling. She needed them now.

Her phone rang. It was O'Connor again. 'I'll just take this outside.' She nodded to Jacob, leaving him to wait for the antiquated computer to wake up.

'Harry.'

'Guv, I've looked into the Brents, like you asked. Neither

have been in any trouble at all, literally not even a traffic offence. Gavin Simon Brent, he works as an app developer and is freelance, often contracting for companies. Thirty-one years old, only daughter, Poppy. He graduated at Birmingham University and has only been married once. He was taken into care as a child. His father was prosecuted for his assault and he and his mother moved away after that. No incidents reported since. Candice Yvette Brent is twenty-eight and works as a dog groomer and that's as exciting as it gets. Officers have just sent the computer from his office in, and tech are just opening it up. Wait...'

'What is it?'

'One of the team has just flagged me over. Bear with me.'

Gina exhaled as she watched through the shop window. Jacob was taking a note of an address and talking to the woman.

'Guv?' O'Connor said.

'What did tech say?'

'It looks like Mr Brent was using the alias BenedictCarnY. They've cracked his computer and he has an account on the Hi There Horny website. He'd been sending abusive messages to Billie. Basically, misogynistic name-calling. It's only been going on for about two weeks.'

'Thank you. Anything else?'

'One more thing. That photo, off Serena's phone. Tech have barely managed to enhance it but given the build and shape of the person, we're veering towards it being a man who was at her house that night.'

'Thank you. Stay with it. Anything else, let me know immediately. Got to go.' She ended the call as Jacob stepped out. 'Where is it?'

'You're not going to believe this.'

'What?'

'The unit is next door to Edward Anderson's. He owns it. He had arranged to rent it directly to Gavin Brent and asked the letting agent to deal with the legalities of drawing up the lease, that was all.'

Gina called the station as she looked at the address on the piece of paper he held up. 'I need officer backup and an ambulance at unit twenty-nine. It's on Talbot Road, Cleevesford Industrial Estate.'

'I'll fill you in on what O'Connor just told me. We have to go, now!'

SIXTY-ONE
CANDICE

As she aimed for his neck, he dodged the blade. Instead, Candice struck the new stainless-steel counter, scraping a line in the shiny surface. The angry line was nothing on Gavin's angry face. She'd missed him. She'd blown her last chance to get out of this alive. Hands trembling, she didn't know what to do as she gripped the handle. She had no option but to go at him again. His smirk told her that he wasn't scared, in fact, it looked like he wanted her to try, like it was a game they were playing.

She ran around the table; he mirrored her from the other side. She went in the opposite direction. The table was the only thing keeping her alive. Reaching out, she tried to scare him back with the knife, but he didn't even move, knowing full well she couldn't reach him. 'You've really surprised me, Candice. You're tough, I'll give you that but you're not going to get out of this one. We can keep doing this all day while you wear yourself out.'

He was right. How many times could she run back and forth around half a table? A man in a fluorescent jacket walked a little way past the window. She ran and smashed her hands into the glass, but the man didn't even flinch. She saw his head-phones and she wanted to cry. 'No,' she yelled, then before she could get back to the table, Gavin was on her.

The next few moments passed in a blur. She tried to duck past him, and he reached for the knife. As they struggled, the weapon fell to the floor, bouncing under the table. His broad shoulders had her trapped. He slammed her onto the floor like she was a doll. Wind knocked out of her; she could see the knife, but it was too far away. If she reached for it, he would get it first. Where did they go from here?

He grabbed the collar of her shirt, strangling her as he pulled her to her feet. She saw his gaze rest on the noose, then back on her. 'I bet you'd love to feel what it's like for one of your dogs, being trapped in place by something that could strangle them to death. Do you get off on the power?'

It wasn't like that. It just encouraged them to stay in place while she groomed them. A dog that jumped around all over the place while she held a pair of sharp scissors could easily be hurt. She also used a belly strap and a calming cradle. She loved the dogs and it hurt her to think Gavin was insinuating that she tortured them like he was torturing her. 'Gavin, whatever you're thinking—'

'Maybe I've lost the ability to think.' He flung her forward and the noose slapped her head. 'Scream for me, just a little.'

Tears fell down her face. Why would he make her do that now? She shook her head.

'Oh well. No chance of a parting memory then.' He grabbed the cord and pushed her head through it, tightening is as much as he could around her neck. She gasped and flailed, arms reaching for anything. He grabbed them and held them behind her back as he pushed her forward.

As her vision prickled, she heard a car skid to a halt outside and Gavin let her go.

He stormed over and threw himself to the floor. She did the same and they both scrabbled for the knife. She needed to stop him. The police would be on her side because she was defending herself. Both pairs of hands grappled for the prize but only one could declare themselves the winner.

SIXTY-TWO

Gina rushed out of the car outside the unit. Two marked police cars pulled up and she could see the ambulance turning the corner, closely followed by a paramedic on a bike. She hurried to the unit and tried to look through the window, but it was reflecting everything. She leaned forward and cupped her hands over her eyes. That's when she saw Gavin Brent lying in a pool of his own blood. 'Man injured on the floor.' His eyes flickered slightly, and he curled his little finger.

A shadow caught her attention. There was someone else in the room with him – Candice. Gina hurried to the door, checked her stab vest one more time and went to open it. 'It's locked.' She banged on the door. 'Mrs Brent, open up.' No one came. She glanced around at the team. Two uniformed officers waited, a battering ram filling the arms of one. Gina lifted the letter box but kept back, not knowing what might greet her. 'Candice, please open the door. Are you hurt?'

The woman wailed from inside. Gina fidgeted in her stab vest, hot to the core and burning up with the early afternoon temperatures. 'Mrs Brent, stand back. We're coming in.' She turned to the officers. 'I'm going to stand at the window. When I say go, get that door open.' She walked back to the window. 'We need to get in there, assess the situation and once safe, the ambulance crew can treat Mr Brent and assess Mrs Brent.' She stared through the window again. The swaying dog noose made her shiver. There were ropes scattered on the floor, empty bottles of water and a dirty old sheet against the far wall. Some fight had gone down. The shadow remained in place. If they were to slam the door down, Mrs Brent was out of the firing line. 'Go.'

The officers banged repeatedly. The heavy industrial door creaked before it finally gave in, bouncing off the wall as they entered. 'Police.'

Gina followed and the police waved the paramedics in. She spotted Mrs Brent facing the far wall, sobbing. She'd covered her ears with her hands. 'Candice?' Gina reached for the woman but all she did was yell and cower. 'Please come with us.' She led the trembling woman out of the room and onto the sunshine covered tarmac where a paramedic led her to a wall to sit on. That's when it clicked. Gina knew. She knew why, who, how and when. Especially now that they had Mr Brent's computer.

Her phone rang, it was Bernard. She might be in the thick of it but whatever Bernard had to tell her, it had to be urgent. He wouldn't call if it wasn't. She listened to what he had to say and if it wouldn't seem inappropriate, she'd have jumped with joy. He'd just confirmed what her mind had been putting together and the clue was in BenedictCarnY on the Hi There Horny site. She knew who Ben was.

She watched as Mr Brent was brought out on a stretcher, his eyes pressed together and an oxygen mask covering his mouth. He half opened his right eye, and he held a finger up and wiggled it, like he was gesturing for Gina to come over. She walked over to him as the paramedics put him in the ambulance. She tried to listen to what he was saying behind the mask, but it was all garbled. 'Can we remove the mask?'

The paramedic shook his head. 'Sorry.' Mr Brent jerked and began to fit. 'I'm going to have to ask you to leave. He's critical and we must get him to a hospital, now.' Gina gestured to a uniformed officer who got in with him. With that the doors were closed, and the ambulance pulled away.

Gina stepped back into the dog parlour. The scene had been messed up good and proper by them all going in. She pulled out some boot covers and gloves from her pockets, and continued, careful to avoid the corner with the sheet. That's when she spotted something out of place above one of the eye level wall cupboards. Reaching up, she grabbed the flat, hard, item and held it carefully, using it as a tray for the items that were shifting on it. One tablet and three phones. It had to be Billie's two phones and Nadia's. She called an officer in. 'Can you find out if forensics are on their way?'

She nodded and left the scene. Jacob peered around the corner. 'They've nearly patched Mrs Brent up. She has a few injuries, but nothing is broken, well except one of her teeth. She'll need a dentist to fix that, but the bleeding has stopped, for now.'

'Jacob?'

'Yes.'

'Can you get me some evidence bags?'

He hurried out and she heard his boot open and slam. He came back, his shoes covered, and he in turn opened each of the bags as she popped the devices in. 'Are these what I think they are?'

'I hope so. We need them logged in and then taken to the station for immediate processing. I'm not going to mess with anything else here. Forensics need to scour the scene so let's get out. Time to speak to Mrs Brent.' She whispered a few words to Jacob, and he nodded in acknowledgement.

As they stepped out, Gina watched as the paramedic closed her kit up and headed back towards her bike.

'He was going to kill me,' Candice stuttered. 'I had no choice. It was him or me. He killed Billie and he took Nadia.'

Gina sighed. Bernard had found a speck of latex amongst some of the smashed items in Billie's kitchen. The tiniest bit of latex from a glove, not one they used. The colour was wrong, and not one of them would have pierced that glove with their long, chipped, red nails. BenedictCarnY was an anagram of Candice Y Brent. Mr Brent had the username AppGuy. She had been monitoring her husband's internet use and had come across the Hi There Horny website. She'd used his internet history to see exactly what he'd been looking at, then she'd read his private messages showing him arranging to pay Billie for sex. Billie hadn't been keen, hadn't wanted to but Gina remembered all those debt letters piled up. Gavin had offered her double what she charged. That's when Candice had set up her own account and sent Billie that message. 'Sluts get what they deserve.' Why she'd taken Nadia, Gina still didn't know but she was about to find out.

'Candice Brent. I'm arresting you on suspicion of the murder of Billie Reeves, the kidnapping, false imprisonment and attempted murder of Nadia Anderson and the attempted murder of Gavin Brent. You do not have to say anything. But it may harm your defence if you do not mention when questioned something which you later rely on in court. Anything you do say may be given in evidence.' She paused as she watched a stream of blood and saliva drip from the side of the woman's mouth. 'Can someone please get Mrs Brent a tissue?' The paramedic came back with a wipe and a pack of tissues. Candice cleaned the mess away and left the used tissue on the wall.

'But it was Gavin and he tried to kill me. I was just defending myself. He killed Billie and took Nadia. It was all him. He kept Nadia here, then he stabbed her, and he took her to the woods and left her to die. He was going to kill me. It was him or me.'

'You'll have your chance to tell us everything, down at the station. Please hold your wrists out.'

Candice Brent held them up and Gina slapped the handcuffs on her.

'I didn't do it.'

'Mrs Brent, Nadia wants to make a statement. She was there the whole time.' Gina knew the woman had been sedated but she was sure of the evidence they did have. It was enough to arrest Candice Brent. Mr Brent wasn't going anywhere for now. Looking at him, Gina doubted whether he'd last the rest of the day. She glanced at Candice's car, and she was sure that would tell a story of its own. Her phone buzzed with a message. 'I need to make a call.' She glanced up to the police officers and Jacob. 'Can you make sure Mrs Brent gets into the police car safely and is processed as soon as you get back to the station. I'll be there to interview her shortly?'

Gina walked past Mrs Brent's battered car. The bonnet had caved in and one of the lights had been knocked out. She grabbed her pencil torch and shone it in the gap, that's when she saw the polythene splayed out. The heat and scent of fear made her recoil. She grabbed her phone and called Kapoor. 'Hi, so what has Nadia said?'

'She's awake, guv. She seemed a lot livelier, and she said that Candice took her. Mrs Brent came to her house and attacked her in her garage, then she forced her into the boot of her car. She took her to the unit next door to the one her husband owns in Cleevesford, and she kept her there. She doesn't know how long as she forced her to take a couple of tablets that made her sleep. She woke up and Candice stabbed her then bundled her into a car. She can't remember anything after that.'

'The cherry on the cake. We've just arrested Candice.'

As Gina ended the call, she watched as Candice shouted with rage and kicked out at the officers. It was hard to believe she was looking at a murderer. Gina had believed that Mrs Brent was the one in danger, that Gavin was their murderer, not the mumsy woman in front of her.

The forensics van turned the corner and pulled up. Jacob's face lit up as Jennifer stepped out, her dyed plum hair in a bun at her nape. The look Jacob was giving her was a look that Gina would never again receive from Briggs.

She thought of poor Kayden, his mother taken from him cruelly. She couldn't bring the young mother back, but she could deliver the justice he'd need, and she wasn't going to let that little boy down.

SIXTY-THREE

With cuffed hands, Candice Brent took a sip of water and flinched. Jacob stared ahead and the tape was rolling. The duty solicitor looked at Mrs Brent and then said, 'My client wishes to cooperate fully.'

Gina imagined that Mrs Brent's broken tooth was causing her a bit of pain. The standard issue track bottoms and T-shirt were a comedown from the pretty blouses and dresses. Gina couldn't help but stare at the woman's broken nails. All samples and fingerprints had been taken when she'd been booked in, and it was only a matter of time before that tiniest bit of nail was matched to Mrs Brent's sample. They had Nadia's statement and something in it made Gina shiver. Nadia said that someone had been coming into her house and moving items around in William's doll's house, they left her wine and a key that had recently gone missing on the kitchen table. A ball that had been in her garden had been rolled outside her bedroom door. She blamed Edward Anderson to begin with.

'Tell me about the night of Billie Reeves's murder.'

Mrs Brent burst into tears. 'I didn't mean to kill her. We were arguing. I confronted her over Gavin. I'd seen the messages with my own eyes, but she denied it. She denied he'd messaged her or come to her for sex, but I could see it in her eyes. She told me to go but something inside me snapped. This woman ruined my family, my life, Poppy's life and this rage burned inside me, so I pushed her and called her a couple of names.

'I remember feeling rushed as I had to collect Poppy from school after her club. It was okay for Billie; Kayden had left early after the school play. I thought that would be it, but she pushed me back and started yelling at me, telling me that it was my fault for putting up with such a lousy husband. I just saw red. The next moment, I'd grabbed a small chopping knife from Billie's worktop and plunged it into her chest.'

'The word slut was written on her wall in red marker pen, the same type that was found in your husband's office. So, you killed Billie and still enraged, you wrote on her wall.'

She let out a couple of choking sobs. 'I hated her. The pen was in my bag with a load of other pens. Poppy likes to use them to draw with. It was a stupid thing I did in the heat of the moment. All I could see was this woman who had broken my family up. I wanted her to pay but I didn't go there intending to kill her.' She paused. 'It just happened.'

'What happened after that?'

'I, err...' She stared as if she was thinking. 'I came around the back and I left through the back. I remember taking off my top and turning it inside out to hide the blood spray. Then I panicked, knowing that Billie's phone and tablet would show that Gavin had paid her for sex. There were too many messages, and I didn't know if he'd been calling her too. I rummaged through the house until I found the tablet upstairs and two phones in the living room. I nipped home, changed, got Poppy and went to Nadia's house as planned.'

'You left her bleeding to death and then went to another friend's house?'

'Yes, but I didn't intend to kill her. I told you. It was an accident.' The solicitor stared into his hands, knowing that Candice Brent had just lied again.

'If you didn't intend to kill her, why did you take latex gloves? You took them with the intent of trying to cover up any fingerprints that would have been left by your visit, didn't you?'

She shook her head and hiccupped another sob.

'That knife was yours, wasn't it?' Gina had no proof of that, but Candice was crumbling.

She yelled out a piercing scream. 'Yes. I'm sorry. The night before, Gavin wasn't in. I know I said he was. I kept calling him. I read his messages and I knew he was visiting her. It hurt like nothing I've ever experienced. I made him my everything and that's how he repaid me, paying that filthy slut for sex.' The solicitor whispered in her ear, but she dismissed him. He shrugged and leaned back.

'By her, you mean Billie Reeves. Is that correct?'

She nodded.

'For the tape, Mrs Brent has just nodded in agreement.'

'He even told Poppy a bedtime story over the phone because she wouldn't go to sleep without him, and he told me he loved me.' She balled her fists.

Gina couldn't help but feel sickened by how calculated Candice Brent's crimes were. She'd hampered their case by mentioning a knife that she heard Nadia and Edward Anderson talking about, knowing that it would be linked to the case as she knew exactly how Billie had been murdered. She'd also quite happily implicated Serena Reeves. Then, she'd tried to blame her husband. Gina could see where Candice's reaction had come from with Billie but not Nadia. 'Nadia Anderson, your other friend. You took her spare house key; you used it to go into her house and rearrange things to unnerve her. Is that correct?' Clenching everything, Gina hoped Candice would cooperate at this point. She had no proof of this but from what Nadia had said, it looked likely.

'Yes,' she said, hands covering her sobbing face. 'I only wanted to scare her to begin with.'

'What changed?'

'A conversation.'

'Okay, go on.'

Mrs Brent took a tissue and blew her nose. 'I couldn't get what I'd heard out of my head. We knew what Billie was doing but Nadia had to go on and on about it to the other parents at the school gates. She said that she only told me and Meera, but she lied. She tells everyone everything.'

'Were you worried that she was going to gossip about you?'

A fresh stream of tears began to spring from Candice's eyes. 'I saw her looking upset and she was sitting with someone on a bench, one of those circular benches around the trees at the school. I had a while to wait for Poppy, so I sat the other side. All I caught was Nadia getting emotional as she said that people had to watch their husbands. That Billie had crossed a line and her secret money earner was going to ruin friendships. I heard the other mother probing her, asking for more information but Nadia said she didn't want to say anything at that moment, but she supposed that everyone would find out soon. It was only a matter of time. She was waiting for the right moment to bring my family down. I knew she meant Gavin and I couldn't let that happen. It was her big mouth that started all this. If she hadn't told me Billie's secret and I hadn't told Gavin, this would never have happened. We all caved like a falling card tower.'

Gina knew that when Nadia had said all this she was thinking that her husband was having an affair with Billie. She wouldn't have known it was Meera and she was obviously toying with what to say and who to tell or confide in.

'Nadia's known as a gossip, and I knew she wouldn't be able

to keep her mouth shut about Gavin. I don't know how she knew.'

'So, you sent her the messages?' Gina had seen the messages in Candice's outbox. The woman hadn't even deleted them.

'Yes.' Her bottom lip trembled.

'And you stalked her?'

'It all just went too far.'

'Then you saw her come home that day. You went in through her utility room door, knowing that she left her gate open, and you hit her with the rounders bat we found at your industrial unit?'

'I didn't know what else to do,' she replied as she bawled.

'Forensics have been through your car. You went to her house, ready with plastic sheeting in the boot, which shows that you intended to take her. Why didn't you kill her there and then, like you did with Billie?'

'Because I didn't know what to do with her. Billie took my husband and ruined my life. Nadia knew and she would have told everyone.'

'Nadia didn't know. She thought it was her own husband who was sleeping with Billie.'

'What?' The realisation hit Candice and Gina could see the shock in her face.

'When she was mumbling on about not knowing, I didn't believe her. I still don't. She's making it up.'

'Why would she do that?'

'To make me look bad.' She brought her bottom lip over her top lip and leaned back.

Gina sighed. 'To make you look bad.' She pressed her lips together. The poor solicitor looked like he'd given up. 'What did you do with Nadia once you had her in your car?'

'I drove her to the unit, tied her up and gave her some sleeping tablets while I decided what to do next.'

'Things had already gone too far, hadn't they, so you stabbed her and left her for dead by the Mutt Trail?'

'I didn't know what to do.' The woman stood and ran towards the door, banging it hard with cuffed wrists. 'I want to get out of here. I need to see my daughter.' She stood at the door. Gina knew Candice couldn't see the enormity of her situation. A strand of her fiery-red hair fell to the floor as she sobbed like a child.

'Interview terminated at twenty-three hundred hours.' Perpetrator or not, it would do more harm than good to the case if Gina didn't get Candice Brent seen by a medic and then a dentist. They had all they needed, for now. Candice had it all. A lovely home, a lovely husband and family, then one shaky moment in the relationship had turned her into a murderer.

The woman peered through her hands before wiping the snot and tears away.

'Mrs Brent, sit back on the chair.'

The woman stopped crying and looked up in anger at Gina. Everything she did was an act, but she did sit. 'Can I see Poppy?'

Gina shook her head. 'No, not at the moment.' The next time Candice would see Poppy was during a prison visit.

Someone knocked at the door. Gina hurried out and Wyre pushed it closed before speaking. 'We have word from the hospital.'

As Gina digested the news, she took a deep breath and walked back in.

'What are you going to do about Gavin? He took me and he tried to kill me?'

She exhaled. 'Nothing, I'm afraid your husband has just been pronounced dead.' Gina could see that a fight had gone down at the dog-grooming unit. Bernard told her that there was evidence of Nadia and Candice being kept in the boot. Maybe, just maybe, Candice could claim self-defence. They'd never get

Gavin Brent's statement now. She scrunched her brows as she looked at the woman.

'Good.' The woman smirked, then began to laugh. 'It started with him, and it ended with him. You like it tidy, don't you, Detective?'

The case had been anything but tidy and now that she had all she needed for the moment from Candice Brent, she needed to see what Nadia had recorded and hidden on Billie's tablet. With Edward Anderson claiming to have been stabbed by his wife and Nadia Anderson having the photos of her own injuries, Gina needed to explore this further. She had the one photo, showing an injury that was impossible to self-inflict but she felt the video was the key to everything.

SIXTY-FOUR

Sunday, 19 June

As Gina took the long walk down the hospital corridor, she forced herself to replay Nadia's video in her head. Hands shaking, she stopped by a window and leaned on the ledge, taking in the courtyard below. A couple of patients strolled around, dragging drips along as they walked. Nadia had lived in fear of her life, just as Gina had when she'd been married to Terry. She remembered that feeling of walking on eggshells, trying to avoid him when he was drunk, upset, angry; thinking she was the cause which made her do anything to appease him. The video had left chills working their way up her spine and all she wanted to do was go back to her bedroom, crawl under the covers and feel sorry for herself.

Nadia had been crying as she revealed her injuries to the camera, each one of them in a place no one would see. She'd claimed that if anyone was seeing the video, she'd probably been dead a while and the world needed to hear her side. She asked if she'd died in a car accident or while on a walking holiday. After confronting Edward over yet another fling with a colleague, he'd denied it. Their argument had escalated, and he'd gone out and got drunk. He'd come home in a worse mood, punched her in the breast and stamped so hard on her toe she'd heard the sickening crunch. She then went on to describe how he chased her around the house. Her limping, him taunting her and laughing as he blocked off all her exits and toyed with her like a cat. Of course, she could never just walk out that night. William was in bed.

Gina left the window and hurried to the ward where Nadia was recovering. PC Kapoor was no longer standing guard, not since Candice Brent's arrest. The same nurse as yesterday buzzed Gina through. 'She's just had a cup of tea, so she's awake.'

'Is her mother still with her?'

'No, she left late last night. I told her she should get some rest.'

A few plates cluttered as people ate. She passed the ward and headed to Nadia's side room and knocked. 'May I come in?'

'Yes,' Nadia replied as she placed her cup on the bedside unit.

'I thought you should know that Candice Brent has been arrested for your kidnap, false imprisonment and attempted murder.'

'We were friends. Billie was our friend.' She swallowed, a tear slipping down her cheek. 'I wasn't a good friend. I should have kept Billie's secret.' She paused. 'How's William?'

'He's still with your husband's mother and he's fine. Your cat came back home so an officer dropped it off there too.'

'Thank you. They'll be okay with Lacey, she's lovely, not like her son.'

Gina cleared her throat. 'Can we talk about your husband?'

'What about him?'

'Billie's phones have been entered into evidence, along with her tablet. Your husband is claiming that you stabbed him. We've seen your video. The one you left hidden on Billie's tablet. We also have a catalogue of photos on a memory stick that we recovered in your locker and a photo of a bruise under your arm. We found that hidden in a book in your bedroom.'

She let out a tiny sob. 'I was trying to keep evidence for when I left him, but he got good at finding things and it would make him angrier. He said if I ever tried to take William from him, he'd find a way of helping me have an accident or worse, he'd say that I was hurting him.'

'But you made that video. Can you talk me through it?'

She nodded. 'If he killed me, I wanted my version of what happened out there. Ed kept reminding me that he had the knife. It had my prints on it and his blood. He had the scar to prove he was stabbed and if I ever tried to leave, he'd say I tried to kill him. We've been stuck in this deadlock since, but his bouts of anger were getting worse and more violent.' She huffed and shook her head. 'Of course, he never hurt me in places people could see but some days were so scary, when he was at work, I made videos or took photos. With the video that you saw, I uploaded it to a private YouTube account online and then I knew I needed someone to be the custodian of the link. I saved it in a message, then I needed to get rid of that message as he read all my social media stuff and texts. I was at Billie's, and I quickly messaged the link to her while she was in the toilet. Her tablet was out so I opened the message and saved the link deep in Billie's documents, amongst a year's worth of to-do lists. Billie never deleted anything. I don't know what I was thinking really.'

'Can you go over the night he was stabbed?'

'He punched me, broke my toe and when I tried to escape, he chased me around the house. I've never been so scared. I thought he was going to kill me, like he'd promised. I thought, maybe he's found some of the photos I've been keeping but no, it was all because I asked him about some texts. He cornered me in the kitchen. As he was about to bring his fist down on me, I grabbed a small knife from the block. I only wanted to scare him. I couldn't hurt anyone. He almost broke my wrist as he guided that point to his own arm and cut it. I was in shock, then he bagged the weapon up with my prints on it. He then laughed, claiming he had all the evidence he needed to get me arrested. He said he'd hide it somewhere safe and if I ever stepped out of line again, he'd use it against me, and I'd lose William forever. I've been looking for that knife for ages and he knew. I can't lose William.' She began to sob as she clutched the white sheet.

'I will need to interview you at the station when you're discharged.'

'I get that. I'm hoping to be out of here soon.'

'Nadia, did you cause any of the injuries in those photos to yourself?'

'What? Why would I do that? He said I hurt myself, didn't he?'

'We have to check everything out.' Gina felt horrible for having to ask.

'No. I have no history of self-harm. I'd never in a million years hurt myself.'

'Some of the photos you took show injuries that you couldn't have done yourself.'

'I can prove what I said is all true, about Ed stabbing himself. I didn't want to go down that route, but my son needs me, and I need him. William saw what happened with the knife. Ed didn't see him, but I saw my terrified little boy peering from the gap between the door and door frame. I didn't want him to have to relive that night, but he saw it all.'

Gina gave the woman a sympathetic smile. She hated having to question a young child but as Nadia had agreed, it would help them get to what had happened that night. That's something they would arrange once Nadia had been formally interviewed.

Not all cases had a tidy ending. This one certainly hadn't and as Gina left the hospital, it grated on her that there was still so much to tie up. It upset her more because a little boy as young as William had seen something so horrific. It hurt that Kayden had lost his mother and that Poppy had one parent that was heading to prison and another who had just died. She almost wanted to cry for those poor children. Their lives turned upside down, mostly because of Mr Brent's indiscretion, which led to Candice Brent's murderous reaction. An abduction that had uncovered more secrets of which Nadia was half keeping and half gossiping about, and the discovery that Edward wasn't sleeping with Billie, he was sleeping with Meera. The tangled web of lies, gossip and secrets had ruined them all.

EPILOGUE

Three weeks later

As Gina said her goodbye to Kathleen Reeves, she glanced back at Kayden and the boy stared up at her with pressed lips. In about twenty minutes, he would get to meet his other grandmother and after speaking to Beryl Brock, initially the woman had been shocked, then she was overcome by the fact that she had a grandson.

'Thank you for the update. I still can't believe it was her.' Kathleen leaned on the door frame as Gina stood on the garden path. 'She's not going to get off with it, is she? That woman needs to rot in a cell forever after what she did to my daughter... I still can't believe Billie's gone. If only she'd come to me for help.'

'I'm so sorry you've been through this, Mrs Reeves. Your daughter's killer has confessed to her murder, amongst other violent crimes. We'll keep you updated with the case and sentencing but she won't be free for a long time. Is Serena okay?'

'She's contacted the university, in the hope that she can get back onto her course. It's looking likely so that's something to be thankful for.'

'Nanny, I'm hungry.' Kayden gripped his grandmother's legs.

'Thank you for everything.' The woman half-smiled with watery eyes as she closed the door.

As Gina reached the car, she watched as Beryl Brock stepped out of a taxi and took a deep breath. 'Are you okay,' Gina called.

The woman exhaled and nodded. 'I'm nervous.'

'He's a lovely boy and I know he'll be happy to meet you. Just take it slowly. He's been through a lot.' Gina was glad that the Reeveses had wanted Beryl in their lives. They too had been upset that the poor woman had never known her grandchild.

'I can't wait to meet him. I don't know what's going to happen to my Shaun, but I can never forgive him for taking five precious years from me. I'm not going to visit him in prison. This little boy is going to be my life now.'

Gina knew that Beryl might change her mind at some point in the future. Once he received his sentence for kidnapping Kayden, he'd do his time and he'd come out. She hoped that he'd come out a better person.

'How is he?'

Gina smiled. 'He knows you're coming. He's a little shy, a little nervous but he really wants to meet you.'

The woman repositioned her handbag on her shoulder and ran the other hand through her thick grey hair. 'Wish me luck.'

'You won't need it.' Beryl was lovely and Gina knew that it wouldn't take long for Kayden to see that. She hung back watching as Beryl knocked and Kathleen let her in.

Gina got into her car and instantly started to perspire in the midday summer heat. The air con would take ages to start getting cool. She remembered her doctor's appointment and snatched her phone from her pocket, tapping it into her diary. If they could do anything to help with the flushes and sweats, it would make her life more bearable. She couldn't manage these symptoms any more.

After Nadia had recovered, Gina had gone over to William's grandmother's house and in her presence, and with Nadia's permission, she had spoken to William. In his childlike way he had confirmed that he saw Daddy prodding himself with a knife and it had upset him and eventually Edward Anderson had caved and confessed. There was too much stacked against him and Gina knew that his solicitor had advised him that it would look better for him in court if he cooperated. Nadia, William and Fluffball had since been reunited but she'd moved out of the house, not wanting Edward Anderson to know where she now lived. She mentioned that Meera had tried to call on numerous occasions, but her actions had been unforgivable.

Four friends. Four families ruined. One of them murdered. She glanced back at Kathleen's house. But there was hope.

Her phone beeped with a text message, and she smiled. It was Jacob.

I've spoken to Jennifer, and she said she'd love a rabbit and we would like to have Thumper. That's if you still want to part with him.

She tapped out her reply.

I'll deliver Thumper later.

She smiled. Things were looking up even more. Doctor's appointment. Rabbit rehomed. Her cat would be thrilled to have Thumper out of their lives. A wash of sadness turned her smile into a frown. The only thing that hadn't been resolved was her fallout with Briggs.

The air started to run cold, so she pulled away. Something Kayden had said while she and Kathleen were talking in the kitchen brought a slight tear to Gina's eye as she mulled it over. He said that Mummy had made him a promise that she was going to take him on a holiday and buy him lots of toys because of her new job. Gina knew ultimately that was her deadly promise. The need to live, the need to make her son happy in a world where it's too expensive for so many families to even exist without food banks or expensive payday loans killed Billie. It forced her into desperation and Gina knew for sure, the cost of living crisis was going nowhere and there were many more Billies out there suffering. She wiped the flood of tears that streamed down her face, wishing she could do more but knowing that she could do nothing. As soon as she got home, she was going to call Hannah and speak to little Gracie. On Sunday, she was going to visit and take her granddaughter to a park or a soft-play centre. With all the bad that she'd seen, Gracie's happy face would cheer her up.

As she pulled up outside her house, her heart began to thrum. Briggs's car was there and he was sitting on her doorstep. Had he come to dish out more anger or had he finally realised that she was telling the truth all along?

She opened the door and a suffocating heat hit her like a slap around the face. It was only set to get hotter, and a heat-wave was predicted. She wasn't prepared in the slightest for the heat or for whatever Briggs had to say.

A LETTER FROM CARLA

Dear Reader,

I'd like to thank you massively for reading *Her Deadly Promise*. If you enjoyed *Her Deadly Promise* and would like to keep up to date with all my latest releases, just sign up at the following link. Your email address will never be shared, and you can unsubscribe at any time.

www.bookouture.com/carla-kovach

I couldn't ignore the fact that Gina is going through the menopause. Throughout previous books her anxiety has got worse because of perimenopause and her PTSD, but now, it's come to a head. Her sweats and flashes are starting to hit like a train, rendering her unable to ignore her symptoms any longer. Half of the population go through this and I'm so glad it's being discussed more in the media and by celebrities, too. Thank you, Davina McCall. Long may we continue to talk openly about it.

I also wanted to feature the cost of living crisis in this book. Poor Billie couldn't afford to make ends meet and I know so many people are suffering at the moment. I wanted to explore what a person might do when pushed into extreme debt and how that might make a person cross a boundary they'd never have crossed if they had a choice. I found myself feeling really upset for Billie while I was writing this book. She was proud, not wanting to take help from her friends and family. It saddened me to write Gina's closing thoughts on the matter. Gina would know that Billie wasn't unique in what she did. There really are Billies everywhere and we need to be aware, and we need to be kinder to each other than ever.

Whether you are a reader, tweeter, blogger, Facebooker, TikTok user or reviewer, I really am grateful of all that you do and as a writer, this is where I hope you'll leave me a review or say a few words about my book.

Again, thank you so much. I'm active on social media so please feel free to contact me on Twitter, Instagram or through my Facebook page.

Thank you, Carla Kovach

 facebook.com/CarlaKovachAuthor

twitter.com/CKovachAuthor

 instagram.com/carla_kovach

ACKNOWLEDGEMENTS

I'd like to say a massive thank you to everyone who's helped bring *Her Deadly Promise* to life. Creating a book is a team effort so thanks a million.

Helen Jenner, my editor, is an absolute star in what she does. In fact, I don't know how she does it. The edits she provides always amaze me and I couldn't do all this without her. Thank you!

The Bookouture team are fabulous. From the rights department to accounts. They keep me updated and informed in every way. I'm truly grateful.

When people see a book, they see a cover and I adore what Lisa Brewster did with this one. It's amazing and much appreciated.

The Bookouture publicity team are wonderful. Noelle Holten, Kim Nash, Jess Readett and Sarah Hardy work super hard making publication days special. I'd like to extend my gratitude to them.

Bloggers and readers are wonderful. With all the books out there, some of these lovely people chose mine. For that I'm always grateful. I know how much time it takes to prepare a review or blog post, so here's a huge thank you.

Thank you to the Fiction Café Book Club. I really feel as though I'm part of a fantastic book-loving community. While I'm mentioning community, I'm grateful to be a member of the supportive Bookouture family. Thank you to all the other authors.

Beta readers, Derek Coleman, Su Biela, Brooke Venables, Anna Wallace, and Vanessa Morgan, are all lovely people and I'm grateful for the time that they've given me. I need to add in a special note of gratitude here again to Brooke Venables who writes under the name Jamie-Lee Brooke, as well as Julia Sutton and Phil Price who are all authors. We are in a mini support group and it's fantastic how the four of us spur each other on. Long live the Writing Buddies group.

I need to say a great big thank you to Stuart Gibbon of Gib Consultancy. He answers my policing questions and without his knowledge I'd most definitely be stuck. Any inaccuracies are definitely my own.

Lastly, huge thank you to my husband, Nigel Buckley, for the coffees and encouragement. I'm eternally grateful for his support.

Lightning Source UK Ltd.
Milton Keynes UK
UKHW010058061222
413407UK00007B/1618